Ryan managed to stagger to his feet

"Leave him," Crow said softly. "He has every right to be angry. But he's no danger to us now."

The words became strung out and distorted as the drug took effect. Ryan swayed on his feet, trying to reach for his SIG-Sauer, but every movement seemed to take an eternity, and his numbed hand failed to respond. He could see J.B. fumble with his Uzi, falling forward to the ground before the blaster was fully in his hands.

The world narrowed and darkened around Ryan. The one thought that cut through his befuddled mind was why hadn't they been chilled then and there?

Other titles in the Deathlands saga:

JAMES AXLER

DEATH LANDS®

Salvation Road

A GOLD EAGLE BOOK FROM
WORLDWIDE®

TORONTO • NEW YORK • LONDON
AMSTERDAM • PARIS • SYDNEY • HAMBURG
STOCKHOLM • ATHENS • TOKYO • MILAN
MADRID • WARSAW • BUDAPEST • AUCKLAND

First edition June 2002

ISBN 0-373-62568-5

SALVATION ROAD

The world is his, who has money to go over it.
—Ralph Waldo Emerson
1803–1882

THE DEATHLANDS SAGA

This world is their legacy, a world born in the violent nuclear spasm of 2001 that was the bitter outcome of a struggle for global dominance.

There is no real escape from this shockscape where life always hangs in the balance, vulnerable to newly demonic nature, barbarism, lawlessness.

But they are the warrior survivalists, and they endure—in the way of the lion, the hawk and the tiger, true to nature's heart despite its ruination.

Ryan Cawdor: The privileged son of an East Coast baron. Acquainted with betrayal from a tender age, he is a master of the hard realities.

Krysty Wroth: Harmony ville's own Titian-haired beauty, a woman with the strength of tempered steel. Her premonitions and Gaia powers have been fostered by her Mother Sonja.

J. B. Dix, the Armorer: Weapons master and Ryan's close ally, he, too, honed his skills traversing the Deathlands with the legendary Trader.

Doctor Theophilus Tanner: Torn from his family and a gentler life in 1896, Doc has been thrown into a future he couldn't have imagined.

Dr. Mildred Wyeth: Her father was killed by the Ku Klux Klan, but her fate is not much lighter. Restored from predark cryogenic suspension, she brings twentieth-century healing skills to a nightmare.

Jak Lauren: A true child of the wastelands, reared on adversity, loss and danger, the albino teenager is a fierce fighter and loyal friend.

Dean Cawdor: Ryan's young son by Sharona accepts the only world he knows, and yet he is the seedling bearing the promise of tomorrow.

In a world where all was lost, they are humanity's last hope....

Chapter One

The broken wheel weighed heavily on his chest, the sharpened and splintered spokes beginning to feel uncomfortable as they poked into his flesh. He pressed himself back into the ground, feeling the sharpness of the small rocks and pebbles in the red dust as they formed a hard, compressed mattress beneath him.

He breathed in short, shallow gasps, trying to extract the maximum amount of oxygen from the minimum movement of his chest muscles. He figured that the axle of the wheel would keep it aloft enough to prevent it penetrating the cloth, skin and flesh and breaking bone and mashing internal organs into a pulpy mess. The balance of the wrecked wagon was delicate, but he hoped that the bulk of its contents would stay on the far side, with just enough weight to lift the broken wheel and prevent it from tilting slowly and inexorably into his all too frail human frame. He would have tried to move, to wriggle out from beneath the spokes, if not for the fact that they already had him delicately pinned, moving almost with the breeze that blew dust and grit into his eyes, making him blink.

Everything was otherwise still. The delicate swirl

of the wind and the almost whispered creak of the broken wagon as it shifted was all that could be heard.

He couldn't remember exactly how the accident had occurred. A vague blur of action as the wagon hit the half-buried rock, the vast majority of its bulk being hidden beneath the loose earth, the terrified cries of the horses as the reins and harness pulled on their muscle and sinew, the wagon suddenly brought to a dead halt by the obstruction. The arrested force pulled the animals back and snapped the neck of one while the other tore free of the frayed leather and ran on, disappearing from view behind an outcrop, the sound of its terrified flight fading into the distance. His own flight, propelled by the force of the impact and pulled forward by the momentum of the reins he had been loosely clutching, had been too swift to recall.

He remembered the impact of his fall, the bone-crunching jarring of his spine on the earth recording indelibly that journey into his memory. The wagon had eventually rolled over the dislodged rock after balancing for a moment in midair, poised to fall with the full weight of twisted and splintered spokes onto his body. The weight inside the wagon, shifted to one side by the impact, had prevented the descent of the deadly wooden stakes, and thus a swift oblivion.

But perhaps this was worse.

He moved again, shuffling beneath the pointed ends of the spokes, which seemed to push back against him and pin him further, as if to emphasize their mastery over his aching, pain-racked frame. The heels of his boots tried to dig into the dust and push back, but found no purchase in the loose earth.

"Emily...my love, are you all right?"

His voice was little more than a whispered croak, the light clouds of dust that eddied around him drying out his mouth even more, making him choke. The coughing racked his body, the spokes responding by pushing harder, biting into his body, their sharpness now more than uncomfortable through his clothing, which, he realized with an obvious but still despondent resignation, offered scant protection.

There was no reply from inside the wagon. His wife had been in the back with their two children. Young Rachel would be all right, but the boy, Jolyon, was little more than a babe in arms, and Doc Tanner was worried that the child would be hurt.

But no more worried than he was about his beloved wife. Doc's world revolved around Emily; that was why the university-educated academic was making his way across country to begin a new life, moving from the civilized and educated east to the still untamed wilds of the West.

For a moment, as he considered this, a flicker of puzzlement and worry crossed Doc's brow, making him forget his current predicament, his mind switching to another gear.

But surely that didn't make sense? Why was he alone with the wagon? Not alone in the sense that he had his young family with him, but alone in the fact that there seemed to have been no other wagons traveling with them. Yes, it would be true to assume that he could have become detached—lost, to be more blunt—from the rest of the train. It would be a reasonable assumption, if not for the simple truth that he couldn't, for the life of him, remember any other wagons traveling with them at any point in the journey. In point of fact, Doc was as sure as he could be that he had no recollection of even beginning the journey.

"Emily? Please answer me, my sweet. Please talk to me. Rachel, are you there? Is Jolyon all right?"

The only answer was silence.

Tears prickled at the corner of Doc's eyes. "Please…please let this end. Let this not happen again."

"Why should you get off light, Doc? Least ways you're still alive, right? Not so lucky…"

If it had been possible to do so beneath the shattered wheel without impaling himself on the splintered spokes, Doc would have physically jumped with shock and—yes—a tinge of fear at the sound of the voice.

Footsteps came to him across the ground, moving around from the blind side of the wagon, the high heels on the delicately sculpted white calf boots still managing to click, even on the relatively soft carpet of dust. Twisting his head, Doc could see the boots and the shapely denim-clad legs that moved up from the tops of the boots in a sinuous, smoothly moving line to a pair of snaked hips. Above, a slim torso was clad in a short fur jacket, the blank face surmounting it a mask of impassivity, the big, blinking eyes focused on his prone figure, the waves of blond hair flowing like honeyed gold over her shoulders.

"Lori?"

She nodded.

Doc squinted, the fear and uncertainty fluttering in his chest, a cavity that was also being filled with pain as the spokes moved and bit deeper.

"But you're dead."

"Uh-huh." She nodded. "So's your wife and your kids, Doc. We're all dead. But you're not. That's why you've got to go on suffering."

Despite the fear and agony, a wry smile crossed Doc's face. He had often considered that those who had perished were the lucky ones. Lori Quint, found in a redoubt in Alaska and rescued from the dysfunctional family of a "father" that used her as a toy for his own gratification, only to perish along the way.

Suddenly, Doc was no longer afraid. He knew he wasn't trapped under a wagon in the West. He wasn't in his own time... In fact, he had no time to call his own. He had long since left Emily, Rachel and Jolyon behind. They had their lives, lived out to whatever span, without ever knowing what had happened to him. How could they? How could nineteenth-century gentlefolk ever comprehend the perverse science behind Operation Chronos, that part of the Totality Concept that had snatched Doc from his own time and propelled him into the 1990s, before his dissension and desire to return to his own time had forced his captors to send him into a future that, ironically, had preserved his life. For while he had leaped over the nuclear holocaust known in his new time as skydark, those very scientists whose Totality Concept had helped form it were to perish.

And in that dark new world of the Deathlands, Doc had met Lori and lost her.

But despite it all, despite the physical strain of being propelled through time, and immense mental torment that made him feel as though he had descended into insanity, emerged the other side and gained the ability to dip his toe in and out of those murky waters of madness, he had survived. He and his traveling companions.

And the journey wasn't yet over.

"Do what you must," Doc said simply.

Lori Quint nodded blankly and walked over to the wheel, poised over Doc's chest.

"Sorry," she said as she began to push the wheel down…gently at first, but then with more force, the effort showing on her face.

"It doesn't matter…it just, ah—"

Doc's ability to speak was taken from him by the rush of pain as the splintered wood bit deeper into his flesh, breaking the skin and tearing the flesh and sinew beneath, the resistance of his ribs making them almost audibly creak before the sharp snapping sounds of bone giving way to a greater force.

Doc looked up into Lori's face as the periphery of his vision grew dim, the black edges spreading across the whole of his vision.

"It just has to carry on...." he whispered as all darkened, and the pain grew to encompass all.

"Doc LOOKS in a pretty bad way."

Ryan Cawdor hunkered down beside the older man, whose white, straggling hair matted in sweat-soaked strands to his head. He was stretched out on the floor of the mat-trans chamber. His limbs jerked in spasm, and his open eyes flicked the whites up into his skull.

Doc was always Ryan's main concern on arriving at a new destination. The mat-trans chambers were located in secret predark U.S. Army redoubts that were dotted across the ruins of America, in the lands now known as the Deathlands. None of the fellow travelers knew how to program the computer-triggered matter-transfer machines that were at the heart of each base; they knew only that closing the door triggered the mechanism and set the old comp tech working that was left in the depopulated bases. Each jump was a gamble. The vast land and weather upheavals that had followed the long night of sky-dark had changed the geography of the old Americas irrevocably, so there was always the risk that they would land in a mat-trans chamber that was crushed beneath tons of rock, or flooded so that they would instantly drown.

So far they had been lucky—either that, or the automatic default settings on the remaining working comps would only transfer at random to redoubts where the chambers were still able to receive. That wasn't something that Ryan could assume.

But the redoubts offered them a way to move vast distances across the scorched earth. However, everything had its price. Although it gave them an advantage that few, if any, could share, it also carried its own cost. The jumps were a nightmare experience where every atom of their being was torn apart, flung across vast distances and then reassembled. It made them all feel as though they had been ripped slowly apart, each sinew stretched to snapping point, all organs squeezed tightly in an iron grip…and gave them a worse hangover and comedown than the strongest shine or jolt.

Some of the group adapted to the jump better than others, and it seemed to be reliant on something genetic rather than just fitness and strength. Although the fact that Ryan was always the first to stir after a jump could lead to that initial conclusion, for he was the most obviously physically fit specimen in the group. He stood more than six feet tall, with a mane of waving, dark curls that framed a square-jawed and handsome face, that was only somewhat marred by the patch that covered the empty left eye socket. The livid and puckered scar that ran down his cheek bore testimony to the manner in which the eye had been lost. The one-eyed man was a fighting machine, his whipcord musculature developed by years of action.

Hearing a murmur behind him as he crouched over Doc, Ryan turned to find his son, Dean, regaining consciousness and rising to his feet. Just as his father had checked the razor-sharp panga strapped to his thigh and the 9 mm SIG-Sauer P-226 pistol in its holster when he came to, settling the Steyr SSG-70 across his shoulder, so Dean automatically checked and holstered the 9 mm Browning Hi-Power that was his preferred blaster. Apart from the fact that he was still in possession of both eyes, Dean could have been a mirror image of his father. Now twelve years old, the boy was developing into a fighting machine that would one day be the equal of his father.

Ryan looked away from his son and back to the prone old man.

"Doc looks bad," Dean remarked, joining his father.

Ryan nodded. "Mildred should be conscious soon. Mebbe she'll be able to do something."

Krysty Wroth was also beginning to stir from the stupor brought on by the mat-trans jump. She groaned as she raised her head, her long fur coat wrapped around her shapely and finely muscled body, tendrils of her Titian red, sentient hair, uncurling from around her head and flowing freely as she felt the danger recede. Krysty had the ability to sense danger, and her mutie senses were trusted by Ryan in tight spots.

The woman rose to her feet, her blue, silver-tipped Western boots clicking on the smooth floor of the chamber. Without pausing, she checked her .38-caliber Model 640 Smith & Wesson, holstering it as she strode the short distance to where Ryan and Dean were hunched over Doc.

By now, Dr. Mildred Wyeth was coming around, as was J. B. Dix. As usual, the pair made the jump side by side, their hands touching. Neither was the type to show his or her emotions, but each would put the other before him- or herself.

Mildred's dark skin was nearly ashen with the shock of the jump, her breathing labored but regular.

"Shit, I never even used to get hangovers that bad," she muttered, her beaded plaits shaking around her downturned face as she tried to clear her head. "That's the worst jump I can remember for a long, long time."

"Uh-huh, I'll second that," J.B. whispered hoarsely from beside her. His lean, almost gaunt face was set in an expression of intense discomfort, broken only by the out-of-focus set of his eyes. His bony hand reached for the wire-rimmed spectacles he kept securely in his jacket pocket during jumps. Placing them on the bridge of his nose, he blinked as his still clouded eyes adjusted to consciousness. Where Mildred carried a generous covering of flesh on her frame, J.B. was wiry and thin, belying his strength and stamina. Known as the Armorer, J.B. had met Ryan when they traveled together as sec men for the Trader, the legendary figure who was foremost among the breed of traveling merchants who kept alive what little economy and trade could exist, sniffing out caches of predark supplies and using them for barter.

J.B. was an armorer by trade and natural inclination, his fascination and thirst for knowledge on all weapons matched only by his ability to get the best out of even the most neglected and damaged blaster. He rose to his feet, dusting himself down out of habit, even though there was no dust in the static-free atmosphere of the chamber. Bending, he picked his battered fedora from the floor and placed it on his head, not feeling properly dressed until he had done that. He then checked his Tekna knife, the M-4000 and Uzi that were his preferred blasters and trusted companions.

Beside him, Mildred had also risen to her feet and checked her own blaster, the .38-caliber Czech-made ZKR 551 target pistol. Although not the most powerful of the handblasters that had run through the hands of the companions during their time roaming the Deathlands, it suited Mildred perfectly, being the model she had used in her days as an Olympic-grade shooter.

For Mildred was, like Doc Tanner, a relic of the past who should not, by rights, have been alive in the Deathlands. She had spent Christmas of the year 2000 in hospital for routine surgery on a suspected ovarian cyst. While under anesthetic, Mildred had developed complications that saw her vital signs sinking fast with no apparent way to revive her. She was cryogenically frozen until this seemingly minor problem could be solved.

Ironically, it was the act of dying that kept her alive, for while she was frozen the superpowers executed the military and nuclear maneuvers preceded skydark and the resultant nuclear winter that created the landscape of the Deathlands.

When Ryan and his traveling companions stumbled across the facility where her frozen body was stored and managed to successfully revive her, she found herself in an incomprehensibly different world to the one she had left behind.

Unlike Doc—whose body and mind had been prematurely aged and ripped apart as a result of being flung through time—Mildred had kept a grasp on reality and adapted well to the harsh new world. Her medical skills were sometimes blunted by the lack of resources, but she had proved herself invaluable to the band of travelers by her ability to apply her knowledge in even the most exceptional circumstances.

Mildred's first move after clearing her head from the aftereffects of the jump was to join Ryan and Krysty over Doc's slumped body.

"You know that one day this is going to be once too often for the old fool," she commented as she thumbed back Doc's flickering eyelid to get a better look at his wildly rolling eye. She felt his sweat-plastered forehead. "Not too much of a temperature, though," she said, almost to herself. Rummaging in the pockets of her jacket, she produced a battered stethoscope that had been salvaged from the ruined medical bay of a previous redoubt. She opened Doc's shirt, roaming the end of the stethoscope across his chest until she picked up his heart rate. It was fluttering and irregular, but even as she listened it began to settle into a more regular rhythm.

"Hell, I think the old buzzard might even last this one out," she said to the others, a smile flickering at the corners of her mouth.

"Mebbe he'll even outlive Jak—well, at this rate it seems likely," Dean commented wryly as he glanced over his shoulder to where Jak Lauren had risen to his knees before retching and puking a thin string of bile onto the chamber floor.

Jak looked tiny swathed in his multipatched camou jacket, and cut a pathetic figure as he coughed and spit out the last of the vomit, spasms jolting his body. But this impression was belied by the fact that the teenager—an albino from the swamps of the bayou whose pale face was covered in the scars of innumerable battles—was a born hunter and fighter, his slight frame almost entirely consisting of wiry muscle stretched over his skeleton.

Despite the vast reserves of strength that he held within his wiry frame, Jak was the member of the group who was hit hardest by the mat-trans jumps, always taking the longest to recover, his senses reeling and his body racked by pain.

"Right now be glad see Doc last longer." Jak coughed in between gulping down breaths of air, his red eyes beginning to focus on the rest of the group. "Feel like already long chilled," he added with a rare grin.

As Jak pulled himself to his feet, and Dean and Mildred helped a dazed and confused Doc to his feet,

Ryan, J.B. and Krysty moved across to the chamber door. This particular chamber had teal-blue armaglass walls; most of the chambers they had encountered, whatever the color of the armaglass, had been opaque. And although that was a good thing because it meant that they couldn't be observed from the outside, it also meant that exiting from each chamber and into the redoubt was fraught with the possibility of being open to an attack they couldn't predict.

Ryan paused by the door and looked at Krysty. Her Titian mane was flowing free, not curling close to her head.

"Feels good to me, lover," she said simply.

Ryan spared her a smile, his single eye sparkling. "Mebbe I'd gathered that," he replied, indicating her free-flowing tresses.

"So take it yellow but still alert?" the Armorer interjected. It was a question, as Ryan was the undisputed leader—there had to be one in any group if they were to survive—but J.B. was as experienced as his old friend, and just needed the one-eyed warrior to confirm what he suspected he was thinking.

Ryan nodded. "Check the others. Are we ready?"

He looked over the rest of his people. Dean was now alert and ready for action, while Doc was recovering rapidly, attended by Mildred.

The younger Cawdor nodded assent at his readiness. Mildred muttered a swift yes before looking at Doc, who also nodded assent, leaning heavily on his lion's-head sword stick but looking stronger with each passing second. Already he had the unwieldy but effective LeMat pistol sitting easily against the heel of his hand.

That just left Jak. The albino was resilient and strong, and he had already moved over to where Ryan, Krysty and J.B. were poised by the chamber door, his .357 Magnum Colt Python already in his hand.

"Ready," he said shortly.

Ryan nodded and reached out for the handle on the interior of the door. It was a simple handle, seemingly too simple a lock mechanism for something that would seal a doorway against the outside world while matter transfer took place within.

Ryan's muscles tensed perceptibly in the fraction of a second it took for the door to swing open, his easy stance replaced by a steeled spring that took him into the anteroom outside. J.B. swung into position behind him, his Uzi up and ready, covering his friend.

Ryan took in his surroundings with one swift circular glance, years of training in the art of survival meaning that every detail of the area was imprinted on his sole retina.

The comp control room was deserted, with the remaining comp consoles covered in a thin layer of dust despite the gentle hum of the air-conditioning, suggesting that the plant that cleaned the air was at least still partly working.

Ryan rolled, clutching the Steyr by stock and barrel, shielding it from harm with his body as he came up on his feet, hunkered behind one of the consoles that provided scant cover.

He looked around. The area outside the chamber was lifeless and empty, and it seemed apparent that there was little, if any, life in this part of the redoubt. It was an impression gained from the slight buildup of dust and dirt by the sec door leading to the corridor beyond.

"Safe down here," Ryan called, rising and noting in passing that the light on top of the sec camera that stood in the top left corner of the arena was dead, "and we can't be seen by anyone."

Relaxed but with a residue of tension that never left them, the rest of the group exited the mat-trans chamber and dispersed into the comp control room. Dean and Krysty, who both had gained an interest in old tech, went over to the still blinking console that controlled the mat-trans chamber.

"Any idea where we landed?" Krysty murmured to Dean.

The youth shook his head. "We need some kind of direction indicator, mebbe a map with it. I guess it's down to J.B. and the stars."

The Armorer expressed his acknowledgment of Dean's comment with a twitch of the lips that may have been a smile or a grimace. It was true that often the only way they knew what part of the Deathlands they had landed in was when the Armorer was able to get outside the redoubt to take a reading on his minisextant from the sky above. It was ironic that, with all the old tech around them, it was something so simple and ancient was the most reliable location finder.

It also amused the J.B. for the simple reason that, before they could get the reading, they would have to reach the surface. And that, as they all knew from past experience, wasn't a foregone conclusion by any means.

"May I suggest, my dear Ryan, that if the redoubt is in all probability empty, then we try to make a rapid if secured progress and ascertain if there are any supplies to be salvaged?"

"Why don't you just say let's look to see if we can sleep and eat?" Mildred added.

Ryan suppressed a good-humored smile. The opportunity to relax enough to make jokes was rare, and if the atmosphere could be maintained by circumstances, then it would benefit them all to rest and eat before taking up their guard once more and taking a look at the outside. And there was only one way to do that.

"Okay, people," the one-eyed man said, "let's take a look outside. Once we get the door open, then it's triple red. Let's keep it tight until we know what we're dealing with."

In many ways it was unnecessary for Ryan to say this, as they had stayed alive for so long by following their instincts and taking such actions as a matter of course; but by saying it, Ryan helped focus himself and his companions on the task ahead.

Forming up as Ryan punched in the sec code to open the automatic door, Krysty was next in line behind the one-eyed man. Jak came next, with Doc sandwiched between the albino and Dean. Mildred fell into line ahead of J.B., the Armorer bringing up the rear. All seven were silent, their senses tuning into the stillness and quiet around as they psyched themselves up to spot the slightest change. All stood easily, yet the observant eye could see that each had shifted his or her balance in such a way that everyone was poised for the optimum reaction.

The door hissed slightly as the mechanism opened, leading onto the corridor beyond.

From their long experience, they knew that the vast majority of redoubts that housed mat-trans chambers were built on the same basic plan, which put them on one of the lower levels. Many redoubts were buried underground, running sometimes hundreds of feet deep. Sometimes, the entrances could be found built into the sides of mountains or hills, or cut into the sides of valleys, so that they were sheltered but still at ground level. The armory and general sec supplies and barrack facilities were on the higher levels, with a quicker access to the entrances, while the middle levels usually housed sleeping and recreational facilities, including the mess halls and kitchens.

All levels were accessed by the corridors, each of which was equipped with a series of sec doors that could seal off sections when required. The levels themselves were accessed by a series of large elevators, some of which were designed for large numbers of personnel, and some of which could take equipment and smaller vehicles. A series of stairwells served as an emergency backup for possible power or circuit failure on the elevators. These stairwells were accessed by sec doors, and were of bare concrete and sparsely lit. The elevators had sec risks for the companions, but from bitter experience they were all aware that the stairwells were traps from which there was less chance of escape.

So they would always choose the elevators if possible. Thus it was that Ryan led his people toward the elevator. All his senses and instincts were telling him that the redoubt was deserted. There was no sign of life anywhere on this level, and indeed it seemed that the level had seen no activity since skydark. And experience told him that, if the redoubt was in any way occupied, sheer curiosity and the search for jack and loot to trade would have led the occupants down to this level.

The companions were relaxed but still alert as they reached the end of the corridor and the dulled metal doors that closed over the elevator shaft.

Ryan studied the electronic panel. ''Looks like it's still working,'' he muttered. ''Let's see....''

The one-eyed man tapped the call button, and the friends stood in complete silence, listening intently for the gentle purr of the mechanism as it approached.

''Sounds like the shaft's unaffected,'' J.B. mused.

The elevator reached their level, a muted shuddering announcing its halt. As the doors opened smoothly onto the empty car, Jak said, ''Mebbe luck change...for once.''

Chapter Two

With a muted hiss, the doors of the elevator opened onto the next level. Ryan and J.B. were poised with blasters ready, their companions ready to move to defensive positions and return fire. Their conditioned stance was met with an almost mocking silence. The corridor ahead of them was as deserted as the one they had just left.

Both Ryan and the Armorer relaxed, the one-eyed warrior turning to the others as he did so.

"Looks like this one has never been breached," he said. "Guess we should take a look around and see if they left anything behind before they evacuated."

"If we're lucky," Mildred added, "there should be food and medical supplies."

"Hot pipe, more self-heats," Dean commented. The tinned units of food that had been standard military issue were usually somewhat tasteless, but they did have the advantage of staying edible for a long time, were easy to transport and had the extra advantage their name suggested of being able to be heated in the pack at any time due to the self-heat mechanism they contained.

Which didn't stop them being a last-ditch emergency.

"Never mind, young Dean," Doc commented as he strode out into the corridor, stretching limbs cramped and weary from the jump. "Perhaps we can find some other comestibles in the kitchen areas that can be used for a more, ah, passable repast before we avail ourselves of the showers—always assuming that the water supply is still constant and the heating works in this relic of the past."

"You're something of a relic yourself, you old buzzard, so watch what you're dismissing," Mildred cut in. "Besides, why do you always talk so much?"

"Just because we live in times of darkness and despair, my dear Doctor, there is no need for us to stop exercising our intellect and imagination—as I'm sure you are too well aware, if you can desist from the desire to extract humor from me at every opportunity…" His tone was harsh, but there was a twinkle in his still clear eyes.

"Let's stop arguing with each other and just get to business," Ryan suggested.

"Yeah. Could use sleep," Jak commented.

The Armorer nodded. "And I'd like to check out the armory as soon as possible. If they left this place more or less intact…" He let his words trail off, but the implication was obvious. If the facilities on this level were as complete as its desertion would suggest, then there was a chance that the armory would also have been left in a fully stocked condition. Not only would this give them all a chance to replenish ammo stocks and perhaps pick new weapons, but it would also satisfy his desire to examine another fully-stocked predark arms dump.

"But first things first," Krysty remarked, pulling off her fur coat, which was proving stifling in the temperature-regulated atmosphere. "Shower, food, sleep."

"Go to it," Ryan replied, indicating that she should take the lead now that they were as sure as was possible of the redoubt's safety.

While Krysty headed for the showers, Mildred made her way to the medical bay. As the only member of the group with pre-dark medical training, she was always keen to loot as many drugs, dressings and medical supplies as possible from a still stocked redoubt, filling the capacious pockets of her jacket with as much as it was possible for her to carry. Many of the drugs had been vacuum sealed with the intention of lasting for a long duration underground, and if she was able to find undamaged stocks of drugs, then it was a bonus that could prove invaluable in the outside world.

Leaving Krysty to some privacy in the showers, Jak, Dean and Doc made their way to the kitchens to see what they could find. Jak detoured to check out the dorms, his mind fixed on some much needed rest, and a deep sleep untroubled by the need to stay on the alert.

J.B. hung back to speak to Ryan.

"This looks good. Food, showers, beds and no intruders."

"Yeah. A bit too fireblasted good."

"You thinking what I am?" the Armorer queried.

Ryan nodded. "You find a redoubt this good, chances are that's because no one can get in."

"So what do you reckon it'll be? The upper levels are trashed in some way and impassable—"

"Or the outside is too hostile to support any life."

"Or has blocked us in," the Armorer finished.

Ryan twitched a half smile. "There's always another jump if we can't get out. Mebbe enough here to let us stay and rest up a few days before."

The Armorer assented. "We're okay for now. You go see Krysty. I'll see if Millie needs any help."

"That's only because you don't want to venture near the kitchens if Dean and Doc are in action," Ryan said wryly.

J.B. didn't answer, only remarking after a pause, "I'll resist the urge to go straight to the armory," before heading off to the medical bay.

Ryan watched his longtime friend disappear around the bend in the corridor before shaking his head and allowing himself a smile.

"NEED A HAND?"

Mildred stopped rummaging through the cupboard. "You could get the rest of these things open and see if there's anything worth saving," she replied.

J.B. moved across the large bay, past the row of couches that were designed for those who needed to be laid out while being treated, and joined Mildred at the far side of the room. He opened the cupboard door. "Looks like you hit the jackpot," he noted, casting an eye over the medical supplies within.

Mildred agreed and enlisted his help to empty the cupboards onto the couches, so that she could more easily survey the cupboard's contents. It took them several trips to empty the array of cupboards.

J.B. stood back and let Mildred take the lead. He knew a little about medical supplies from his time with Trader. The old man had insisted that all his people know the rudiments of first aid, and there had also been a thriving trade in the few medical supplies and drugs that could be salvaged and used for barter and trade. But Mildred was the expert.

Her plaits swinging around her face, masking her expression as she muttered to herself, Mildred sifted through the vacuum packs of drugs and dressings. Some would be of little use on the outside, and those that were for minor ailments, such as the inoculations against the flu virus, were dismissed. People had to be hardier, and there was too little space for those drugs that couldn't be termed lifesaving. Besides, many of the smaller bugs and viruses from predark times had mutated into something that could no longer be combated by the old drug.

The medicated dressings were always useful, and Mildred had to decide which to take on the matter of size: were they easy to stash in her jacket? Would they be too small to be of any practical use? Taking all the larger ones was no answer, as once the seal was broken they were rendered useless and no longer sterile, so it would all too easy to waste so much.

J.B. waited patiently while Mildred made her choices and placed them carefully in the pockets and bags sewn into the coat, turning it from just a protective garment into a walking repository.

When she had finished, Mildred looked up at the silent Armorer. "Guess this'll be you tomorrow when you're in the armory, right?"

J.B. nodded. "Different thing, same purpose," he said simply.

RYAN DECIDED to shower before eating. Like J.B., he couldn't face the thought of Dean and Doc in the kitchens before relaxing with a hot shower—assuming that the water-heating system was still operative.

The one-eyed warrior made his way to the shower rooms, noting the sound of running water as he drew near. It was unlikely that Krysty would be showering under a cold stream, so he felt assured that the heating system was fine.

Entering the communal area where Krysty's clothes lay discarded, Ryan picked a towel from the pile that was stacked in an open cupboard space. He shook it vigorously, and a fine rain of dust was released into the air. It was an indication of the gradual failure of the air-conditioning, but was nowhere near enough for any of them to worry about.

"Come on in, lover, the water's fine," Krysty called from in the shower.

"How did you know it's me?" Ryan replied, as

he left the towel on the bench that ran around the walls and began to strip off his clothing, putting his blasters down first and unstrapping the panga from its sheath along his thigh.

"Who else would it be?" Krysty replied with a laugh in her voice.

"That's a fair point," Ryan answered as he stepped into the showers. A long stall with several showerheads supplying the hot water, some of them were partially stoppered with scale and so spluttered intermittently, while the majority sent streams of almost scalding water onto the one-eyed warrior's leathery skin. He shuddered involuntarily as the pinpoint needles of hot water hit his aching muscles, releasing the tension within them. Steam swathed their bodies as he moved closer to Krysty.

"Feels good to get the sweat and dirt off, doesn't it?" she said, her mass of Titian hair plastered to her scalp by the running water, her strongly muscled but still shapely frame glistening with the wet.

"Feels better to get the tightness out of my muscles and feel them relax," Ryan replied, turning his face into the jet stream of one showerhead and feeling it run down his face, his good eye closed against it, the water pounding a tattoo on his eyelid. "We need this now and again. Need this respite, this chance to relax and rest up."

"Need it for a lot of things," Krysty whispered, moving closer to him.

Ryan opened his eye and found himself looking

directly into Krysty's green eyes, opening directly into her inner being.

Ryan Cawdor was a man of action, a practical man not given to flights of fancy, but he knew that Krysty's mutie genes gave her abilities that were beyond everyday comprehension. One of the things Ryan had read in the fragments of old texts that he was sometimes lucky enough to find was something about eyes being "windows to the soul." It was a notion mostly too fanciful for the bleak realities of the Deathlands.

But looking at Krysty, Ryan could believe that it was sometimes so, and that she could somehow see into him—whether he wanted her to or not.

And right then he wanted her to.

JAK HAD CHECKED the dorms and found an array of beds and also a supply of fresh clothing, untouched since before the nukecaust. Satisfied that they could all rest comfortably and refresh some items of clothing, he made his way back to the kitchens, his guts grumbling, reminding him that it was too long since he had last eaten.

The four corners of the kitchens—large enough and well enough supplied to feed a full complement of personnel for an indefinite period in the event of a nukecaust—had been scoured. There was a plentiful supply of self-heats and bottled water, which would be plundered by all the companions in order to carry emergency supplies with them on a trek into the unknown. There were also other foodstuffs which, if not perishable, had a shelf life that would see them stale. Unwilling to use any of the self-heats, which were barely palatable, Doc and Dean had tried to concoct something edible from what was available to them. Neither was a particularly good cook, but between them they hoped to pull together a meal that would be both nourishing and, at least in some degree, palatable.

Despite the fact that the meal was a bizarre stew of vacuum-packed rice, frozen vegetables of indeterminate origin and a meat substitute made presentable by a liberal use of spices and seasoning, it was good enough to keep the rest of the party happy. Even Jak, who had a propensity to complain about any food that came his way, was able to enjoy the meal.

With the medical supplies sorted by Mildred, and the self-heats and water sorted by Dean and Doc, it just left the armory to be dealt with.

"I'd like to get a look right now," J.B. said, stretching, "but I figure it'd be better if I showered and slept first."

Mildred looked at the Armorer in amazement. "John, I never thought I'd hear you say that. Maybe I should look at you in a professional capacity."

"That what you call it?" Jak commented.

At that they parted company. Jak, Dean and Doc took showers and slept. Mildred and J.B. cleaned up before locating their own private room. Ryan and Krysty had already located theirs, and took the rare opportunity to make love before sleep engulfed them.

IT WAS MORNING when they all awoke. Although the redoubts were artificially lit and could change from day to night at the flick of a switch, the companions had their wrist chrons to help them keep track of time in the outside world. They knew it was midmorning by the time they had risen and breakfasted on the remains of the edible food left from the night before. After finishing, they made their way to the armory.

"Need plas-ex more than anything else except spare ammo for the blasters," J.B. commented as he punched in the sec code for the door, which opened with a purr. "But if we find any blasters that are more powerful and mebbe in better condition than ours, we should load up on what we can carry."

As the door opened and the extent of the armory became clear, the normally taciturn Armorer pursed his lips and blew out a low whistle.

"Bet this hasn't seen the light of day for a century," he said with a touch of genuine awe in his voice as he almost crept into the room, surveying the boxes of oiled rifles, the machine blasters still cased in their constituent parts, the handblasters that hung on the walls alongside the rows of grens and the boxes of plas-ex that were stored in one corner.

Ryan stepped into the room behind him. "I know you could spend days looking over this, but I reckon that mebbe we should get up top as soon as possible, see if we can get out and find out where the fire-blasted hell we've landed up this time."

J.B., snapped out of his reverie by his friend's

words, nodded. "Yep, reckon so. Let's get loaded up here…"

While the companions searched the armory for spare ammo to fit their respective blasters, J.B. restocked the body belts and pouches in which he carried enough grens and plas-ex to start and finish a small war, which sometimes he'd had to do.

Ryan allowed him some time to pore over the weapons after the others had finished restocking their own supplies of ammo. Although there was a plentiful supply and variety of blasters, there was nothing that hadn't been seen before, and they each individually elected to stick with the weapons they knew and trusted.

The one-eyed warrior gave J.B. extra time not just because he knew the Armorer was like a kid in a prenuke candy store with a fully stocked armory, but also because it gave J.B. time to asses the full range of the armory and pick out the weaponry with the maximum possible efficiency and use.

Eventually, he finished his task and turned to Ryan Cawdor.

"Okay, let's see where we are," he said simply.

Chapter Three

The sec door leading onto the outside creaked and groaned as it began to open.

"Think it'll make it?" Dean asked his father.

Ryan shrugged. "Should do. The corridors haven't been twisted enough to warp the frame. Mebbe some plas-ex if it gets stuck?" The last was directed, as a question, at J.B.

The Armorer paused, squinting at the slowly rising door and at the surrounding tunnel. Ryan was right to a certain extent. After leaving the armory and making their way up to the top level, they had stopped and looked at each level. It seemed that there had been some earth movement within the redoubt, but not enough to cause any collapse in the tunneling, nor to cause any breaches or rifts within the redoubt. But right up at the top level, it seemed as though something had pushed against the entrance, causing the door to warp slightly, and making its ascent difficult. It wasn't from the inside.

"Plas-ex could be tricky," J.B. said at length. "There's nothing inside, so mebbe the problem is on the outside. And if we've got a real heavy rockfall, then the blast could get directed inward."

Ryan listened to J.B., trusting his judgment on the

use of any weapons, and nodded as the Armorer concluded. "Okay, we'll see how far it rises first."

There was a tense silence among the companions, relieved only by the glimpse of daylight that pierced needlelike through the widening gap, casting a swath of light across the mouth of the tunnel that was blinding in comparison to the muted electric light inside the redoubt.

"No rockfall," Jak murmured, "so why door stick?"

"That is a thorny question, my dear Jak," Doc replied. "A multitude of possibilities await, and yet how can we be prepared for any unless we prepare for all?"

"Hot pipe, Doc, you talk some real shit sometimes," Dean muttered, standing beside the older man.

Doc smiled ironically. "A trifle crudely put, young Dean, but you do have a point."

"Well, I'd say we're about to find out just exactly what that problem may be—out of all the myriad of possibilities, of course," Krysty interjected with a touch of sarcasm.

"One thing for sure, it was no rockfall," Mildred added, taking in the panorama before them.

The door of the redoubt was now fully retracted. Before them was nothing more than an azure-blue sky, with little sign of any chem clouds within the area framed by the portal. A couple of large, dark birds circled at a height that would appear to have

been several hundred feet, indulging in a complex
series of maneuvers that presaged a savage battle.

The sun was a burning orange globe surrounded
by a haze that betrayed the fact that, although there
were no chem clouds in sight, the atmosphere was
still tainted by the remnants of the nukecaust. The
swirling, skeetering figures of the large birds flew
across the globe, lost momentarily in the light, far
too bright to stare into. In less than the blink of an
eye they were out the other side, and the ritual dance
had ended.

The bird at the front turned, whirling suddenly in
the air in a tight movement that swung him around
to face the oncoming assailant. But his attempt to
catch the following bird was doomed. The second
bird ducked beneath the first bird as it turned, moving
underneath, then jabbing swiftly and sharply, its beak
tearing at the momentarily exposed belly of the leading bird.

The squawk of surprise and pain, harsh and gut-
tural with an undertone of fear, carried across the still
morning air, reaching them as the first bird began to
fall, the slightest darkness in the sky betraying a rain
of blood as something vital was torn.

The fight was that swift, that sudden, that savage.
As the first bird fell, the second bird wheeled in the
sky with an almost deceptive leisure, heading for its
falling opponent. It swooped beneath the plummeting
bird, jabbing at it so savagely that it changed the
course of its fall. It followed it down, slowing the
momentum of the fall by pushing it from side to side,

sometimes jabbing so savagely and with such force that it propelled the now chilled bird upward for the slightest moment. The corpse, which had given one last harsh cry, was now disintegrating as it fell, ripped apart by the attack of its rival.

"Welcome back to the real world," Mildred murmured.

Ryan walked to the lip of the tunnel and peered over the edge. The tunnels and corridors on the top level of a redoubt always sloped upward, but suddenly he realized that the angle of ascent had been slightly more than usual. Looking out over the land, he could see that it was a bare desert, with very little scrub cover, and the reddish-brown earth dry and loose. It was also some fifty feet below them, with a rock face that fell away from the mouth of the tunnel.

J.B. joined him, pushing his spectacles up the bridge of his nose as he looked down.

"So it was a rockfall, but not how either of us reckoned," he observed.

The one-eyed warrior assented. "Looks like this redoubt was another one set into a mountainside, and when some of that mountain moved—" he gestured to emphasize his point "—the redoubt moved up, and the road in moved down."

"Still, it's not much of a climb. Even Doc should be able to make it."

"Please do not mock me, John Barrymore," Doc said, eyebrow raised as he peered over the Armorer's shoulder. "It would seem to be a simple descent."

"Probably, Doc, but we don't know how safe it is

yet. If the rocks have settled loosely, then…'' Ryan gestured how the rocks would part.

"Then we are buzzard fodder,'' Doc finished. "A fair point.''

"Exactly.'' Ryan turned to the others. "We'll take it one at a time. I'll go first, then Krysty, Jak, Mildred, Dean, and Doc. J.B. last.''

"Sounds fine to me,'' Mildred stated, staring down at the steep slope of loose rocks. "Sooner I get down the better.''

"Then let's get to it,'' Ryan stated.

The one-eyed warrior stepped off the lip of the redoubt entrance and onto the rocks, pressing hard with the ball of his foot to test the security of each rock before resting his weight.

He turned and faced the rocks, using his hands to steady himself. The slope was deceptive. Although the descent seemed steep, the slope of the rocks was less sheer, the outcrops providing plenty in the way of foot- and handholds. The problems arose from the fact that the rock face was composed of many individual rocks rather than one slab. And until the descent had been made, there was no way of knowing how secure were the actual rocks.

Ryan took the descent slowly, searching for handholds and testing each rock. His feet stamped rocks, knocking some away from the face, landing firmly on others and using them to define a path. He was watched intently from above by the others, all of them making a note of the path for when they would come to use it. This was made easier by the falling rocks that had been rejected as footholds, which almost outlined Ryan's route.

It was slow but not difficult, and Ryan's progress was relatively easy. Despite that, he had to stop several times to wipe the sweat from his brow before it ran into his good eye, the occasional drop stinging his eyeball and making him blink furiously. He felt a sheen of sweat on his body, soaking into his clothes, and wondered how hot it would get at the height of the day.

THE DESERT SEEMED to stretch indefinitely in every direction, and although they had good water supplies Ryan would feel happier when J.B. had taken some readings and worked out roughly where they were. They knew the characteristics of the Deathlands better than most trading parties, having traversed great distances with the help of the mat-trans units.

If it was going to be this hot, then they would need to preserve water and work out the direction in which a ville or some kind of vegetation would be likely.

All of this crossed Ryan's mind while the greater part of his attention was focused on his feet and hands. Any attack from around them—natural or otherwise—didn't bother him as he knew J.B. would be on triple red while he was so exposed. Neither did he notice how far he had reached, so it was a pleasant surprise when one foot, groping for a rock, hit dirt.

Ryan stood at the bottom of the rock face, looking up at the path he had created. Krysty had already begun her descent, following his trail. She was swifter, having only to follow the path rather than create it. She set foot on the bottom and turned to the one-eyed warrior.

"So far, so good, lover," she said simply. Ryan nodded, watching Jak begin his descent. The rest of the companions followed in rapid succession. J.B. immediately took readings with his minisextant.

"So?" the one-eyed warrior asked.

"Some old stamping ground," J.B. said, squinting at the sun. "Not quite what they used to call New Mexico, but near enough. Kind of near to where they had that old fort—the Almo?"

"The Alamo," Mildred corrected. "Then we're in what used to be Texas."

"Yeah, which I guess means it's gonna get hotter," J.B. rejoined.

"So we need to find some shelter, and soon," Ryan stated. "But where? That's the big question."

Chapter Four

Ryan had felt that they were in a no-win situation as they set out away from the remains of the hillside where the entrance to the redoubt had been situated. It was likely that their explorations would turn up nothing of interest, yet their boundless curiosity compelled the companions to investigate the area around the redoubts they jumped to.

Ryan consulted the Armorer about their position.

"We face the hill, it's east. Away from it's west. The rest is easy enough to guess."

So, with a rough bearing and nothing in view of the horizon, the one-eyed warrior had to decide which way to lead his people.

"Jak, you know the old New Mexico better than all of us, and I guess that's the nearest point we've traveled before. Much chance of us hitting hospitable land within a few days?"

The albino shrugged. "Depend where are now."

"And we really don't want to be out in this any longer than need be," Krysty added, voicing all their thoughts as she gazed up toward the burning sun. Already, just standing in the glare, they were beginning to sweat valuable salt and water.

"My dear Ryan, I know that this is a far different

land from the one in which I was raised," Doc began, "but I feel that perhaps yourself and the inestimable John Barrymore perhaps underestimate your own knowledge of the land. After all, you did spend a fair proportion of your youth traversing its length and breadth with Trader, did you not?"

J.B. shook his head. "Trader went where the jack was, which meant villes, right? These areas…"

"But surely," Doc persisted, "you must have traveled across such areas in order to reach the areas of population?"

Ryan shook his head, sucking his breath through his teeth. "I appreciate what you're saying, Doc, but J.B.'s right. Trader used to say that every stretch of land that was empty was another tank of gas wasted. He used other traders' mistakes, things he picked up in bars, to find ways to scout around areas like this and pick up jack and trade along the way."

Dean's brow furrowed. "Yeah, but if he knew to avoid the areas, he had to know where they were, so he must have had some kind of map."

J.B. smiled. It looked foreign on his usually implacable countenance. "Trader kept most things in his head. Made him more valuable to anyone alive than dead. The biggest jack of all is knowing, he said to me once. I didn't understand then, but now…"

"All of which gets us nowhere," Mildred said. "Look, Dean's got a point. Did you ever trade in these areas?"

Ryan and J.B. thought long and hard. Finally, the one-eyed warrior spoke. "Yeah, I see what you mean. J.B., can you give me a rough idea of how many miles to where Jak's old place is?"

The Armorer shrugged and took out his minisextant. Using the position of the sun, time of day and his knowledge of prior readings in other places, J.B. calculated that the ranch Jak had briefly called home, before his wife and daughter were brutally slain and he rejoined the group, was some six days away in a southwesterly direction.

Ryan greeted the knowledge with a grunt. He squinted his single piercing blue eye to the horizon in a southeastern direction.

"I remember Trader taking us somewhere over there. I also remember, from what he said, that this is a fireblasted big desert we've landed in…but I figure we should hit a group of villes about three days away. There are some old blacktops that still run through parts of here, as well. If we hit one of those, we might hit an old gas station for shelter at night."

"It's our best option," J.B. commented.

Mildred fixed him with a stare. "John, it's our only option," she said steadily.

"'Fraid so," Ryan said. "Either that or risk another jump."

Jak shook his head. "Not want do that soon. Rather fry."

But there was no way he could have anticipated the intense heat of the day.

It was the perpetual dilemma of traveling across scorched earth. Did they try to keep up a rapid pace, hoping that their water would see them through as they lost more water from exertion, or did they keep to a slower pace, and hope that they could fend off sunstroke at the height of the day?

And then there were the nights... Desert nights could kill. They chilled to the bone and caused hypothermia to set in and take effect long before the morning sun could warm frozen flesh. In many ways, the nights were more dangerous, more insidious. During the days, temporary shelters could be constructed, any scrub used to give some kind of shade during rest periods. At first the cool of evening would be welcome, lulling the unsuspecting into a false sense of security before the bitter cold took hold. The scrub was even more vital at these times, as a source of firewood.

But there was little scrub and little chance to shelter. The chem-scoured and rad-blasted skies above them afforded no respite from the burning ultraviolet of the sun, and the deep freeze of the moon. Time began to lose meaning as there were no landmarks along the way, no visual relief from the unrelenting monotony of the desert, spreading all around in brownish, red dust that soaked up the rays of the sun and beat them back out. The heat burned the soles of their feet even through their heavy boots, radiating through the heavy clothes they used to cover the ground when they rested in whatever shade they could find or manufacture from their surroundings.

J.B. had taken regular readings to try to keep them on track. It would have been too easy to end up wandering in circles in a place where there were few landmarks. They kept heading in the direction they had chosen, but by the time they reached the remains of the road even Ryan began to wonder if somehow they had wandered off track and would end up frying in the desert dirt.

Doc was the worst hit. His time-trawl-ravaged body needed water at regular intervals, intervals that began to grow shorter with even greater regularity. He began to lean heavily on the lion's-head swordstick that also doubled as a cane, and Dean hung back to aid him.

"Don't worry, Doc, it'll soon be better," he said at one point.

Doc's answer chilled him. He fixed him with a blank-eyed stare and said, "Jolyon, you've come back to me at last. How is my dear Emily? And Rachel? Is my hell finally over?"

Dean didn't know what to say, but his eye met Mildred's, and he could see that the woman was concerned about the way that Doc was deteriorating.

In ordinary circumstances, the water supplies they had taken from the redoubt would have lasted them more than a week. But here, the sun was hotter, the lack of cloud cover and the way in which the baking earth absorbed then released the heat made the journey almost intolerable. Even when they stopped and tried to raise some kind of rudimentary shelter, it was almost impossible to escape the heat. All the companions were sweating out more water and salt than they could afford to lose, and when the cold night drew in they huddled around the small fires they could build and filled up on the self-heats. As most of these were soup- or stew-based foods, they supplied some more water for the dehydrated bodies, as well as supplementing the salt tablets that Mildred had plundered from the medical stores.

So the road, when it came, was met with a sense of elation—although all were too hot and exhausted to express this in any other way than a massed sigh of relief, shot through with the uneasy knowledge that even though they had reached the road Ryan had gambled upon, there was still the dilemma of choosing which way to follow the cracked blacktop.

The shimmering surface of the road, the aged macadam almost melting in the intense heat, was visible from a few hundred yards away, and the companions exchanged glances as they, as one, noted the landmark for which they had been searching. They were too exhausted to speak until they had tramped the last few yards to the edge of the road, where they drew to a halt.

"Why don't I feel excited that we're actually here?" Krysty said in a hoarse, cracked voice. Her sweat-plastered red hair clung to her head, the long ends clinging like tendrils to her neck and shoulders. Her fine skin was covered with a layer of dust, and her lips—as cracked as her voice—betrayed her attempts to conserve the rapidly shrinking water supply.

"Because this is still only the beginning," Ryan replied in a voice that had been reduced by thirst to a dry whisper. "First we work out which way to go, and then we hope we hit some kind of old wag stop, or mebbe a ville if we're lucky.''

"I think we've got a better chance of a wag stop," Mildred commented. "Who the hell could keep a ville going out here?" she added, turning her head slowly, sun-blasted muscles aching, to survey the long blank stretch of the road in each direction.

"Mebbe just over the horizon." Dean shrugged, following Mildred's stare.

J.B. said nothing. He took out his minisextant and took a reading to confirm their position, then extrapolated it to an overall direction for the road.

"I'd say that we head due west from here, following the road," he said in a voice made drier than his usual tones by the heat and attempts to save his water. "I'd reckon that going east just leads us back."

Ryan assented. "If I remember right, then there were some villes headed that way. We should rest up a few minutes, mebbe take some water and a salt tablet, then head that way," he said softly, lifting his arm to indicate a westerly direction. Even lifting his arm made the muscles ache, the buildup of lactic acid unable to dissipate with his dehydrated state. His skin was burning, but covering up made him sweat too much, losing more fluid and salt. Like all of them, he was trying to balance perspiration with the dangers of sunburn and sunstroke.

But it was Jak who was having the greatest problem. As an albino, he had no pigment in his skin to combat the harsh rays of the sun, and his face was almost scarlet, the scars that crisscrossed his countenance standing out lividly. His arms were red and raw, and the amount of sun he was absorbing was making him susceptible to sunstroke, and he was swaying dangerously as they stood still.

Mildred had some sunblock originally designed for desert maneuvers by the predark military that she had taken from the redoubt, and she offered one of the tubes to Jak.

"Not doing good," he said in a distant voice as he took the tube from her.

"It's all there is," Mildred replied. She watched as he applied some of the cream to his raw skin. They had all used the block, but she had saved extra for Jak, only too aware of the problems he was left open to by his albino condition.

Ryan noted the concern in her voice. "How much of that do we have left?" he asked.

Mildred shrugged. "Not enough. Maybe two, three days' worth. It's like the water and the self-heats. This damn sun is making us use more than we could have estimated."

Ryan nodded but said nothing. It was a cause for some concern that all their supplies, taken from a rich source, were being used far too fast. He squinted his good eye and took a long, hard look down the road in the direction in which they would travel. The horizon shimmered, but even in the haze there was little sign of even a hallucination that could be construed as shelter.

"Okay. Let's just see...."

THEY SPENT the rest of the day making slow, agonizing progress along the old blacktop. The surface was too broken and scarred to use. The uneven tarmac could cause a sprained ankle or worse, and the sticky, almost melting surface would slow progress and take too much energy as it dragged and pulled at their aching leg muscles.

The sun, with an almost interminable slowness, gradually sank. Night fell, and the sudden drop in temperature caused them to shiver uncontrollably, making it hard when they stopped to light a fire from the sparse brush, using a flare to ignite the blaze and add a burst of heat. The self-heats were difficult to handle with their spasms, and precious water was spilled.

"We have to try to sleep," Mildred said when they had finished eating. "Try to get as much rest as possible."

"If I sleep, then I fear that I may never wake," Doc said in a sudden burst of lucidity. "If this is life, and nothing more than a waking dream," he added as an afterthought.

"Nightmare, more like," Dean said, his voice betraying a slide into sleep.

"Have to get through this," Ryan said as they huddled together to keep warm and preserve valuable body heat. "There could be a ville just over the horizon."

"Or a wag stop," J.B. added. "Anything…"

THE RISING SUN WOKE them next morning, the lack of atmospheric cover causing the ultraviolet rays to immediately scald them.

"Another day, another adventure," Mildred muttered sarcastically as she stirred beneath her jacket. "I just hope that we find something today...." She let the sentence drift, not wanting to add that they didn't have the water and salt—even as carefully rationed as they dared—to last much beyond.

They began the slow march to the west, trudging heavily along the side of the road. The sun beat down steadily and with an ever growing intensity, and after a few hours it was all any of them could do to keep their heads up. Ryan took the point, J.B. the rear, and they straggled out into a line with Dean propping up Doc in the middle, while Krysty and Jak followed close to the one-eyed warrior, with Mildred staying at the rear with the Armorer.

They couldn't bear to look up in the glare of the sun, and their aching neck muscles couldn't support them in their attempt to stare ahead, so it was the sound that came to them first, floating across the empty air and breaking the intense concentration that enabled them to keep one foot going in front of the other.

It was Jak, with his heightened senses that made him such a keen hunter, who heard it first. Despite his fatigue, he snapped his head upright, red eyes burning brighter than the bloated orb above them.

"People."

Ryan stopped, the line closing behind him as they banded together, coming to a halt. Jak's statement, and Ryan's sudden halt, instantly broke them from their own personal reveries. They all listened intently, staring as they did so into the shimmering haze that became more indistinct as it approached the horizon.

There was no mistaking the sound. Voices—at least four men, maybe more. And the sounds of hammering and some kind of work activity.

Under the intense light, it was harder to make out the view, but there seemed to be some kind of building moving in and out of the edges of the haze, standing at the side of the old blacktop. It was too indistinct to see, but it seemed to be obvious that this was where the sounds emanated.

"A wag stop, and people," Ryan husked, his voice almost destroyed by the dry heat.

"I don't believe it, even though I see it," Mildred said, even the husky and croaking tone of her voice failing to hide her elation.

"Let's get to it," Dean said, "before we can't make it."

J.B. was, as ever, the voice of caution. "Don't know that they're friendly, though," he pointed out.

Ryan nodded. "Good point. Triple red, but try not to let it show. We'll be a shock for them, coming out of nowhere… No need to spook them more by looking ready for a firefight." He coughed as he finished the speech, his voice almost wasted by the amount of words he had to use.

He indicated that they move rather than speak, and as the companions moved forward they all checked their blasters and brought them to hand. The instincts that had kept them alive for so long enabled them to smoothly bring their favored blasters to hand and chamber shells in case they should need to fire on the human beings ahead—the first they had seen for days, the ones who could save them if they had water and food, and the ones who could give them shelter...if they were friendly. And there was no guarantee of that in the Deathlands. No, not at all.

The last thousand yards would be the hardest.

IT WAS A SMALL cinder-built blockhouse, the adjunct to an old truck stop that had long since perished. The raised floor and foundations were all that remained, and it was on these remains that the men had their camp while they worked on the blockhouse. The roof had been removed and an upper story added. It was made of old sheets of corrugated iron, insulated against the sun by loose sheets of an aluminum foil, which deflected the blazing sun from the iron, which would otherwise trap and magnify the intensity of its heat. The roof had been replaced on top of this, its sloping tiles giving the appearance that with one chem storm they could slide off at a bizarre angle.

It was to this problem that the work party was now addressing itself. To one side of the blockhouse lay an abandoned site that marked an extension to the existing building, while the eight-strong work party was either on the roof itself, or was swarming up and down the three ladders that stood at the sides of the building unattached to the new extension.

There were four more men: three were sec men, heavily built and wearing broad-brimmed hats to protect them from the worst ravages of the heat. They stood at points that covered the area surrounding the building. All held blasters, muzzles pointing down. Two had Heckler & Koch G-12 caseless rifles, while the third was carrying an Uzi. All weapons were in fairly good condition.

The fourth man stood out among the others. Standing at somewhere around six-four or six-five, he was sparsely clad, with a loose cotton shirt open to the waist, loose cotton pants that ended around his shins and leather thonged sandals. He was slim, with the loose clothing hiding most of his body, but the open shirt revealed a tightly muscled chest and stomach. He had long, raven-black hair that fell in a single thick plait almost to his waist, the plait shot through with threads of silver-gray that betrayed the encroaching middle age of its owner. On his head was perched a black stovepipe hat with a few oily feathers from a desert buzzard attached to the crown. The brim shaded his eyes, throwing them into shadow, and making the aquiline sweep of his nose and the thin, impassive set of his lips the only clues to his mood. He had walnut-brown skin, tanned and textured like supple leather, and his coloring betrayed his ancient Native American roots.

Yet despite all this, the most striking thing about him was that he carried no blaster. Even the eight-man team swarming over the roof had handblasters holstered and attached to their clothing. But this man, standing as still and silent as a ghost in the burning desert air, carried only a long-bladed knife of his own making, with a finely honed blade and an intricately carved handle that appeared to be of bone.

The sec man covering the area to the east turned and hollered across the space between himself and the silent giant.

''Yo! Crow, y'all ain't gonna believe this, but there's a whole bunch of people walkin' out of the desert.''

The giant said nothing, but the shout led to hilarity from the men working on the roof.

''Shee-it, you been chasing them desert mushrooms again, Petey?'' yelled a thickset, heavily scarred man with sandy hair thinning on his scalp, not pausing in his task of rapidly resetting the thick asphalt tiles as he spoke.

''Shut up, Hal,'' the sec man countered. ''Just take a look-see.''

The sandy-haired man stopped momentarily and looked up. Squinting into the desert haze, he could make out the straggling line of the companions as they approached slowly.

''Well, I take it all back, Petey,'' he said. ''Where in hell did they all come from?'' He looked down to where the impassive giant stood. ''Hey, Crow, y'all hear that? And they got blasters out,'' he added.

There was a pause—not long enough to denote that the giant was ignoring the exchange, but long enough to impose his sense of authority. Something that was emphasized by the manner of his reply.

"I heard. They'll all be exhausted. Must've walked for days, no matter which way they come. And they don't know if we're friendly folk. They'll be too exhausted to be a threat."

His voice was quiet and low, almost a rumbling whisper that carried across the hot desert air despite the almost inaudible volume.

It was a voice that commanded respect.

"What you wantin' me to do about them?" Petey asked.

The giant spoke again without turning. "Let them come. Keep your blaster ready but down, like theirs."

"How the hell you know that?" Petey asked, looking back at the approaching line to double-check.

There was the ghost of a shrug from the giant, but his voice was still impassive. "'Cause we're as suspicious of them as they are of us. Stands to reason. We don't spook them, they'll be fine."

"'Kay, you're the boss," Petey said, turning back to them.

"Sure am—and you boys on the roof remember," the giant continued, indicating by tone alone that he had noted the way in which the work crew had stopped in order to watch the approaching line.

The hardness in his tone made them start work with alacrity.

"THEY GOING TO BE a problem?" J.B. whispered, his voice barely audible.

"Looks like they're wary rather than hostile," Ryan called over his shoulder.

"Let's hope it stays that way," Krysty added. "I don't think any of us are up to a firefight right now."

"I'll second that," Mildred commented.

Ryan continued on, his people following, until he was a few hundred yards from the waiting sec man. Noting that the large and muscular sec man had his blaster held across his chest but with the barrel pointing down, Ryan took one hand from his Steyr and waved slowly and carefully. He called out in a hoarse and cracked voice that barely carried across the space between them.

"Hey! We've been in the desert for three days. We don't want a firefight, just a little water and direction to the nearest ville...." His voice petered out into a cough, the sheer number of words too much for his damaged and dry throat.

"Okay," the sec man replied, his voice strong and clear across the distance. "Y'all just put those blasters down and leave them before you come any farther, and we'll be just fine."

Ryan stopped his people and held ground at the distance. Coughing heavily and hawking a dry phlegm ball that made it hard to speak, he croaked, "'Fraid we can't do that, friend. I appreciate you don't want strangers coming on you with blasters out, but we can't just leave ourselves defenseless."

The sec man didn't reply at first. The one-eyed man's refusal, albeit in a nonthreatening manner, left him nonplussed. Ryan took note of the work party's leadership order by the way in which the sec man looked toward the tall, dark figure who had been standing all the while with his back to them.

The giant turned slowly and took in the companions with a long, slow gaze. Despite the distance, and despite the fact that the giant's eyes were ostensibly hidden by the shade cast from the brim of his hat, Ryan felt his eye and those of the giant meet. He felt that he was being assessed and hadn't been found wanting.

The giant spoke to both the sec man and the companions, and the quiet voice carried across the still desert air.

"It's okay, Petey. You people can keep your blasters, just holster them and don't move too fast. The sec boys here can be a mite jumpy."

Ryan paused for a second, then assented. "Okay, we'll do that," he said simply, swinging the Steyr across his shoulder. Behind him, the rest of the companions holstered their blasters. Ryan waited until they had all complied, then turned back. "Okay to come on now?" he asked.

The giant nodded. It was the slightest of movements, but against the stillness of his stance was an almost shocking movement. "I appreciate your caution," he added cryptically.

As they began to move the last hundred yards to the cinder-block house, the workers on and around the roof stopped to watch. Sensing that they wouldn't work properly until their curiosity was satisfied,

Crow called a halt to their work and the beginning of a rest break.

The men had all descended and were in the shade of a camp built to one side of the newly begun extension, the tentlike structure forming a shelter from the blazing sun. They were drinking water from large drums that had been insulated to keep them cool.

Crow strode away from the men and toward the oncoming group. His stride was lengthy, his gait loping with an easy animal grace. Ryan noted that the man carried no blaster, but was sure from the look of him that he would be no easy competition.

The giant Native American held out his hand to Ryan.

"They call me Crow, and I'm the foreman here. You screw with me and I'll chill you before you know what's happened. But you treat me and my boys with respect, and we'll help you if we can."

Ryan took the proffered hand, noting the strong but easy grip. In his weakened condition, Crow could easily have ground his knuckles to dust, but he didn't take the advantage. Ryan immediately felt sure that he could trust the man not to chill them out of hand. But he also knew that the Native American would take any precaution necessary to defend his position.

"Name's Ryan," the one-eyed warrior returned in a painful whisper, then naming all his party.

Crow introduced his party by name. Apart from Petey, the other sec men were Coburn and Bronson. Turning to where the work party were gathered, he pointed out the others as Hal, Ed, Mikey, Molloy,

Tilson, Rysh, Hay and Emerson. To the tired and dehydrated Ryan, the members of the work party were hard to distinguish from one another. They were all muscular, scarred and tanned. They all looked like men who had built muscle from hard work and could more than hold their own in hand-to-hand combat. He also noted that they all had blasters on their hips.

In their current condition, his people would stand no chance if they really were in any danger...and despite the fact that he trusted Crow not to chill them, there was something that niggled at him.

"So how come you people end up out here in the middle of nowhere, looking like buzzard food?" the bronzed giant asked.

"Damn wag we traded for jack and food back in New Mexico," J.B. said before Ryan had a chance to answer. "Tank was rigged so that they could fool us on the gas, and the engine bearings were shot to shit 'cause the oil was full of crap. Had to leave the bastard thing or die with it."

Ryan smiled inwardly at the sudden outburst from the taciturn Armorer. It was a good cover story, as all of them knew the importance of keeping the mat-trans system as secret as possible. His own cover story would have been similar, but he was surprised at the sudden acting talent shown by his old friend.

Crow settled a level gaze on J.B., trying to assess his story.

"Seems to me that mebbe you're not that stupe," he said finally, "cause y'all seem too battle-wise to be taken in that easily. On the other hand, I guess we all get screwed over sometimes. So where were you headed?''

"Anywhere," Ryan answered. "We don't belong to any particular ville, and I guess we're just looking for somewhere. We were headed in this direction when we got stranded, so I figured that we'd just keep going. There was nothing for several days back, so we just kept going forward. Bastard of a place to get stranded.''

Crow nodded slowly. "Uh-huh. Just unlikely to see anyone coming out of that desert alive. There are old stories from way back beyond skydark about that place among my people. Travelers don't come back.''

"Mebbe we just got lucky," Ryan said evenly.

Crow nodded again. "Mebbe. And mebbe the best thing you can do right now is get some salt and water into your bodies, mebbe some rest.''

Ryan assented. "If you don't take offence, we'll take our rest in shifts. You can never be too careful, right?'' And he fixed the giant with his piercing blue eye.

Crow returned the stare evenly. "I can see that. Join the others and eat. Take water. We have a supply delivered from Salvation every two days.''

"Salvation?''

"The ville we come from.'' With which he led them toward the sheltered area where the workers were drinking and eating from a pot of some indistinct stew that bubbled over a small heater. "Please, partake with us," he said, indicating the food and water, and also deflecting any further inquiries about Salvation.

The companions took dishes from a small table, and also plastic cups that were beaten but well scrubbed, despite the dust that seemed to drift into the shelter from the air outside. They took food from the pot and water from the insulated tank.

"Water running low," Jak remarked to Crow as he scooped a cupful. "You sure this okay?"

"Delivery's due," the Native American answered simply.

Jak nodded and joined the others as they sat and ate between mouthfuls of water that tasted sweeter and more intoxicating than any brew that they may ever encounter.

"I fear first watch may be beyond me," Doc said weakly. "In point of fact, I have a notion that I may not even reach the end of my meal."

"It's okay, Doc, I'll cover you," Dean said.

"I don't think any of us are up to it," Ryan husked, his throat raw despite the soothing coolness of the water. "But anyway, I'll take first."

"I'll go second," J.B. put in.

"Play it by ear from there," Mildred added, addressing Ryan. "I don't know if you could really plan a watch right now, as some of us may be more heat affected than others."

Ryan agreed, casting a glance at Jak, who was beginning to fade into semiconsciousness even as he tried to eat and drink.

"Reckon as you're right," he said. But even as he spoke, he became aware of a leaden feel in his limbs that hadn't been there before—a numbness that was beginning to spread. His speech had been slurred, which it hadn't been before, despite his fatigue.

He looked at Krysty, but the Titian-haired beauty was already beginning to fall into the same state as Jak. Changing the direction of his gaze, which in itself seemed to drag, as though he were moving in heavy, deep water, he could see that Doc had slumped into unconsciousness.

"Dark night," he heard J.B. curse. Slowly, like dragging himself through molten lead—an impression heightened by the burning fatigue in his limbs— he looked to the Armorer.

J.B. had noticed Jak slide into unconsciousness and Dean begin to shake his head slowly, as though trying to clear it. The boy tried to rise to his feet, but slumped forward as his legs failed him.

"Tranks...in the...in the water...or the food..." Mildred stammered, her plaits shaking in futile motion as she tried to clear her head.

"Fireblast, Crow," Ryan cursed. "Why did you lie?"

The giant Native American shrugged. "Got the boys to slip something into what was left of the water. Couldn't take any chances. You'd do the same," he added.

Ryan knew the foreman was right, and he was more angry at himself than at the giant. He should have known this would happen. The only excuse he could give to himself was that his acute sense of danger, and his survival instincts, had been dulled by the dehydration and the effects of the sun.

But that would be no consolation if they were chilled.

Ryan managed to stagger to his feet. From the corner of his rapidly blurring vision he could see the workmen going for the blasters they had holstered, but they were stayed by the subtlest of hand gestures from their foreman.

"Leave him," Crow said softly. "He has every right to be pissed. But he's no danger to us now."

The words became strung out and distorted as the drug took effect. Ryan swayed on his feet, trying to reach for his SIG-Sauer. Every movement seemed to take an eternity, and his numbed hand failed to respond, even though his arm did move, albeit at an incredibly slow rate. He could see J.B. fumble with his Uzi, falling forward to the ground before the blaster was fully in his hands.

The world narrowed and darkened around Ryan. The one thing that cut through his befuddled mind was why they hadn't just been chilled there and then? What did Crow intend for them?

As the blackness descended, even that question became an irrelevancy that drifted into the void.

Chapter Five

The pounding in his head made J.B. open his eyes. He knew that the light pouring in would hurt like the darkest night, but he figured that if he could see who the rad-blasted hell was pounding his skull he could at least fight back against them.

The outside world was a blur as he squinted and gradually opened his eyes, but at least he was soon reassured of the fact that he wasn't under attack. There were two shapes in front of him that stood out from the light around—one was stocky and light, the other tall, thin and dark. Neither was in an attacking position, as both were several feet away from him.

The Armorer furrowed his brow in concentration as he tried to recall what had happened. Everything was clear up until the time that they had been fed and watered by the workers they had stumbled upon. After that, there was only drowsiness, the insanity of the nightmares that troubled him and the thumping at the forefront of his skull.

J.B. groaned, and not only from the pain. It suddenly occurred to him that all of them had fallen for the oldest trick going. While low and in need of water and salt, unable to really focus or concentrate, they had been disarmed by the apparent friendliness of the workers and hadn't questioned the willingness of the party to share valuable water.

But why weren't they chilled?

His speculations were halted by Crow's low yet penetrating voice.

"Is that a groan because you're hurting, or because you were duped?"

The Armorer groped instinctively in his breast pocket for his spectacles and registered surprise that they had been carefully placed—obviously with some thought—where he usually kept them when they weren't being worn.

As he pushed them up the bridge of his nose, he noticed that Crow was smiling, almost to himself.

"Better now you can see? You're the first to come around, so I guess you didn't drink as much as the others. And I wouldn't try that yet, either," the foreman added as J.B. tried to raise himself to his feet, finding that he hadn't recovered enough equilibrium to do more than make the covered shelter spin dizzyingly around his head. J.B. slunk to the floor again.

"I guess I should mention now that we stripped you of all your weapons when you were unconscious," Crow continued, "just in case you get a little angry when you try and check for them. Left you all the medical supplies, though. I'd love to know where you got them, but I guess you'll tell us if you want. You're certainly a mysterious group, and if you thought I bought that story about the wag, then you didn't reckon much to me—"

"Why not? I'd believe it," J.B. interjected, tacitly acknowledging his lie.

Crow laughed, a deep, rumbling sound. "Sure, you would. So would some of these boys. But they— and you—weren't bought up on the legends of this area before skydark."

J.B. gestured his acknowledgment, then asked, "So why aren't we chilled? That'd be the obvious thing."

"If that was the idea, then I tell you, my friend, that you wouldn't have got within a hundred yards of this site. I would've let the sec boys cut you down afore you had the chance to raise your blasters. And let's face it, you were in no shape."

"Okay," J.B. said, rubbing his aching forehead and looking at the ground intently as he tried to focus his spinning vision. "So what do you want from us?"

Crow shrugged. "Don't want anything from you, really. I meant what I said. I don't want to have to chill you, and I guess if I'm honest I didn't like having to trick you. But you've got to understand that I know jackshit about you, and I couldn't let you walk around with all that hardware. And let's face it, there was no way on this or any other world that you were ever going to give them up without a struggle. By the by, my friend, I take it from the amount of ammo, plas-ex, grens and blaster power that we took from you that you're the dude who keeps this outfit in working order when it comes to the hardware?"

J.B. nodded. "You could say that."

"Then you're a talented man, my friend, and I'd sure as shit hate to be on the opposite side to you in a war. I take it that the one-eyed dude is your leader?"

"Kind of. We don't call him that, and he doesn't call him that, but it amounts to the same thing."

"Then I guess you're a formidable outfit, and I'd sure as hell hate you to take against us just because I was kind of cautious. I'd be grateful if you'd explain that to him when he comes around."

"Why don't you do that?"

"'Cause I've got work to do. That's why we're here. I'll be back later, but in the meantime my friend Petey here will be just outside, and the kind of jack he's on to do a good job, then he may be just a little trigger-happy if you do something rash. We've got a lot to do, and not a lot of time, so the bonuses are good and we can't afford interference."

"Just what is it that you are doing here?" the Armorer asked as Crow turned to leave.

The foreman didn't pause, just said, "I ain't going to waste breath. I'll be back here when the day's work is done, and when you're all in a fit state to listen. Use the food and water," he added, gesturing to the barrel and table in the corner of the shelter. "That ain't drugged, take my word...there's no need for it, now."

J.B. watched him go, followed by Petey, who stopped just beyond the last sheet of material covering the shelter. The Armorer then turned his gaze to his still unconscious companions.

It was going to be a long day.

RYAN WAS THE FIRST of the others to come to, and the one-eyed warrior experienced much the same symptoms as the Armorer.

"Fireblast, what the rad-blasted hell hit me?" he complained, raising his head and opening his eye to be greeted by his old friend standing over him.

"A heavy-duty trank," the Armorer replied without humor, "and a hell of a shock if you look for any weapons." He went on to explain the situation as quickly and concisely as possible, before Ryan had the chance to check for his blasters or his trusty panga and the red mist of fury descended.

"Guess we'll just have to trust what he says," Ryan mused when J.B. had finished telling his tale. "I knew there was something about him that set me on edge, even though most of my instincts said to go with him."

"Figure you were right in the long run," the Armorer said. "I can see his point."

"Yeah, and just mebbe I would have done the same thing," Ryan added.

The two friends and longtime traveling companions decided that there was nothing to do but sit back and wait to see what happened when the day's work was done and Crow returned to them. In the meantime, they had to wait for the rest of their party to awaken.

The amount of time it took for the others to come around depended on their individual physical condition and how much of the water they had drunk.

They were all extremely fit, even Doc. Despite the ravages of his enforced time travels, which had made his late-thirties frame seem several decades older, Doc was still extremely fit. There was no way he would have survived if not. His mind was another matter, and how it would react to this shock, when he had already been delirious from the desert trek, was something that they had to ponder. Also, he had been the most dehydrated, and Mildred had made sure that he had drunk a larger amount of the water than any of the other companions.

Jak was next to awake, and he reacted to the drug and the enforced sleep in much the same way as he did to a mat-trans jump, by vomiting heavily. But he recovered his strength, and was aided by Mildred, who came around next and was able to feed him a solution from one of the packs taken from the medical bay at the redoubt which quelled his stomach spasms.

Krysty surfaced and showed her strength by gracefully uncoiling from her sleeping position and rising in a fluid movement, standing upright and still while her balance and equilibrium settled.

Dean took some time, as he had drunk copiously, and Doc wasn't far behind. But while Dean was fine, Doc was another matter. Mildred crouched over the prone old man as he began to regain consciousness, muttering and twitching as though in the throes of a fit. His eyes stared blankly from his head, and he failed to respond to any stimulus.

"Is there anything that we can do?" Ryan asked Mildred.

She looked up and shook her head, the grim set of her face showing her concern. "Not that I can think of. Trouble is, I just don't know what's going on up here," she said, tapping her head to indicate Doc's mind. "Whatever else, it's just more shit for him to deal with."

Mildred and Krysty made Doc as comfortable as possible, and while the others paced the confines of the shelter, careful not to attract the attention of the sec man outside but feeling confined like caged animals, Doc responded to the cold compresses applied to his fevered brow and the sedative injection Mildred gave him. It was one of the few sealed needles that Mildred had salvaged from the medical bay, and as she was usually loath to use such items, she wasn't surprised at the quizzical look Krysty gave her when she broke the seal on the packet.

"I know, I know. I'm not that keen, either," she said in answer to the unspoken question, "but I don't know what else to do. The trank has unbalanced him even more than the desert, and this is so mild that it should just keep him under long enough to get more rest. There's not a lot else that could work," she added, shrugging.

And sometimes desperate measures could be the most effective, for after a couple more hours of deeper rest, Doc suddenly opened his eyes and said in a clear, firm voice, "I feel as if I have been asleep for a thousand years, and have awakened to the strangest feeling that I have said that, or something akin to it, quite recently." He raised himself on one elbow. "Now, would it be possible for someone to tell me what on earth is going on, and how we got to be here, for I have to confess that I have not the slightest idea of where, or indeed how."

The relief Ryan felt at Doc's recovery was shown by the smile that flickered at the corners of his mouth as he replied, "We can fill you in part of the way, Doc, but for some of it we'll just have to wait and see."

"Until when?"

Ryan looked out of the shelter and at the darkening sky as twilight closed in on the old wag stop.

"Not long, Doc. Not long at all."

THE WORKERS CONTINUED to labor until the light was almost gone and the temperature had dropped from the blistering heat of the day to the bone-numbing cold of night. Petey had come into the shelter, cradling his H&K, and lit a number of oil lamps that were suspended from the poles that also held up the protective sheeting.

"How long do you usually work?" Ryan asked the sec man.

Petey shrugged, keeping a wary eye on the group but showing no great hostility. "Depends on the light, but it's more or less around this time. We get about fourteen hours of work a day."

Dean whistled. "That's pretty intensive."

"Eh?" The sec man paused, staring at the boy.

"I mean it's a lot of time and doesn't give you much chance to rest," Dean explained.

Petey shrugged again. "Sooner we get done, sooner we get paid, and the more jack we get. Baron Silas is generous if you play straight and work hard. Mean-eyed fucker if you don't."

"Baron Silas who?" J.B. asked disingenuously.

"You don't catch me out that easily," the sec man said with a wry grin. "Crow'll let you know all you need when he comes in. And that won't be too long, so you just be patient," he added, leaving them alone.

The sec man's assumption was correct. It was less than half an hour before Crow led the workforce into the shelter.

"Glad to see you're all awake and well. I'd guess that the enforced rest may even have done some good after your long journey," he directed at them before turning to his own men.

"Bronson, you, Rysh and Hal are on sec duty tonight."

The three men took food and water from the supplies for the sec men who remained on guard duty, taking them their meal before settling to their own. While they did this, the remaining workers took their own meal, discussing with one another the day's work and their individual performances. The companions, listening to them, all noted that the main topic of conversation was getting the work finished and collecting the large bonus for a quick finish; the men were graphic about the manner in which they would spend the bonus in a gaudy house, casting glances at Krysty and Mildred as they did so.

The two women were the last people to be worried and shocked by such talk, which was obviously the intention, and Ryan noted that Crow was watching their reaction. The foreman did nothing to halt such talk, although he was silent and impassive as he took his meal. The one-eyed warrior guessed that the foreman said nothing as he wanted to test both the resiliency of the women, and the ability of their male companions to keep their peace. A swift glance at his team showed Ryan that they wouldn't be found wanting.

The tone of the conversation continued when Hal, Rysh and Bronson returned from their task and also began to eat. It continued until Crow had finished his repast, at which point he decided that enough was enough.

"I hope," he said, his quiet and deep voice cutting through the talk and silencing the others despite its lack of volume, and directing his comments at the companions, "that you have also partaken of our food and water?"

Ryan assented. "We appreciate you sharing your supplies with us. And I can appreciate why you did what you did. I figure that mebbe I can trust you people not to chill us—otherwise you would have done it already. What I'm wondering now is what you want from us, and who you are and where you come from. Oh yeah, and why you're working out here in the middle of nowhere on an old wag stop."

Crow allowed a rare touch of emotion—a barely contained humor—to creep into his tone. "Sure there's nothing else?"

"Not yet," the one-eyed warrior countered.

"Okay, let's take it from the top," Crow began. "We all come from a ville called Salvation, which lies about three days from here along the remains of the old road. Salvation is run by Baron Silas Hunter, who's the man who pays our jack."

"Good jack, by the sound of it," J.B. interjected.

"Certainly is, especially if we finish on schedule or ahead."

"Finish what?"

"This way station. There are a number of old wag stops along this route that date back to beyond sky-dark, and our job—and the job of other teams like ours—is to get the way stations ready for when the well is open again. 'Cause Salvation is built around the remains of an old oil well, and the refinery that went along with it. Baron Silas's folks have always been around these parts, and they've spent a long, long time trying to get the well and refinery going."

"And he has?" Ryan asked. When Crow affirmed this, Ryan whistled. "Fresh oil, refined—that's big jack. How did he manage to get the thing going?"

"Baron Silas has a deal going with the barons of all the villes in this region. They've bankrolled him in return for a share in the fuel he produces. That's real power. And they need stops along the road to pick up and rest up on their way to and from the well. So here we are. Most of us working here are from Salvation. That's not so on other stops. Guess you could say part of the payment is in manpower."

All Ryan's people exchanged looks. Like anyone in the Deathlands, they knew how important fuel for wags would be. There were few vehicles left, and those that had survived were always short of fuel. To have such a source would give whoever possessed it, or formed an alliance, immense power.

"So where do we come into it?" Ryan asked finally.

"You don't as such," Crow replied. "You just happened to walk in. You can either walk away and take your chances, or you can join us and work. If we get this finished all the quicker because of you, then I guess we can spare a little jack. Plus you get your weapons back and mebbe the chance to see Salvation."

"Mebbe?"

Crow shrugged. "Where you go after we finish is up to you. What do you say?"

Ryan considered the options. The desert offered nothing but chilling. They couldn't get their weapons back from the workers by force, as they were unarmed and outnumbered, and just mebbe there would be something of use to them in Salvation. Baron Silas Hunter sounded as though he could be interesting.

"Tell you what," the one-eyed warrior said eventually, "you take us to Salvation when we finish this job and give us back our weapons, and we'll gladly work our way. Hard work is no problem, but that desert is a bastard."

Crow nodded. "I figured you'd see it that way."

Chapter Six

The work party rose with the sun, and at first light the next morning they began to stir under the covers that protected them from both the sun and the chilling night. Crow was one of the first to awake, as though snapped awake by the first glimmerings of the day.

The giant rose to his feet and looked at the sprawled figures around, huddled under blankets or coats. He noted that Krysty and Ryan were sleeping close together, and likewise J.B. and Mildred. He then glanced over his still slumbering workers and remembered the comments of the night before. Although it didn't show on his impassive visage, he figured that he would have to watch closely for any trouble, as it was almost certain to arise.

The foreman began to stir his workforce awake, and after he was sure they were rising for the day's work, he turned to the companions.

"I see you're already awake," he said generally, as they were all rising.

"My dear sir, although you are as silent as a spirit walking, the combined noise of any amount of people within such an enclosed space would make further slumber an impossibility."

"Don't mind Doc," Dean added, "he never likes to use one word where a hundred could be."

The Native American allowed himself the flicker of a smile. "Betrays a good brain," he said. "I just hope he can work as well as he can talk."

"Despite my apparent age, I shall not be found wanting," Doc uttered.

The foreman nodded. "Okay, eat, take some water and join the others outside. You have twenty minutes," he added.

Playing it the way it felt, the companions allowed the workmen to wash themselves down and freshen up before taking their morning meal. It meant hanging around and taking the stares directed at the women, but in their current position it was best to play possum.

"Hey, you think those gaudies gonna get their skin on show when they work?" Hal asked Emerson.

Emerson, whose dark hair was tied back in a ponytail, and whose beard was flecked with gray, studied Mildred and Krysty through hooded eyes.

"Hell, I hope so," he drawled. "Them bein' two colors'll make it look real nice."

He directed his next comment to the men in Ryan's party. "Hey, I bet you boys have some fun, there."

Jak's red eyes pierced through the heavily set workman. "More fun in chilling scum," he said quietly.

The albino teenager was nearly a full foot smaller than the workman, was unarmed and was slight in build compared to the burly Emerson. But still, there was something cold and diamond hard about the youth that made the workman look away without saying anything further.

An uneasy silence hung over the room after the workforce had finished and walked out into the sunlight, leaving the companions alone.

"This isn't going to be easy," Ryan said slowly. "Not easy at all."

WITH THE ROOF NOW securely in place, and the newly finished two-story blockhouse in place, the remaining task was to build the extension onto the existing structure. The new wag stop would then have storage space for fuel, food and water, as well as accommodation for a regular attendant and a few travelers.

The foundation for the extension had been completed, and the task in front of the workforce and the companions was to construct the one-story building and insulate the interior walls of the storage space, in order that any fire in the interior could be contained, and an exterior fire wouldn't be able to penetrate the walls and ignite the fuel stores.

Wags from Salvation had carried out the building materials needed—a salvaged amalgam of brick, cinder block, sheets of metal and some sand and cement that could be mixed with some of the precious water in order to meld the whole together. The insulating materials were salvaged from old buildings, and were carefully wrapped to prevent the asbestos in the mix from spreading dust into the air.

Crow directed the companions to their tasks. Ryan and J.B. were to help lay the cinder-block outer walls, while Dean, Jak and Doc were to assist in the building of the interior walls and the installation of the insulation. Mildred and Krysty were spared the heavier work, and were to mix the concrete. When J.B. asked how Baron Silas Hunter had amassed an amount of something that was simply no longer made, Crow informed him that one of the villes that were investing in the baron's scheme had an old cement works within its boundaries, and the supplies for all the wag stops on the route had been plundered from those bags that hadn't been split or had leaked over the past century, and had so gone hard.

"It was tight, but I reckon as how we've got enough," the foreman said thoughtfully.

"You're an expert?" J.B. asked.

"I make sure I know what's going on if I'm to do my job properly," Crow replied. "I went to the works to assess what there was, and checked up in some old predark building manuals that Baron Silas had acquired.

"He's a thorough man," Crow added simply, but heavy with a hidden threat.

The Native American's putting Mildred and Krysty onto the concrete mixing wasn't a gesture toward their sex, but rather a shrewd move, which Ryan appreciated, to forestall the need for them to shed too many clothes through exertion in the heat.

If they stayed fully clothed and away from the main body of the workers, then there would be less chance of conflict between Ryan's people and Crow's workforce.

But it wasn't to be that easy.

"SAY, BOY, have you learned what it's like to be a man yet?" Rysh asked Dean as they laid the internal brick wall separating the fuel store from the food and water store.

Dean stopped with a brick poised over a line of mortar.

"Just what exactly do you mean?" he asked cautiously. "I've chilled my fair share and traveled a long way."

Rysh shrugged. "Chilling's just a way of life, boy. I mean, have you ever had any pussy?"

Dean blushed despite himself, and felt the eyes of both Rysh and Emerson on him. The heavyset, dark workman pushed the point home.

"Hellfire, Rysh, just look at the boy, blushing hot as a forest fire. He's been there with them."

"And I'll bet they're good—they'd have to be with those five boys to keep happy," Rysh added, winking.

"Dunno about the old guy." Emerson chuckled. "He don't look like he could keep it up enough."

"I know what you're trying to do," Dean said, keeping his voice as even as possible, "but it's not going to work. There's no way that you'll get anything out of Krysty and Mildred, and we sure as hell aren't going to fight you over it.''

"You saying you a virgin, then, boy?'' Emerson goaded.

"That's my business,'' Dean replied shortly. ''But it's not like that with Mildred and Krysty.''

Rysh looked closely at Dean's hand, at how the brick was trembling in the boy's grip. He decided to push it further. ''I reckon as how those gaudies could pull a train for us when we finish the wag stop. What do you think, Emerson?''

The comment fulfilled its purpose. Dean swung around, the brick still in his grasp and following through in a roundhouse punch that would have caved in Rysh's skull at the temple—if the workman hadn't been prepared for the action, and had already moved away from the arc of the blow.

As one man sidestepped, so the other moved in. Emerson ducked underneath and aimed a giant fist at Dean's solar plexus, which had been left exposed by his stance. On anyone else, the movement would have been quick enough to catch the victim in the guts. But Dean Cawdor was quicker than that, and twisted his body in midflight, avoiding the blow and somehow managing to keep his balance.

Doc saw this from the far side of the building's interior, where he and Jak were erecting the metal sheeting walls that would delineate the sleeping quarters. He was facing the scene, while Jak had his back turned—although both had heard the beginnings of the altercation.

"Jak," the old man said in a low, warning voice.

Emerson flailed and fell forward as the momentum of his blow took him past Dean. The boy was having similar problems, however, as the momentum of his initial swing, combined with the effort to avoid Emerson's attack, had left him off balance and open to an attack from Rysh.

The blond workman had a bloodthirsty twinkle in his eye and was smiling savagely as he raised the trowel he had been using for smoothing the mortar Dean laid bricks upon. Dean was falling toward him and was unable to defend himself in time as Rysh drew back his arm to land a blow.

But the smile was wiped from his face and replaced by a surprised and puzzled frown as an iron grip stayed his arm, steel-tight fingers gripping his forearm and making his fingers tingle and go numb as the blood supply was cut off. He turned to find that Jak had hold of him. Despite the fact that the albino stood several inches shorter than the blonde and was looking up at him, he seemed to swell in Rysh's vision and fill the room.

Jak's scarred face was impassive, his eyes glittering hard but saying nothing. For a fraction of a second the two men were still, but before the blonde had a chance to act, he felt rather than saw the heel of Jak's other hand as it drove into his face, angled upward and catching him beneath his nostrils, pushing the flesh and bone of his nose up into his head, the pressure forcing his head backward.

His head snapped back in agony, and he lost his

balance, falling backward and dropping the trowel from bloodless fingers as Jak released his grip.

Dean was still regaining his balance as Emerson swung back toward him. He felt sure he could balance before the big man came for him, but it was unnecessary as Doc stepped forward, clutching a baton that held together the metal sheeting. That was the real use of the long wooden pole, but Doc drove it into the stomach of the workman, the point hitting home and doubling him over, the air driven from his lungs.

"Boys, you know I don't want any of this."

The five men stopped, staring toward what would be the main entrance to the extension, where the impassive Crow stood watching them.

"Just keep working, and we'll all be happy," he said simply before leaving them.

"SHIT, I KNOW THAT this is supposed to be easier, and keep us from having to strip off and inflame the passions of these poor boys, but I really wish they could put some shade over this bastard. And it's so damn loud," Mildred complained as she shoveled another spadeful of sand into the cement mixer. The predark relic was turning erratically, but enough to mix the concrete that was needed for the construction. The ancient generator that powered it was coughing and spluttering, an ancient relic that was among the treasures amassed by Baron Silas to fulfill his ambition.

"I'm not one to complain as a rule," Krysty said

breathlessly as she tipped another bucket of water into the drum of the mixer, "but I think you may just have a point. There is one thing, though."

"What's that?" Mildred said, wiping the sweat from her brow.

"I'd love to know where this baron got all this stuff."

She put the bucket down and joined Mildred at the side of the drum. They both watched the mix blend inside until it acquired a smooth texture that was thick and gloopy.

"Looks done to me," Mildred said.

Krysty shook her head. "I wouldn't know. This is one thing I can truly say I've never had to do before."

Mildred grinned. "I must've spent a good part of my childhood doing this. My father was a great one for what we used to call DIY—do it yourself," she explained, seeing Krysty's puzzled expression. "Back before skydark there were a lot of people who liked to build and improve their homes as a hobby, and my father was one. Lord, the house always seemed to be like a building site."

Krysty shook her head. "You know, sometimes the more I hear, the weirder the world sounds before the nukecaust. It gets too hard to imagine."

"I guess you just had to be there," Mildred said with a tinge of sadness in her tone. "Guess this looks done," she said to change the subject, switching off the mixer and tilting the drum so that the mix spilled out onto a board laid in front of the mixer. The generator calmed down now that it wasn't called on to power the mixer, and as that machine had now fallen silent, a relative calm fell over the site.

Hal came across to them, pushing a small cart with a shovel at the side. He joined the two women in shoveling the concrete onto the cart.

There was a strained silence between them, which Krysty attempted to break.

"How's the work going?" she asked simply.

From the way Hal looked at her, she immediately knew that it was a mistake.

"Going well so far, as long as you don't hold us up by not working quick enough."

"You got any complaint yet?" Mildred countered hotly.

"Not yet, but it's only the first day, right?"

"So what's the problem?" Krysty asked.

Hal stopped shoveling and looked her up and down. "Ladies, you are. 'Cause that's what you is."

"Say what?" asked a puzzled Mildred.

"Ladies...you sure as shit ain't men," he elaborated.

"Well ten out of ten for observation, dumbass," Mildred hissed. "So what the hell does that have to do with anything?"

Hal looked at her in amazement. "Shit, girl, does havin' a pussy make you stupe or somethin'? You ain't gonna be able to keep up the pace, are you? And if you keep mixing slower and slower, it takes longer and longer to get the wag stop built. 'Cause you got the crucial task, right?"

"Yeah, I can see that," Mildred agreed, "but that don't matter shit, does it? We didn't ask for it."

Hal was dismissive. "That don't matter none. We're on good shit bonuses to get this stop built real quick, and we was on target for a real big bonus. Y'see, we's all been out here a long time now, and we ain't had no pussy. That's all there is to think about out here, 'specially when there ain't none. So the thing we all want is to get the hell back and get us some from a gaudy house."

Krysty looked long and hard at Hal. She could feel her hair creep around the base of her neck, but had to push him to find out exactly what he meant. "What's that got to do with us?" she asked.

The man grinned, showing a row of rotten, stained teeth with a couple missing. "Shit, I shoulda thought that was obvious. Gaudies cost big jack. We don't get the jack for it 'cause you don't get the work done, then I figure we got the right to take out what we're owed in trade."

And before either woman had a chance to react, his hand had snaked out to between Mildred's legs, grasping and rubbing at her crotch.

"Jesus fucking shit," she yelled, leaping back more in surprise than shock. Her arm shot out in a straight-arm punch that hit Hal full in the mouth, breaking a few more of his teeth.

Despite the force of the blow, the workman wasn't put off. He was stronger than he looked, and although his head jerked back, it made him tighten his grip, causing a jolt of pain to shoot up Mildred's groin. She yelped in agony and fell to the ground. Hal was on her before she had a chance to react, and she could feel his groin hard against her, his foul breath on her ear.

"Aw, don't play hard to get, babe. I'm real hot, y'know."

"You'd be hotter if you fried in hell, asshole," Krysty yelled at him, driving the silvered tip of her boot into his ribs, the upward thrust of her foot sending him sprawling off of Mildred and into the remains of the cement.

While this occurred, a group of men had run from their stations working on the outside of the building. Ryan and J.B. were in the lead, acutely aware of what could happen if the other workers reached Hal's aid first, and the women were outnumbered.

All were pulled up short by a short burst of Uzi fire. Sitting up and rubbing her aching groin, Mildred saw Petey and Crow walking over to them. The sec man stayed silent and impassive while the foreman spoke.

"Now, cut that out. As long as they're here, they're not women. And definitely not gaudy house sluts. We all work, we all get what we want. The more trouble we have, the more we fall behind. And that would be bad. Right, Petey?"

The sec man looked as uncomfortable as the others at the sudden steel that had entered the Native American's voice. But he still answered, "You call the shots, Crow."

"Believe it," the giant said softly.

Turning to the workers, including Ryan and J.B., he said simply, "Get back to work. Now."

Then, turning to Hal, he spit at the ground by the dazed workman's head. "Fool. Get your ass up and get out of my sight."

Finally, he said to Mildred and Krysty, "Accept my apologies for this idiot. It won't happen again. And until we finish, it hasn't happened. Are we clear?"

Before either woman had the chance to confirm or deny they understood his meaning, he turned and walked away, while Petey helped Hal to his feet and hustled him away, pushing the cart loaded with concrete that had sparked the incident.

"Him I trust," Krysty said, indicating Crow. "But the rest of them?"

And she shuddered with apprehension.

FOR THE REST of their time working on the wag stop, there was a palpable air of tension. It was obvious to the companions that the workmen felt resentment toward them fueled by the manner in which the women had treated Hal when he tried to assault Mildred. For their part, they all kept their simmering resentment under control.

Ryan spoke with them on the evening of the attack, taking them away from the shelter to discuss the matter privately.

"I know what you all want," he said. "In any other position, I'd agree with you. But we haven't got our blasters, and we're outnumbered, while they're still armed.''

''Beat bigger odds before,'' Jak muttered. ''Mebbe best chill, get out.''

''Our albino friend could have a point,'' Doc offered. ''They will be out to get us now.''

''But we have Crow and the sec men on our side,'' Ryan argued. ''And I really feel that getting to Salvation will be good. If we chill them and get out, then we could have the whole of Baron Silas's sec force on our tail. There's too much time and jack invested here for him to let us go if we stall his plans. Besides where would we go?''

''Much as I hate to admit it, the man has a point,'' Mildred said. ''Lord alone knows I should be the first to blow them away, but it wouldn't do us much good.''

Ryan nodded. ''So it's heads down, people. I reckon as we've got a couple of days' work left here, then we get a ride back to Salvation. I figure we can keep it frosty that long.''

''Mebbe,'' J.B. mused. ''As long as they see it that way.''

THE ARMORER'S WORDS of caution were justified, as the next morning would prove.

The companions found themselves ignored, cold-shouldered by the workforce when not actually involved in the act of construction. And when they were working on the extension, they were addressed only if necessary.

And then the accidents happened.

The first was on the outside of the building, where J.B. and Ryan were working on the outer walls. Those were now in place, and using ladders to scale the twenty-five-foot exterior, the workmen from Salvation were placing roof joists and timbers to take the asphalt tiles that would be laid on top. J.B. and Ryan were shifting the timbers from where they had been stored on delivery, carrying the heavy wood across the short distance to where they were handed up the ladders to Mikey and Molloy, who were placing and securing them across the roof space, flinging boards across the gaps between the tops of the interior and exterior walls, running across to place the joists and poles.

The two workmen had been talking to each other, and also to Tilson and Hal, who were also catwalking across the open space. But all had been pointedly ignoring Ryan and J.B.

The one-eyed warrior planted his foot firmly on the first rung of the ladder, shouldering the weight of the joist that J.B. balanced from the rear.

"Okay," the Armorer said, affirming that he had the joist steady.

Ryan then began to climb the ladder, swiftly and surely ascending. He gripped the joist with a hooked arm, knowing that J.B. would be lifting the heavy piece of wood by its bottom end and following him up the ladder.

Sweat pouring down his forehead, plastering his dark curls to his forehead and making his good eye sting with salt, Ryan looked up to see the silent Molloy standing on the edge of the wall, ready to take the joist as Ryan and J.B. pushed it upward, taking the weight until Molloy had rebalanced it for positioning on the roof.

Molloy watched Ryan impassively, and the one-eyed warrior wasn't surprised that the workman was making him do the maximum amount with the minimum help. That was in line with their behavior all morning, and it wasn't surprising bearing in mind their attitude to the previous day's events.

"Okay," Ryan grunted, partly as a signal to J.B. that they were to push the joist upward, and partly to let Molloy know it was coming.

As the heavy piece of wood was propelled upward, Ryan felt some of the weight taken by the workman, and the passage of the joist became smoother.

Both the Armorer and Ryan began to descend the ladder as the joist left their grasp. At the bottom, J.B. paused for his friend.

"I'll be glad when they've got them all in place. Guess we drew the short straw in this one."

Ryan grinned wryly. "Is that any surprise?" Then he noticed that the flicker of light on J.B.'s spectacles had disappeared.

The one-eyed warrior threw himself backward, rolling in the dust as he hit the ground. Without looking, he knew that J.B. had also noticed the sudden change of light and had acted accordingly, particularly as he heard the Armorer curse as he, too, hit the ground.

But this was drowned by the thud of the joist as it hit the ground at the spot where the two men had been standing a fraction of a second before. The indent it made on the earth revealed that it would have been fatal had it landed directly on the two companions.

"Dark night," J.B. cursed. "What the hell did you think you were doing?" he yelled at Mikey and Malloy as they stood on the lip of the roof, looking down. But even as he uttered the words, he knew they were rhetorical and pointless.

"That's careless," Mikey said to Molloy in bland tones. "They'll have to carry that up again."

INSIDE THE BUILDING, where Emerson and Rysh were still working alongside Doc, Dean and Jak, there were other accidents waiting to happen.

The walls were now in place, and, wearing improvised masks against the dust, Emerson and Dean were insulating the fuel store while the others were fitting shelves and doors.

The rolls of insulation were tied together by nylon cords that were knotted in several places, showing how many times the pieces of old rope had been used and recycled. Emerson had a bowie knife, which he had honed on both edges in order to speed his rate of work, and with it he was slicing through the cords at a rapid rate as they unrolled the insulation rolls. They were old asbestos and fiberglass insulation taken from predark factories, and spilled poisonous dust into the enclosed space.

Dean watched Emerson, distrusting the man with the knife when he was unarmed. Some of the knots on the rope were doubled over, and even with such a finely honed blade the workman was having trouble cutting through the ropes. Dean wondered why Emerson didn't just cut the rope in areas where there were no knots.

It never occurred to him that it was a piece of low cunning.

"Check that roll," Emerson barked, his voice muffled by the mask. Dean started, as it was the first time the workman had spoken to him that day. Emerson glared at Dean and repeated, "Check it—asbestos or fiber?" he yelled.

Dean turned to the roll, thinking nothing of the request. After all, the varying thicknesses of the rolls had been determining their positions on the walls of the room.

But this roll was difficult. It was wrapped in a layer of cotton cloth, suggesting that there was a greater degree of disintegration than on other rolls. Dean bent to examine the roll through a tear in the cotton cloth.

As he lowered his head, he felt a rush of air by his ear and a sound like a stone in water by the side of his head.

"Hot pipe!" he exclaimed, falling to his side. He looked at the roll and saw Emerson's bowie knife embedded into the roll, the shaft still quivering from the force of the impact. He looked at Emerson, who shrugged his shoulders, eyes cold and impassive above the improvised mask.

''Guess it slipped out of my hand on a awkward knot,'' the workman said blandly.

BEYOND THE FUEL STORE, a similar fate was to befall Jak.

In one of the rooms, he and Rysh were putting shelving into what would be the food store. They had screws and bracketing for the shelves, but there was only the one screwdriver between the two of them. The only other screwdriver on site being used by Hay, who was in another room installing doors with the help of Doc.

Rysh pushed a shelf plank toward Jak. ''Pick up some brackets and put it on that wall,'' he snapped.

A gleam of fire showed in the albino's eyes, but he kept calm in the face of provocation and turned to the wall Rysh had indicated. Placing the plank against the wall, he took some brackets from the pile in the middle of the room and sufficient screws from a large earthenware jar.

''Screwdriver,'' he said evenly, indicating his need.

Jak spoke as he turned, and it was only his incredible reflexes that saved him. For Rysh had decided to pass him the screwdriver by the simple expedient of throwing it at him like a knife.

The mutie albino saw the sharply pointed instrument speed across the room, and his hunting and survival instincts took over. For Jak, time seemed to slow almost to a halt as the screwdriver hung in mid-air, his instincts racing fast enough to make the progress of the object in flight seem almost stationary.

Jak's red eyes focused on the screwdriver, and he bought up his left arm, tight to his body and moving at the elbow. The fingers of his left hand opened and splayed, like wraiths of white mist.

To Rysh, it seemed like the screwdriver had vanished from the very air itself as Jak plucked it from its flight, the metal shaft grasped between his second and third fingers, his arm whiplashed downward to dispel the momentum of the flight.

Rysh couldn't help it. His mouth hung open as he gaped at Jak.

"Next time just pass it," Jak said softly, displaying the screwdriver to Rysh as he lifted his arm. Without waiting to see the workman's reaction, Jak turned his back and began to fit the first bracket.

THE PROJECT WAS completed after two and a half days. Crow had instructed the sec man Petey to oversee Krysty and Mildred, in order to keep some distance between the women and the workmen. In addition, he had set them to work on the tidying and clearing of the work sites, which mostly entailed the areas free of the other workers. It had been done without comment, but all the companions could see that the Native American was as good as his word.

As each group finished its tasks, so Mildred and Krysty would move in and clear up the mess. By late afternoon, the workmen were bathing and relaxing while the women put the final touches to the clearing-up process.

"To think they used to protest against this when I was a kid," Mildred said with heavy irony.

"Mebbe we should start again," Krysty returned with a grimace.

But finally they had finished and joined their companions. Crow came over to the group, which had stayed separate from the workforce.

"This is good," he said simply. "We're way ahead of schedule, and the bonuses will be good. I've sent to Salvation and Baron Silas will be sending wags for us tomorrow. He's interested in meeting you."

Ryan and J.B. exchanged glances. "So you've been in contact with Salvation?" Ryan asked.

Crow allowed himself a smile around the eyes, even if the rest of his face stayed impassive. "One of the things Baron Silas has traded with his collaborators is a series of predark two-way radios. They're erratic, like all his machinery right now, but they keep him in touch with all his work parties. And you didn't really think I'd tell you that I had one, did you?"

Ryan shook his head. "Guess you're too smart. So we get to see Salvation tomorrow."

Crow assented. "But first you've got a possible problem. The boys'll want an end-of-work party. We have some brew, and I know for a fact that some of them have jolt, even though they're not supposed to. But they've worked hard, so it's their concern. And yours. There are scores to settle, and I can't guarantee your safety.''

"Then give us back our blasters,'' J.B. said simply.

Crow shook his head. "I can't do that. But I'll be around, and I'll make sure that the sec keep on their guard. Just watch your backs is all.''

Before any of the companions could answer, the giant turned and walked away.

THE WORKMEN WAITED until the sun had fallen before they started the party. The companions left the shelter and set a fire some distance away, figuring that the best course of action would be to give the workmen a wide berth until they had drunk and jolted themselves insensible.

After a couple of hours, the light from the lamps within the workers' shelter was suddenly spread across the desert dust as the sheeting was cast aside.

"Hey, muthafuckers,'' yelled a voice that was unmistakably Hal's, "you gonna come and join us or just be plain unfriendly?''

"A paradoxical statement from those gentlemen, I think,'' Doc murmured.

Hal continued, "You gonna let those lovely ladies come and give us a little pussy to celebrate. Molloy here, he's hung like a mutie horse and he'll make them scream…''

"I wish I had a blaster,'' Dean muttered.

"Leave it,'' his father said softly.

But the companions weren't allowed to leave it.

The light spread farther as the sheeting was parted, broken by the shadows of the workmen as they spilled out onto the desert.

"Trouble," J.B. whispered as the workmen came toward them. The companions rose to greet the potential fight, and weren't to be disappointed. Although the workmen seemed relaxed as they approached, they were clutching bottles. Ryan tensed and knew that as he did, so did all of his people.

The deceptively friendly approach was broken when the parties were only yards apart, as the workmen suddenly sprung into action. There were more of them than there were of the companions, and that was crucial. While the five men took to an opponent one on one, the two women found themselves fighting three workmen. Rysh and Molloy closed in on Mildred and Krysty, and Emerson slipped behind them, forcing them to circle and keep part of their attention behind.

So it was that Rysh was able to catch Mildred a glancing blow on the temple and stun her. Krysty whipped her head around at the sound of Mildred's groan, and in that crucial fraction of a second found herself fall victim to the same tactic.

Rysh and Molloy slung a woman each over their shoulders and headed into the dark, with Emerson covering their backs.

Ryan saw their direction as he dealt with Hay, a short-arm blow finally disabling the armed worker.

Hal whistled, and Ryan's fighters found themselves wrong-footed by the sudden retreat of those they were fighting.

"Millie?" J.B. shouted, whirling around.

"They took them around the back of the extension," Dean cried, his eyes picking out the other workmen disappearing around the corner of the new building.

Without a word, the companions took off after their opponents. Doc lagged somewhat behind, and by the time he had gained the extension, he found the others had searched all the rooms.

"They're not here," Ryan said shortly. "They must have doubled back to the shelter."

"No," Jak snapped. "Trail lead away."

In the dark night, it would seem almost impossible that anyone could pick up a trail, but Jak's finely honed hunting sense had led him to the scent.

They followed him as he set off toward the collection of wags and trailers that contained the construction tools. As they approached, they could hear the sounds of fighting.

Rounding the largest wag, they saw Mildred and Krysty, both still fuzzy but revived by the adrenaline rush of danger, standing back to back. The two women were holding the workers at bay, but it was a losing battle.

Until the cavalry arrived. The battle was short, swift and bloody. Ryan and J.B. were experienced hand-to-hand fighters, and Jak was a white blur of fists and feet. Dean and Doc, although for their own reasons less experienced, had learned from their companions, and the drugged and drunk workmen offered little resistance when taken by surprise.

In a few seconds, the workers were floored, unconscious and battered into submission by the anger and skill of the companions.

"Good."

Ryan whirled to find Crow standing, watching, with the three sec men behind him.

"You watched all this?" the one-eyed warrior asked. When Crow assented, Ryan yelled, "Why did you let us take them alone?"

"If you'd had trouble, then I would have stepped in," the Native American said quietly. "But the fact is, I wanted to see how you'd manage."

"Why?"

"Because Baron Silas asked me to assess you."

"So he could use us if we won? Fireblast, I should chill you where you stand," Ryan spit.

"You won't," Crow answered. "Because you're not armed and we are. And because you're curious. Sure, it'll benefit Baron Silas. But just mebbe you'll get something out of it, too."

Ryan paused, breathing hard and letting his temper settle. Finally, he said, "Yeah, but don't push us too far." With which he turned on his heel and joined his companions in attending to Krysty and Mildred, who were still dazed from the initial assault.

"I wonder how far too far is," the Native American mused quietly to himself.

Chapter Seven

Ryan and his companions had little idea what to expect when the morning came. They had made themselves a camp some distance from the main body of the workforce, and had mounted a watch through the remains of the night in case the workers decided to try to extract revenge. But whether it was a matter of the beaten workers unwilling to continue the fight, or whether it was the efforts of the sec men to keep them apart and Crow keeping his word, there was no further sign of trouble.

When the sun was a dull orange glow low in the sky but already throwing down oppressive heat, the companions were fully ready to face the rigors of the day ahead.

"This should be interesting," Mildred murmured, casting a glance at the activity among the workers as they rose and prepared to leave.

"One way of saying it," J.B. replied. "Think we can trust them, Ryan?"

"We have to—for now," the one-eyed man returned. He was about to speak further when he saw the giant Native American crossing the sand toward them. "Well, let's see what he has to say."

"I would say good-morning, but that may seem

inappropriate," Crow said wryly as he reached them.
"The wag to take us back to Salvation will be arriving in about an hour," he continued, checking his
wrist chron. "It'll also have drivers for the supply
wags."

"You do not trust your workers?" Doc asked with
a raised eyebrow.

"Would you?" Crow returned. "Baron Silas certainly doesn't. Most of these lowlifes would steal
from themselves if they had half the chance. So we
make sure we only use workers who can't drive."

"Anyone can drive," the Armorer interjected cyn-
ically.

"You wouldn't say that if you'd seen one of these
sons of bitches try and steal a wag on the first night
we were here," Crow answered. "That would
change your views. But I didn't come to you to discuss this. Come and eat, take water before we leave.
It's a long, hot journey back."

Krysty glanced over to the camp. "It'll be longer
if we have to see them before the wag gets here,"
she said quietly, her hair curling gently at the ends
around her neck.

"There'll be no need for concern," Crow said.
"These boys know what'll happen if'n they get stupe
about this. They don't want to get chilled before they
get their jack. Mebbe they'll get chilled after, when
they get into a firefight over some gaudy slut, but
that ain't my problem, or yours."

Krysty and Mildred looked at Ryan. He returned
their gaze evenly, and noted from the corner of his

eye that Dean, Jak, Doc and J.B. were also watching him intently. As leader of the group, Ryan knew that they were all uneasy about mixing with the armed workers when they themselves had been stripped of their blasters. He also knew that it would be difficult for Krysty and Mildred to travel easily back to Salvation in the same wag as the men who had wanted to rape them.

But Ryan knew that survival was about playing odds. They needed to get their blasters back, and Crow had told them that Baron Silas Hunter wanted to meet them, possibly with a proposition that would give them both their blasters and some jack. They would also get taken to a ville and out of the inhospitable desert. However hostile Salvation might be, there would be more places to hide, and more places to steal food and water if necessary.

At the end of the rad-blasted day, a few slim chances were better than none at all.

"Okay," Ryan said eventually, "we'll follow you over."

The Native American nodded and turned his back, heading back to the sheltered camp without a backward glance.

The companions extinguished the last embers of their night's fire and gathered their clothing together.

"Not sure 'bout this," Jak said bluntly. "Chilling time."

"Yeah, but not for us," Ryan answered. "I've got a feeling that Crow's under orders from this Baron Silas to treat us like the most precious treasure."

"But why would we be that important? Not that I wish to denigrate our worth in any manner," Doc continued, "but nonetheless, I fail to see why we have suddenly become so precious."

"So do I," Ryan replied. "But if we're worth something, then we stand a better chance there than we do staying out here."

He turned to the women. "It's going to be bastard hard, but we just smile sweetly and chill the fuckers later if necessary, okay?"

Krysty smiled. "If you say so, lover."

"Then let's go, get it over with," Dean added.

So they moved off towards the camp.

CROW WATCHED THEM come across the sand from his position, and turned to his sec men. Petey, Bronson and Coburn had their Uzis in hand, and were positioned across the entrance to the shelter.

"Remember what I said. Baron Silas wants them alive, so if you have to chill every last muthafucker of these scum, then you do it."

"But they're our people," Coburn protested.

Crow fixed the white-haired sec man with a steely glare that seemed to eat through him. "If they don't get back in one piece, then you won't be man enough to call anyone your people."

Coburn winced, recalling the rumors in the sec force about the torturous fates of those who had crossed the baron of Salvation in his single-minded pursuit.

"Exactly," Crow said simply.

THE TIME BETWEEN the arrival of the companions in the tent shelter and the arrival of the wag to take them back to Salvation was tense, and seemed to drag on forever. The workers muttered among themselves, avoiding the subject of the strangers and contenting themselves merely with a few sideways glances at the companions, always aware of the cold eyes of Crow and the Uzis of the sec men who stood facing them. For their part, the companions sat in silence, all straining their ears for the first sign of the wag.

It was Jak who heard it first, his acute sense of hearing much more finely tuned than possibly anyone else's except Crow. "Wag coming," he murmured.

Ryan nodded. "Okay, people, let's keep it triple red while we load up."

It took another five minutes by Ryan's wrist chron before the rumble of the wag on the old blacktop became audible. It started as a distant buzz, then became a fuller, deeper roar as the empty desert became suffused with sound.

The roar of the engine as it pulled into the old wag stop space in front of the cinder-block building made speech impossible, but the attention of everyone in the tent camp was drawn by the click of three Uzis, the higher-frequency sound cutting across the rumble.

The engine cut out, and the silent camp heard two wag doors open and three men get out to exchange small talk.

One of the voices came closer, and the owner of

the lazy drawl pushed his head through the gap in the sheltering material.

"Hey, Crow, y'all ready to rumble?" He cast a curious eye over the companions. "And these are the people the baron wants to see so bad, eh?"

"The answer to both is yes. Now let's go," the Native American answered, rising to his feet and sweeping past the lanky driver.

The workers followed, and as Ryan and his companions rose to join them, they were halted by Bronson, who stopped them with a raised palm, being careful not use his Uzi in a threatening manner.

"No, Crow said as how you were to wait until everything was loaded and the others were already secured."

They sat once more, a feeling of frustration sweeping over all of them at the manner in which they were kept virtual prisoners. It would be easy to overpower the sec man and use his Uzi to even the odds in a surprise attack, but to what end? So they continued to sit while outside the camp was deconstructed, and what little had not already been cleared was loaded onto the wags that had contained the construction equipment.

They still sat while the tent-style shelter was taken down around them, the sheeting rolled and stored in one of the wags, the remaining stores of water and food loaded up to be returned to the ville.

Finally they were left sitting in the open glare of the sun, with everything secured for the journey back to Salvation. Bronson watched carefully while the work party, having finished its final tasks, climbed into the back of the wag that had brought the drivers there and was designed to carry them home.

While the wags containing the construction equipment were rust edged and dust smeared, showing signs of heavy work and a low level of maintenance, the transport wag was another matter. It was like some of the wags that Ryan and J.B. had seen as sec wags during their days on the convoys of Trader. A low, six-wheeled wag with reinforced armored sides and blaster ports on each side, it would be a tight squeeze to take the work party and the companions together, but as a vehicle purely for an eight-man group of workers it would be perfect.

The actual bodywork of the vehicle showed little signs of wear and was kept in good condition. Although it was covered in dust from the journey out, this was a surface layer and not the ingrained dirt of the other two wags. The tires also showed a degree of tread that the other two vehicles didn't share.

"Baron Silas Hunter likes to look after his workers," Ryan muttered to J.B.

The Armorer nodded. "Long time since I've seen a wag that good. These men mean a lot to him."

"Or to be more accurate," Doc interjected, "the work they are doing means much to him. Let us hope he sees us in the same light."

With everyone else in place, Bronson finally turned to the companions. "Okay, let's get ourselves loaded up." And as the companions rose, the sec man moved a little closer and lowered his voice.

"Listen, Crow may think those guys have had enough, but I'm not so sure. I don't give a fuck what the argument is between you. I just got my job to do so's I can keep alive. But it's gonna be mighty close in there, and get mighty uncomfortable. They may try and chance something. I'm gonna be the only sec man, apart from Crow hisself. See, Petey and Coburn'll ride shotgun on the other wags."

"You expect trouble?" J.B. queried.

Bronson shook his head. "There ain't jackshit out here that can live apart from those buzzards and mebbe some lucky scabbies that wander too far and don't chill themselves. But there's a lot riding on this for Salvation—not just the baron—so he don't like to take no chances."

Ryan nodded. "Guess I can see the sense in that. Thanks for the warning."

Bronson's face twisted into something that resembled a grimace. "Hell, I ain't helping no one but myself. That's the way Salvation is."

"It is the way everywhere is," Doc countered, "but we thank you anyway."

Bronson looked away. "Let's cut the shit and get loaded up now," he said simply.

The companions walked to the wag, which had a rear entry. The heavily armored doors were open, and as Ryan and his people came around to mount the back step, they were faced with eight hostile faces, staring at them.

"This is going to be fun," Ryan heard his son mutter from behind.

FUN WAS THE LAST WORD Ryan would ever have used to describe the trip back to Salvation. The interior of the wag was laid-out bench seating along the sides, starting at the back door and running up to where the front seats for driver and sec shotgun rider were placed. The lanky driver named Tex, who couldn't stop talking in the lazy drawl that soon became irritating, was seated along with Crow. Bronson rode in back with the work party and with the companions.

The line of the benches was broken on each side by the mounted blasters that were aligned with the blaster ports. On first climbing into the back, J.B. had checked those visually and could see that the barrels were trapped in the ports, able to move only within the confines of these gaps, and couldn't be used to turn inward to the wag. Given the obvious attitude of their traveling companions, he was relieved.

The work party was seated, four on each side of the wag, at the front end. That left the benches at the rear of the wag for the companions and for Bronson. It was a tight squeeze, but all eight settled themselves.

No one spoke...except Tex. As the wag rolled on through the desert, eating up the blacktop, the nasal, whining drawl became a buzzing irritant that stretched already frayed nerves. For the atmosphere in the rear of the wag was as taut as a piece of elastic stretched to breaking point, and the constant monologue from the driver was like an object that played on the elastic, twanging the stretched material until it would suddenly break.

As with all men of his type, the driver was supremely unaware of the damage he was causing to his passengers' nerves as he kept driving and talking. Behind his back—and that of Crow—the work party kept up a silent campaign of hostile stares at the companions. Ryan and his people did their best to ignore it, but Dean's temper was being pushed to the limit, and of all people the one who seemed to be suffering most was the sec man Bronson, who nervously fingered the trigger of his Uzi and seemed ill at ease with the atmosphere. If Crow knew what was going on—and if he was even listening to what Tex was saying—he kept his peace, his impassive and still figure seemingly unconscious of what was going on behind him.

Ryan felt sure that, if nothing else, the Native American could smell the tension. For the wag wasn't built to comfortably hold that many people, especially on a run in such weather conditions.

The desert sun was now at its height, and although they were spared the direct glare of the glowing orange-red orb, the uninsulated metal of the wag acted as a conductor and storer of the heat, magnifying it and making the interior of the vehicle a sweatbox. The only air came via the breeze stirred by the open blaster ports, and the small door windows at the front of the wag.

The companions had no way of knowing how long the wag journey would be, and it seemed that with each passing minute the temperature in the interior of the wag rose a few degrees, the heat causing everyone effectively trapped within to sweat profusely. Even if the wag had only contained the work party, the atmosphere would have rapidly become close, the heat and smell growing to unpleasant proportions. Doubling this because of the excess number of people crowded into the rear of the vehicle, and adding their mutual distrust and dislike, and it was a recipe for disaster, the brooding, tense atmosphere not helped by the constant whine of Tex's monologue.

It was going to break. And when it broke, it would be violent.

"SO ANYWAYS, I was always telling Slim and Satchel about how you can never trust them damn gaudy sluts down at the Red House. Lord, why Silas don't do somethin' about that place I just don't know. Y'know, I've got nothin' against a good gaudy, 'cause you can just go and have some fun and not ever have to worry about getting' yourself no problems like kids or any shit like that to slow you down, 'cause that's what I always used to worry about since I was with Lula and she had that kid… Course, that was way afore she was killed in that accident back when they was first trying to get the wellhead open and there was that there explosion that chilled twenty. Lord, that must be a few years back now, but I guess you could say that it was one of the best things that kinda happened to me in a way. But anyways, as I was a sayin', I was always telling those dudes not to trust those sluts any farther than they could toss them. Course, it's supposed to be the other way around, but that ain't the point. Point is, they were there doing the do and getting some fun when Satch looked around and found one of the other gaudies had snuck into the room and was diving down his pants looking for his jack. Course, like he said to me, that would've been all right if he'd still been wearing the pants, but he wasn't, so he got real riled and yelled, squirming out from underneath the gaudy on top of him and tryin' to get his hands on this other slut. That would've been okay if not for the fact that Slim still had a part of hisself in her mouth, and as she fell she kinda bit too hard and made the bastard bleed. So there's him cursin' and swearin' and tryin' to beat on her for injuring him, while Satch is trying to catch this other gaudy with nothin' on below the waist—which included his blaster. And dang me if she don't run straight into Waldo, that big retard they use for sec down there. 'Waldo, Waldo, this boy done gone screwed me and don't want to pay,' she says, all innocent and that big lug Waldo pulls out his blaster, and he says—"

"Why don't you shut up," Dean interjected, the heat and incessant noise finally snapping his patience.

The sudden bark of the young man cut Tex short, and in the sudden relative silence of the sweltering wag, there was an increase in tension.

"Why can't Tex say what he wants?" Hal

growled. "Why should some boy tell him what he can and can't do."

"Hell, Hal, I knows I can sometimes get a mite carried away and go on and on without stopping, like a gaudy slut on extra time, and—"

"No, this time you do shut the fuck up," Hal broke in across him, "'cause the way you could talk the pads off a stickie ain't got jackshit to do with it."

"So what has it got to do with?" Ryan answered in a growl even lower and more threatening than the workman's.

"It's got to do with you uppity dipshits comin' in out of nowhere and tryin' to muscle in our jack," Hal returned.

"And nothing to do with not getting our pussy?" Mildred countered.

"You take our jack, we take it out in trade," Emerson rumbled from behind Hal.

"We don't want your jack," Ryan said. "We just want our blasters back and to get on our way."

"Yeah, sure, but if Crow here decides that he wants to divide up the bonuses with you, you ain't gonna say no," Hal continued.

"Think we triple stupe as you look?" Jak said, sneering. Never the best traveler, the confined space, heat and movement of the wag made him feel like puking, and made his temper unnaturally short. This pointless argument was beginning to grate on his nerves.

Rysh decided to take up the argument. He half rose

from his seat, swaying unevenly as the wag raced across the old blacktop, and leaned across to where Jak was sitting, hunched into himself to try to counter the feeling of sickness.

"Listen, you white-faced mutie scum, why don't you keep your views to yourself, 'cause I don't want to listen to the opinions of some piece of shit freak like you. That okay with you, is it?" he said mockingly, leaning almost into Jak's face. He was bent over, legs slightly apart to keep his balance, his left hand gripping the mounting shaft of the blaster that divided the bench seats.

"Oh, dear," Doc murmured to himself.

For Doc had seen Jak tense within his jacket, which he had wrapped around him protectively despite the heat. The multicolored patches, dulled in hue by time and travel, contained tiny pieces of metal that were sewn into the fabric and kept the much repaired camou jacket together. Doc, seated right next to Jak, had seen some of the small metal shapes just shimmer as they moved slightly.

He knew it meant just one thing: trouble.

Rysh's sneering smile was still right in Jak's face when the albino moved. His calf muscles had tensed and pushed, throwing his body forward. This momentum was increased by a nod of his head that brought his cranium forward at the optimum point of his torso's movement, giving his scarred and pitted forehead extra momentum at the point of impact.

It was a sudden and violent movement, unexpected in such a confined space despite the air of tension and the taunting. Jak's stringy white hair flailed around him in strands as his forehead connected with the bridge of Rysh's nose, the crack sounding preternaturally loud in the enclosed space.

The thickset and muscular workman howled like a baby as the bone in his nose splintered beneath the impact, shards of it tearing through the skin and nasal membrane to gush out of his nostrils with the seeming river of blood that flowed freely. His eyes blurred, suddenly distant and out of focus as he staggered back instinctively, his grip loosening on the blaster's mounting shaft that had been helping him to keep his balance.

Tex was unable to resist a quick look over his shoulder, yelling "Fuck!" when he saw what was happening. Despite this, Crow didn't look back, but he did notice that the wag suddenly slewed across the road as the distracted Tex lost concentration for a second. The vehicle jerked as it moved, the sudden change of direction throwing the occupants in the back off balance.

Tex looked back quickly and corrected his course. But the damage was already done. Rysh, with no mounting shaft to steady him, and his senses misted by the pain, staggered in the middle of the wag before falling onto his back. He hit the floor of the wag with a groan as the air was driven from him—not by the impact of the fall but by the sudden intervention of Jak's knees on his abdomen.

Jak was the only traveler in the back of the wag not to be affected by the sudden change of equilibrium. The same innate sense that had made him such an exccllent hunter enabled him to adjust within a fraction of a second to the sudden movements and maintain the poise that had enabled him to win fights against heavier, bctter-armed opponents. Rysh's falling had just made Jak's task easier, for the youth had already launched himself through the momentum of the head butt, his legs uncoiling beneath him, with the sole purpose of driving his larger opponent to the deck and using the man's own weight to make him land heavily and drive the breath from him. The fact that Rysh had already started the fall made it easier.

Too easy for Jak. As the workman lay on his back, straddled by the wiry and immensely strong albino, with his eyes still unfocused and his brain failing to register what was happening through the pain, he was only aware of the fact that he could now taste the blood from his nose down the back of his throat, and it was starting to choke him.

Jak punched him hard, one, two, three times. Each blow was with the full force his forearm, to protect his knuckles, and was aimed at the prone man's temple. Quite simply, Jak wanted to cave in the man's skull at its weakest, most vulnerable point.

The other workmen had been stunned by the sudden ferocity and speed of the attack, but now it was beginning to dawn on them that the albino would actually kill their colleague unless they intervened.

''Nuke shit! Rysh'll buy the farm unless we stop the little fucker,'' Tilson roared. He was the wiriest of the workmen, and also the one who had been the least antagonistic toward the companions. But this was too much for him. With a speed that his wiry frame suggested, he reached for his blaster. A snub-nosed .38 Smith & Wesson, it nestled in a holster in the small of his back, and it was only that fact that saved Jak from a chilling. For it took him a fraction of a second longer to reach to his back than it would have done to reach to his waist. And that fraction of a second was all that Ryan needed.

Tilson may have been quick, but the one-eyed man was quicker. The almost incoherent roar of rage from Tilson had drawn Ryan's eye to him, and as the man's hand began to move toward the small of his back, so Ryan began to move. Pushing himself from his seat, he took an explosive spring step that propelled him past the prone Rysh and Jak. He twisted his heavily muscled torso so that his body began to spread full length across the workers seated on the bench seat. Because Ryan had one big problem—if Tilson had been seated diagonally opposite, then he could have leaped across and tackled him head-on. But the workman was actually seated on the same side of the wag as the one-eyed warrior, and so he had not only to leap from one end of the wag to the other, but also to change direction so as to be facing his opponent.

It was tight, but he managed it. He felt sinews strain as he tried to attain enough momentum, and as Tilson's blaster hand emerged from behind his back, thumb already cocking the blaster's hammer, Ryan was able to reach for the man's wrist and pinion it in his own iron grip.

Tilson gritted his teeth and hissed a barely suppressed yelp of sudden agony as Ryan's muscular wrist tensed, and the fingers like rods of steel closed on his own bony wrist, crushing cartilage and bone and cutting off the blood supply to his fingers.

The nerves in his fingers twitched, enough to make his trigger finger squeeze and loose off a round within the wag. His arm had been forced right back behind and above his head by the sudden action of the one-eyed man, almost wrenching the arm from its socket. His hand now pointed toward the roof of the wag, the muzzle of the blaster almost touching the rounded metal top of the vehicle.

The explosion of the blaster within the wag was deafening, resounding with a ringing that continued for some seconds. The stink of cordite joined that of sweat and fear. The slug hit the roof and ricocheted wickedly, driving across the far side of the wag and almost taking off the top of Emerson's head. The large workman ducked instinctively and overbalanced, falling onto Jak, who was still in the process of beating the now insensible Rysh.

The slug whined back, plucking at the shoulder of J.B.'s jacket as the Armorer's instincts and experience made him calculate the angles and move out of the way, pushing down Mildred as he did so. The ricocheting shell finally came to rest in the leg of Bronson, hitting the sec man in the shin and shattering the bone. He yelled and went deathly white, the color draining from his face at the shock and pain. He dropped his Uzi and grasped at his leg, blood pouring over his fingers as he dropped off his seat beside Krysty.

The Titian-haired beauty would have attended to his wound, if not for the fact that the shot had galvanized everyone into action, and she had to first defend herself and her companions.

Ryan and Tilson were still struggling, the wiry worker trying hard to head butt the man, but not having the momentum to get any real force into it. Their hands were still locked together, though the nerveless fingers of his blaster hand had let the weapon fall behind him with a clatter against the side of the wag. In his attempts to reach across, Ryan had thrown himself against Hal, Mikey and Hay, pinning them to their seats. But only until the initial shock had passed. As soon as they had gathered their collective wits, Ryan found himself under attack and in no position to defend himself. He gritted his teeth and winced heavily as Hal brought his fist down in a rabbit punch to Ryan's kidneys, the pain coursing through his body. He felt Hay try to bend his leg against the knee, and he sharply brought the knee up so that it hit the workman in the chest. But with no real swing, there was equally no real force behind the blow. Mikey was in the middle, and ideally in the position to disable Ryan instantly, as he aimed a blow at the one-eyed warrior's unprotected groin.

He didn't have a chance to make the blow.

As soon as he had avoided the ricochet and had

pushed Mildred down with him, J.B. had risen to his
feet and jumped across the small interior of the wag,
avoiding the grappling bodies in the middle of the
confined space. He had identified Mikey as the man
most likely to disable Ryan in the group, and had no
hesitation in aiming where his first blow was to be
struck. His arm extended rigid as he drove his hand
forward, palm flat to the ground, fingers bent at the
first and second knuckle joint. The ridge of bone and
tissue made by the finger between the first and second joint was rock hard, and drove into the space
between the point of Mikey's chin and his thorax,
driving his Adam's apple up into his mouth so that
he felt his throat was exploding from within. The
excruciating pain caused him to momentarily black
out, and all thoughts of attacking Ryan were lost.

Without pause, and without even having to think
about it, J.B. pulled back his arm and pivoted on his
heel, turning toward the still pinioned Hay, who, having seen the Armorer disable the man next to him
with ease, was now desperately trying to free himself. He looked up at J.B. with an almost pathetic
expression in his eyes, which the Armorer ignored as
he drove his arm forward again, this time with fingers
extended and rigid. The blow smashed into Hay's
face, deflected from its intended path of between his
eyes by Hay's raised left arm. The blow took out one
of his eyeballs, the ball popping from the socket and
resting on his check. The iron-hard fingers of the
Armorer broke the socket bone.

Freed from the attentions lower down his body,

Ryan was able to finish what he had started. Tilson's dead arm went limp in his grasp, and the one-eyed warrior loosened his grip, allowing the useless arm to fall down. His other hand was still locked in a grip with Tilson's other hand, their fingers enmeshed in a grip neither could relent.

It did, of course, leave Ryan with a free hand. He formed it into a fist and drove it twice into the side of Tilson's head, the stinging blows making the man's head ring, and a numbness creep down his face. Stunned, his grip on Ryan's other hand weakened momentarily, and the one-eyed man used this advantage to twist savagely, breaking Tilson's wrist. As it snapped and went limp, another iron fist pummeled the workman's face, and consciousness left him.

This just left Hal, who had been torn between aiding Mikey or Tilson, and as a result had helped neither.

"Sweet Jesus," he whispered as he found J.B. and Ryan in front of him. It seemed as though he would just submit...but then, with a yell that was part savage and part resignation, he threw himself at both of them.

It was a noble but pointless gesture. Both men hammered him in the face and body with a succession of blows as he rose from the seat, and in mere seconds he was an unconscious, bloody heap slumping back to the bench seat.

That left Mildred, Krysty, Dean and Doc to deal with the remaining men. Doc landed a right hook on the rising Emerson that knocked the man into the path of Mildred, and she and Dean finished the burly worker with a succession of kicks and punches that soon rendered him unconscious. Molloy was next in line. He tried to take Doc from behind with a blow from the butt of his blaster—the workers had realized as soon as Tilson squeezed off a shot that the dangers of using blasters in such a confined space made them impractical except as clubs. Doc moved, taking the blow on the outside edge of his shoulder, and caught the worker with an upward blow to the solar plexus that doubled him. A shove from Doc's boot in his ass pushed him toward Dean and Mildred, who finished him off.

It was Ed, the quietest of all the workers, who may have been the most dangerous. He singled out Krysty for attack, and as she rose and turned away from Bronson, she found herself encircled by the muscled arms of the workman, which closed around her in the grip of a crushing bear hug. She felt the breath being squeezed from her, and her ribs start to protest and creak as he tightened the grip.

Breathing in, and pulling in her muscles as much as she dared, she wriggled her arms to free them, and brought her hands together on either side of his head with a clap that resounded down his ear canals, making his eardrums rupture with the combination of force and pressure. Ed roared in pain and let loose his grip, doubling over so that it seemed for a ridiculous second as though he were crying on her shoulder. But only until she stepped back, jerked his head up with one hand, and took him out with a knuckle punch between his shocked and staring eyes.

With their opponents now wiped out, the companions paused for breath. Jak stood up from the now unconscious Rysh, breathing heavily but steadily as he calmed himself.

"Well," Crow said quietly, finally looking around, "that was most impressive. Baron Silas will be interested."

"Why didn't you try to stop it?" Ryan asked.

Crow shrugged. "What could I do?" he said before turning back to face front, impassive and silent.

Ryan and J.B. exchanged glances before hauling the unconscious bodies to the front of the wag, joined by the others taking a workman each. Krysty examined Bronson's wound before Mildred joined her to apply to a dressing. The sec man was thankful, especially when Mildred gave him a painkiller from the small supply she had stored from the redoubt med bay.

"Whoo," Tex drawled finally, his first words for some time and the first thing he had dared to utter, "looks like you got it all cleaned up just in time. Here comes Salvation...."

At which the companions looked from the blaster ports to get their first view of Salvation, home of Baron Silas Hunter.

From first look, they could tell it was going to be an interesting time.

Chapter Eight

As the wags rolled into Salvation, the companions crowded around the blaster ports, trying to get a better view of their destination. The workers were still at the front end of the wag, barely beginning to regain consciousness, so Ryan and his people felt safe turning their backs on them for a few seconds.

The blacktop had taken them through the remains of an oil-town suburb, with deserted and derelict buildings that reflected the residential nature of their old use. There were low-level apartment blocks, houses and rows of shops dotted with the occasional strip mall. All had been deserted since the days of skydark, and gave no indication of what was to come.

For, as the blacktop gave way to an old concrete road and Tex took them on a winding route past the most damaged parts of the old ville, they began to see signs of fortifications. The buildings had been obviously burned and demolished in more recent times, the rubble used to make rudimentary towers from which observation posts could be established. The outer ones were empty, but there were signs of life from those that began to occur more and more frequently as they approached the heart of the ville.

There were also sounds of manual labor—the breaking and hammering of construction, and the rattle and hum of generators. A babble of voices occasionally cut through the constant level of noise. And then, finally, they came to the gates of Salvation.

A wall of rubble had been carefully constructed to provide a walkway on the top and recesses for observation posts, and as far as each group could see from either side of the wag's blaster port slits, the wall traveled on for at least a mile. Ryan guessed that it continued around the whole of the reconstituted ville, hemming it in and protecting it from intruders and, conversely, also keeping the inhabitants safely within view.

"There more than one road in?" Ryan asked Crow, not expecting the taciturn Native American to answer.

"One at each compass point, all like this," the giant replied. "Before you ask, no other exits."

"I think mebbe we'd already figured that one," Ryan murmured. "Baron Silas is a very cautious man."

"Around these parts you don't get to stay baron unless you are," Crow said.

"Same as anywhere," Ryan observed.

Mildred interrupted Ryan's train of thought with a low whistle. "Man, he may be cautious, but he likes people to know who's boss," she said. "Look at that."

"I'm looking, but I'm not sure I believe what I'm seeing," J.B. countered.

For the full grandeur of the gates dividing the wall of Salvation was now fully apparent. The giant structure stood over thirty feet. It was made from pieces of scrap metal that had been smelted and beaten into grotesque and Gothic designs, so that the upward-thrusting poles that had been honed at the top into spikes were joined by wreaths and curlicues of spiked and hollylike wire that kept the gate see-through and yet completely impassable. The two gates were joined in the middle by a simple locking system that was accessible only from the inside due to a protective and decorative plate several feet across that was divided in the center.

But it was at the top that the ego of Baron Silas Hunter became obvious. Over the top of the gates stood an arch that joined one side of the wall to the other, and sat independent of the gates themselves. The arch was composed of two bars, with carefully beaten-out metal lettering between. It said simply Welcome To Salvation. In itself not a particularly egotistical message. However, on top of the arch stood a statue made of bronzed metal, the polishing of which showed that it had not been standing for many years. The statue was of a tall, thin man in a long coat and cowboy boots. He had a drawn, haggard face with an iron-cast jaw that wasn't softened by the beard that had been cast beneath. Even in the statue, there was something about the hooded eyes that made a person wary, shielded as they were by a Stetson hat.

''Baron Silas likes folks to know who he is when

they arrive,'' Crow said, observing the companions' silence on seeing the statue.

Both J.B. and Ryan glanced at the Native American sharply, but he kept his head turned away from them, seemingly impassive.

''If I did not know better than to say so, I could readily assume that there was a touch of sarcasm in that statement,'' Doc murmured.

Crow stayed silent while Tex leaned out of the wag's side window. ''Hey, Lenny, let me back in, you bastard!'' he yelled.

An obscene reply, half-lost on the morning breeze and the sound of work within the ville, came down from the observation post, followed a few minutes later by the man Ryan took to be Lenny. He unlocked the gates and pulled one side open, taking his time to open the other.

''Yeah, very funny,'' Tex drawled. ''Let's see how the baron likes you screwin' me around when I got some booty he wants to see.''

Lenny's reply was as obscene and incomprehensible as before, but the attention of Ryan and his people was taken by the terms Tex had used.

''Is that how we're seen?'' Krysty asked Crow. ''We're some kind of commodity or jack to be used for trade?''

''Not my choice of words,'' Crow replied, ''but everyone is that to some extent. Especially when they work for Baron Silas. And you do.''

''That remains to be seen,'' Ryan muttered.

''It does?'' Crow countered.

Tex put the wag into gear and drove through the portals of Salvation, and into the heart of the ville, followed by the two wags holding the construction materials. They soon lost these wags, as they turned off to head for wherever Baron Silas had his work supplies sequestered. The wag driven by Tex, however, kept heading for the center of the ville.

It slowed considerably as it began to hit the heaving mass of humanity that was crammed into the relatively small area that was the ville of Salvation. In an undertone, to avoid being overheard by Tex or—most particularly—Crow, J.B. and Ryan discussed the ville as they could see it so far.

"Way I figure it, old Silas couldn't devote too much time or manpower to building the wall around the ville to begin with, so they had to make the ville just the size of a few old blocks," the Armorer stated. "That'd account for the fact that the wall is so strong—"

"Otherwise," Ryan concluded, "they would have been wide open to attack while they were constructing it. So as the ville's got richer, and Baron Silas has got more and more people coming in to take up living and working here, then it's got more and more crowded."

"Guess he'll use some of the jack from the oil well to enlarge his barony," J.B. mused.

"Got to get the fireblasted thing working first," Ryan reminded the Armorer.

While they discussed this is undertones, the others kept watching the ville of Salvation go by. It was obviously to the center of the old oil town, and many of the towers that were used in predark days for offices had been pressed into operation as residential. The upper levels hadn't stood up to the ravages of time, and were left empty and derelict. But some kind of maintenance had to have been observed, for the lower levels showed signs of occupation as dwellings. At a level closer to the street, the old shops of the oil town were used for trading and holding markets where goods were bartered or sold. The old bars had been pressed into use as gaudy houses, and there were some that were used as homes by the residents.

Progress through the streets became slower and slower as the crowds grew more and more dense, spilling off the old sidewalks and onto the streets, obstructing the little traffic that passed.

"Doc, have you noticed something?" Dean queried.

"I have, my young friend, noticed many things," Doc retorted. "To which, in particular, do you refer?"

Dean ignored the slight condescension in the older man's tone, and continued. "It's just that, for somewhere that's supposed to have its own fuel well and refinery, we're the only wag that I've seen since we lost the construction wags."

"Too packed for wags," Jak observed. "Waste fuel. Keep wags for outside gates."

Doc nodded sagely. "I think that friend Jak may be right. Think about how much fuel we're wasting right now. By the three Kennedys, this is more packed than Washington on Thanksgiving Day with a free turkey.''

Jak and Dean both looked at Doc, puzzled.

He observed them, smiled sadly to himself. ''A small joke, gentlemen. It would have been mildly amusing once.''

Tex kept hitting the horn, the sound blaring harshly at passersby and obstructions to traffic that did little more than turn and curse him.

''Shit,'' he spit, ''this little jam'll take us all day to get through.''

''Is there no other route?'' Ryan asked. It was a seemingly stupid, but leading question, and elicited the information he wanted from the unaware wag driver.

''It'll all be the same,'' Tex replied. ''See, we don't really have wags in the walls anymore 'cause there ain't the room. Since Baron Silas found that the well still had some oil down in bottom, and he figured out how to get the refinery going, then there ain't been much except people coming from all over to swell up the ville. Some of them come of their own accord, but a lot come from nearby villes 'cause of the deals that Baron Silas done gone and done with them all. Guess as how it's bought a whole load of trade and jack in besides the well, which is nice for guys like me 'cause a lot of these new folk are card players, 'specially the merchants, only they ain't as good card players as me. That right, ain't it,

Crow?'' he added, glancing at the giant Native American.

''Shut the fuck up,'' Crow countered with soft menace.

But the rambling monologue had revealed exactly what Ryan needed to know. He looked out of the blaster port again. People walked in the streets because there were stalls laden with goods on the old sidewalks. The traffic in the roads comprised more than just pedestrians: there were bicycles weaving in and out, and men and women pushing barrows laden with different goods that were either for sale or were in the process of being delivered from one dwelling to another. The crush of people spelled success for the ville. Each person had jack, and each person represented some piece of trade that either had gone on, or was about to.

Salvation had become a rich ville very quickly. And maybe there was the problem: Baron Silas had a large number of people within a very small space, and no room to expand the ville. To deconstruct and then remake the walls around the old boundaries of Salvation would take time and manpower that couldn't be spared right now. Not with the vast amount of work that was taking place along the old blacktop linking the villes that were involved in the refinery reconstruction and giving them a route to the outside world, and not with the vast amount of work and manpower that was also being invested in the refinery that was the point of the alliance.

The sec forces of Salvation had to be stretched to

the breaking point coping with the extra people and the extra work. As with most villes, particularly larger ones, Ryan could see at a glance that all the inhabitants that passed him by were armed, blasters hanging easily from holsters or cradled in arms as they walked.

So many people in such a small space. Tensions would be bound to arise. And if they did, they would be concentrated within the boundary walls, unable to diffuse outside.

Although he felt uneasy about their being deprived of their own blasters, Ryan felt sure that they would soon regain them. The way in which Crow had been ordered to deliver them to Baron Silas, and the way in which he had allowed them to be tested in unarmed combat could only point to one thing…

If they were to move on, then they had to first become part of Salvation's sec force.

"THIS IS IT," Crow said simply as the wag pulled up.

"As if I couldn't have guessed," Mildred observed, surveying the building in front of them. It was a large, ornate stone building that had probably stood since the founding of the old oil town from which the ville of Salvation had been forged. The white stone had become discolored with age and the old balustrades, cornices and carvings were now covered in a creeping vine of ironwork that spread tendrils of barbed and decorated dark metal across the front and sides of the building, as far as they could see. There were no breaks for the windows, the decoration also acting as a protective bar to any access other than through the ground-level doors.

The large stained-wood doors to the building were reached via a short flight of stone steps, impressively constructed with a tapering sweep to reach a pinnacle by the doors, the wide base of the steps marked at each corner by a plinth that had, at one time, housed statues that were of the same stone as the building. These had long since been replaced with statues in beaten metal that were obviously Baron Silas Hunter, as they were identical to that which stood on the arch over the gates to Salvation. If there was a similar arch at each entry, then there were four statues surrounding the ville, and now at least two within the walls.

Baron Silas Hunter was obviously a man of some ego.

"So we get to meet the great man at last," Ryan said to Crow as he stood in the back of the wag and stretched muscles cramped by too long a confinement after their explosive bout of action.

"Yeah, as soon as we deal with these assholes," the foreman said, jerking a thumb at the still semiconscious workers in the back of the wag. "Wait there."

"Nowhere else go," Jak mumbled in reply. But if the Native American heard him, he failed to respond as he dismounted from the vehicle and joined Tex in walking around to the rear doors. Inside, the companions heard the lock being sprung, and then the doors were flung open, admitting light into the back of the vehicle that caused the pile of beaten flesh to stir a little more. It also caused Bronson to awaken, the mild sedative and painkiller administered by Mildred having made his journey a little easier.

"Help him out," Crow said, taking Bronson by one arm. Ryan took the other, and the sec man was so disoriented and such a deadweight from his injury that it took all their strength to get him from the wag. While they did this, the doors to the building opened and a squad of sec men came down the steps. Three of them—armed like all the others with Uzis—took over from Crow and Ryan, and Bronson was taken into the building.

The companions climbed out of the wag and stood to one side under the eye of the sec squad. The seven-strong squad stayed silent, but kept their hands thoughtfully on their blasters.

"Hell, they're okay," Tex drawled, observing this, "but you should see what they did to those good ol' boys in back." He chuckled, indicating where the workmen were beginning to surface, groaning in agony.

"They're with me," Crow said dismissively of the companions, indicating them with a gesture. Then, turning, his attention to the wag, he pointed in. "Those stupes, on the other hand… Get them out and send them home. They'll get their jack when they're fit enough to come and get it on both feet."

He left the sec squad to decant the still groggy workmen and send them to their homes to recover.

While Tex moved around to the front of the wag in order to take it to the wag bay where all Baron Silas's vehicles would be stored, Crow began to mount the steps.

"Follow me," he commanded without looking back.

Ryan exchanged glances with his people, and fell into step behind the Native American after whispering, "Triple red," to the others, who all made small gestures of acknowledgment. Although they were unarmed, they could still be prepared to meet any danger as best they could, and without thinking they fell into formation, with Krysty and Dean followed by Doc and Mildred, J.B. bringing up the rear.

But there was little sign of danger once they entered the building. The doors were closed behind them by two armed sec men, but once they were in, there was little sign of any overwhelming sec presence. Instead, they took in the ornate plush with which Baron Silas Hunter had decorated his baronial palace. Rich hangings and plundered paintings sat over a rag bag of antique furnitures plundered and traded from many points. And always the intertwining wire and smelted iron rails that ran in decorative yet secure form across every window and opening.

"Hell, he doesn't need strong sec inside, not with that armor outside," J.B. murmured to Mildred.

"What worries me is what it keeps in right now, not what it keeps out," the doctor replied.

They followed Crow up a red-carpeted staircase that ended in a pair of off-white wooden doors. As they approached, the doors opened and a man appeared, staring down at them.

There was no doubt who he was, as he was dressed exactly as the statues had portrayed him. When he smiled, it was as icy as his eyes.

''Welcome to my home, good people. Welcome to the heart and soul of Salvation.''

Chapter Nine

Baron Silas Hunter led the companions and Crow into the sumptuously furnished room from which he had emerged. There were windows on all sides of the long, hall-like room that had a long, polished oak table as its centerpiece. There were a dozen chairs, six on each side of the table, with a large, gilt-covered throne at the head. The light from the windows, depleted as it was by the ironwork that covered the glass, was augmented by a plethora of candelabra scattered around the room, resting along the length of the table, as well as reposing on the mantel and on plinths and small tables that lined the room's walls.

The heels of Baron Silas's snakeskin cowboy boots click-clacked on the tiled floor as he walked easily along the table before gliding into the throne, swinging up his legs in one easy move so that his heels rested on the tabletop, feet crossed at the ankles. He pushed the Stetson hat back on his head and eyed the companions coldly, following in his wake. He gestured at them to be seated, and so they took positions, with Ryan, Krysty and Jak on one side, J.B., Mildred, Dean, and Doc on the other. Crow slipped into a position beside Jak.

They waited in an expectant silence for the baron to speak.

"So these are the hombres you spoke so highly of, Crow," he began.

The Native American nodded.

"They don't look that mean to me."

"Mebbe we just don't have to," Ryan declared. He could see from the manner in which the baron was appraising them that the man's intent was to spur some kind of reaction so he could judge their individual and collective character.

Ryan didn't appreciate those type of games. He had come thus far for a reason, but he couldn't be pushed...and wouldn't allow his people to be pushed.

"Well," drawled the baron, "mebbe you do and mebbe you don't. You've come to Salvation, and this is my ville. I make the rules."

"We've come here because we wanted to," Ryan returned.

The baron watched the one-eyed man with glittering snake eyes and smiled a gimlet grin that contained no humor.

"Wanted to come here rather than wanted to take your chances in the desert?"

"If need be," Ryan answered. "Let's lay those cards on the table. We willingly gave up our blasters and worked for you in return for food, water and shelter. We agreed to come back here rather than stand and fight out there. And if you've taken any notice of what your man here has said," he added with a gesture toward Crow, "you'll know that we could have taken the blasters from your workmen and then taken your sec."

"Easy to say," the baron rejoined.

"Easy to do," J.B. said softly from where he sat, opposite Ryan.

"You let your monkeys speak for you? Hell, even a benevolent son of a gaudy like me doesn't do that," the baron said gently, steeling this with a firm glance at Ryan that didn't flicker toward J.B.

Krysty felt Jak stir at the insult and knew that although the albino mutie would show nothing on his scarred and impassive face, every muscle would be tensed for an angered attack. She gently moved her hand from her own lap to Jak's arm and squeezed his wrist. She didn't look away from the baron as she did this, but knew she had the intended effect when she felt Jak's tension relax against her grip.

Crow had noted this group interplay and ruminatively scratched his chin. That would be something to mention to the baron later.

Across the table, Dean had also reacted to Baron Silas's words, and Mildred spared him a glare while Doc laid a hand on his arm. The younger Cawdor had yet to learn the cool of his father. The flicker in the corners of Baron Silas's eyes gave away to the one-eyed warrior that he was watching them all intently, and Ryan grinned before he spoke again.

"These people aren't monkeys, Baron," he said easily. "We've all been together a long time, and I'm leader 'cause someone has to make the decisions.

But we watch for each other, and act for and with each other. That's how we survived, and that's why I figure we're valuable to you.''

Baron Silas cracked his impassive features with a raised eyebrow that could have indicated surprise. If it did, nothing was given away by his still frozen eyes.

''Now, why do y'all think you may be valuable?'' he asked in a flat tone.

''Because if we weren't, or you didn't think that we could be, then we would have long since been chilled,'' Ryan answered.

Baron Silas considered that for a moment, then said, ''That's a damn good point, and one that can't rightly be answered that well. So I guess I'll have to give you that.''

''In which case, sir,'' Doc piped up after noisily clearing his throat as a preliminary to speech, ''you may perhaps see fit to do us the justice of some manner of explanation. After all, from what our acquaintance Crow has told us, it would seem that you have taken some time and effort to build up this ville. Pray where do we fit in?''

For the first time since he had stared to speak, Baron Silas took his full gaze away from Ryan and settled it on Doc.

It was all Doc could do to avoid recoiling. The cold eyes and stone face were all too reminiscent for him of Jordan Teague, baron of Mocsin and the man who had been Doc's torturer when he had first been flung into the world of the Deathlands. Both men shared the ability to make one feel like an insect in amber, being appraised by a superior intelligence and being.

Baron Silas noted this instinctive recoil and remembered it for future reference.

"I'll tell you," he said finally and in almost hushed tones. "But first, I think we could all do with food. Hell, I know I could…"

The baron clapped his hands three times, and the double doors opened. Two armed sec men came into the room, then exited again when they saw Hunter nod.

J.B. looked at Ryan. They were both thinking that this had to be some kind of arranged signal. If so, the big question was had the baron arranged this to impress or overawe them in some way… Or did he actually live in this manner?

Before either had a chance to say anything, the doors opened again and the sec men reentered, standing one on either side of the double doors. Following them came a procession of women, each carrying a silver tray containing dishes of food. The women, all of whom were well clothed in a variety of low-cut frocks and had similar physical characteristics—were all redheads either naturally or by dye and were large bosomed and small waisted although of varying heights. They were obviously picked by Baron Silas to follow his own preferences and weren't just employed as serving girls. As they placed the trays on the tables, they stood back against the walls. They were followed by more girls with pitchers of wine brewed from locally grown fruits, and water. Plates, cutlery and goblets were laid before the companions, Crow and the baron.

"Interesting staff you have here," Krysty murmured, taking in the similarities between the serving girls, and also their differences. Despite the shape and the hair color, some of them were black, Hispanic or Native American in ethnic origin. It made for a bizarre mix of the similar and the different.

"All my girls are handpicked," Baron Silas said, indicating them with a sweeping wave. "I only go for the best—like in everything," he added pointedly. "They're available if you wish...always assuming you don't have your own arrangements," he said with a brief glance at Krysty and Mildred. "Now eat, drink and then I explain."

J.B. looked at Ryan and then cast an eye over the food and drink that lay on the table. There were meats, vegetables, and some strange breads and biscuits that seemed of uncertain origin. Ryan's eye met the Armorer's over the top of the man's spectacles.

"Crow," Baron Silas said, noticing their exchange and grasping the meaning.

The Native American and the baron both reached for food and also took some of the wine. They began to eat and drink, and only when they had observed this did the companions join them.

"You disappoint me," Baron Silas said through a mouthful of bread. "I'd expected less overt distrust."

"Sometimes the obvious can pass you by," Ryan answered.

"But what good would it have done?" Baron Silas continued, washing down the bread with some wine.

"Didn't have to do any good—mebbe just a little prod," Ryan replied.

The meal continued with little small talk. The companions exchanged a few words with one another about the meal, and any attempts by the baron to draw Ryan further were met with a bland response. They were too aware of the serving girls, who could possibly catch any comments that the baron or Crow may miss. The Native American, for his part, ate his meal in silence.

When they had finished, the serving girls gathered everything that was left on the table and took it away. The two armed sec men—who had remained impassive in the doorway throughout—followed them out and closed the doors behind them, but not before the Native American had joined them. To all the companions, the fact that Crow had also departed meant that the real business was about to begin.

They sat for a few moments in silence, the baron composing his thoughts.

"So do we get to hear why we're here now, or is there a cabaret?" Mildred asked.

Baron Silas fixed her with a stare that indicated that, for the moment, he wasn't sure whether she was serious. Then he began.

"Salvation means a lot to me. A hell of a lot. Not just because it's made me rich, with more jack and booty than I know what to do with—which is never a bad thing—but because it's something that's taken a long time for me to build. I was just a kid when I first came here. My daddy brought all of us from a ville called Dallas that used to be a big predark place. 'Cept as how there wasn't much left of it after, on account of all the oil wells and refineries firing the whole area after the nukecaust. When it was okay to settle again, there just wasn't much left to settle.

"They tried to farm that land, but my daddy always had this theory that the old wells shouldn't be dry. They weren't used up in the days before skydark, so why shouldn't there be some left, and why shouldn't we all exploit that, seeing as how fuel is the most valuable thing that there is these days?"

Doc pursed his lips, blowing through them. "That is a sound piece of reasoning, I would say. And surely any baron who was sitting on such a potential source of trade and jack would jump at the chance?"

Baron Silas allowed himself the luxury of a small grin that made him look as friendly as a sidewinder. "Well, now, you'd think it might, and mebbe it would have if there was any sense to anything. But Baron Angus Eddison of Dallas didn't want that. It was a small ville, and he couldn't devote time and manpower to getting the wells investigated or opened again."

"So why not form alliances as you obviously have?" Krysty asked.

"Because there ain't no one in these parts who'd pitch in unless they knew as they were onto a good thing, and there ain't no one who Baron Angus'd trust anyways. Stupe thing is that the only man he ever trusted was his son, Christian, and it was Christian who had the old man chilled so as he could take over. I've got an alliance with Christian, but I can't say as I'd trust the fucker. Then again, he'd be a fool to trust me,'' Baron Silas added reasonably.

''So how end up here?'' Jak asked, his piercing red eyes trained on the baron.

Baron Silas met his stare with an equally piercing gaze. ''My daddy was convinced that he could find a well to work and get rich, mebbe become his own baron. If Angus wasn't going to let him look for one in Dallas, then mebbe he'd just have to get out and find his own. He knew this land like his own skin, and so he knew that if he came here he had a chance of getting a well. There were some people here then, but it was so small that they didn't even have a baron as such.

''Well, it took a long time to build a reasonable place for my ma and me, and then get the trust of the locals enough to start the search. They had some machinery and stuff that they'd salvaged, and they used wag parts for trade and also used their knowledge of how wags worked to barter their way with passing trade convoys. So they had some time when they wasn't doing so much work that they couldn't help. I guess my daddy had a vision of what he wanted to find, and what he wanted to make of it. And I guess the folks of Salvation were stupe enough to believe him and greedy enough to work at it.''

''Stupe enough?'' Mildred broke in.

''Yeah, mebbe they were at that. After all, there

was no real proof that any of the wells were actually capable of being worked. Shit, even if you found one with oil, how the hell were you supposed to get that refinery and plant working to get it out and make it into fuel…liquid jack?''

"Workable enough given their mechanical skills," J.B. mused.

"Guess that was it." Baron Silas nodded. "Anyways, it took years. I grew up, and my daddy taught me all he knew, and showed me the old documents he used to piece together the knowledge he had for finding and testing the old wells. Shit, they're big enough to find, all right, if you've got a map reference, but actually seeing if they had anything left… That can sometimes be a dangerous business. You try and get the damn things to gush and if they do, then you run the risk of firing the bastards. That's what happened to Daddy. He was caught in the backdraft at a well and fried.'' He fell into a thoughtful silence.

"And that's the well you're working?" Mildred asked in the sudden pause.

Baron Silas shook himself out of his reverie. "Hell, no. That's the irony of it all. It was another dry one, with just enough to fire up, then fizzle out. It burned for about ten minutes, long enough to chill any poor bastard near enough, and fuck all else.''

"So you took over the search?" Ryan prompted.

"That's about the size of it," Baron Silas nodded. "I had the know-how, and I had the people behind me. When he died, my daddy wasn't baron—there still wasn't one. But I made sure everyone knew that if the search was gonna continue, then I had to be baron and had to have the whip hand. It'd need a strong man to handle what would happen if we actually found a well.

"So they made me the baron, and after a little more searching I finally found the motherlode. By this time we were a lot richer in Salvation anyway, 'cause word gets around and there's too many folks who'd want to be on that train when it starts rollin'. They don't wanna get left behind, and so they're all too willing to start paying you favors."

"But they always want payback," Ryan pointed out.

"Oh yeah, and they know they'll get it," the baron agreed. "And finally I hit paydirt, about two years back. Found a well, found it was still capable of a good yield and got it capped. But that's when the real work begins. You see, in order to get a well like that working, and to get that raw shit refined into usable wag fuel, that takes a lot of machinery. And to get that all built and working takes jack and manpower. Now that's something we didn't have enough of in Salvation. Y'all probably saw how small we were…still are."

"You mean the walls?" J.B. mused. "They're an impressive construction."

"And necessary—not just now," Baron Silas said. "Back in the day when we were still basically a wag-repair town, there was a lot of jack coming in, and a lot of valuable supplies. We also had trade convoys who were completely at mercy because they were being serviced. So sec was always a major concern. And when we were a small ville, we built the walls around where we lived and worked.''

''But now?'' the Armorer queried.

Baron Silas shrugged. ''When we capped the well, that's when I knew that we had to get outside help. There was no way that we could pay or trade for all the materials we needed on our own, and no way that we had enough people in the ville to work on the well and refinery and still keep enough trade going to keep the ville alive. So that's when I started to make alliances. 'Cept that alliances means more people, and we ain't got the room. And there's nothing like that for making people a mite testy.''

THE MIND of Baron Silas traveled back momentarily to a few weeks before, when there had been a meeting in that very room of the barons involved in the alliances concerned with the well.

As always, Baron Silas was at the head of the table. Standing behind him were two armed sec guards. He hated having armed sec in his own baronial halls, but figured it was a necessary precaution as all the other barons in attendance had their own armed guard, and to be without would be foolish. And Baron Silas Hunter didn't maintain his position by being foolish.

There were eight barons in attendance, from the far-flung villes that had formed the alliance to reap the profits of the revitalized well. The bargaining had been hard, but the agreement had been forged over the amount of jack and manpower that each ville had guaranteed to the project, which in itself was determined by the size of the ville and its proximity to Salvation.

Nearest Silas on each side of the table were Baron Silveen from Mandrake, and Baron Lord from Hush, curiously named because of the valley in which it was situated, which seemed to deaden all sound coming out and kept it secure from outside prying eyes. Next down were barons John the Gaunt from Haigh, and Red Cloud from Running Water. The latter was the ville from where Crow had originated, the foreman coming to Salvation as part of the project and being adopted as a close associate of Silas because of his qualities. Farther down the table—as they were farther from Salvation—came Baron Abraham and Baron Cay from the villes of Carter and Water Valley. Farthest away was Baron Howard from Baker, and the baron of Dallas, Eddison. Baker was the farthest distance of any ville from Salvation, yet Dallas was one of the closest. But, as in the days of Silas's father, the farmers of the new Dallas were skeptical of the oil well of Salvation.

The eight barons were all leaning over the table, arguing and shouting at and over one another and at Silas, their angry voices a confusion of sound, a cacophony from which it was difficult to determine anything that resembled sense. The tense and fraught atmosphere had also transferred from the barons to the sec men who stood to the rear of them, all of whom were fingering a variety of automatic blasters, from Uzis to H&Ks and Thompsons. It seemed to Silas as he sat back and watched that any moment the atmosphere could crack, and violence erupt.

"Gentlemen, please," he yelled above the racket, trying to make himself heard. But there was no letup in the bickering. So Baron Silas rose to his feet, slipped one snakeskin boot from his foot and banged the heel on the table repeatedly. The piercing clatter of the heel on wood cut through the noise and silenced the barons, who stared at Baron Silas in amazement.

"That's better," he said in a quieter tone, slipping the boot back on. "Now, if you'll all stop playing stupe games to see who can shout louder than the other, let's address the issue at hand here."

"Sounds good to me," Cay said, his voice bluff and deep, ridiculously so for a man who stood at barely five feet. "What's it all about, that's what I want to know."

"You standing or sitting there, boy?" John the Gaunt muttered, directing the piercing gaze of his skeletal face to the rival baron. "Never can tell with you, just as I can never tell if you're asking a good question or talking shit."

"What did you say?" Cay exploded, rising to his feet, which in truth didn't make him much taller than when seated. "I—"

"Cool it, dude," Baron Lord murmured with a dismissive wave of the hand. "Let's leave the rivalries at the door while we're in this. If the well gets screwed, then we all go down together.''

"Which is exactly why I don't understand what's going on,'' Silveen blustered, thumping the table with his large, raw fist. "Who the fuck is sabotaging all our work?''

"And you think I don't want to know?'' Baron Silas countered. "Who stands to lose the most out of this? Yeah, sure we all lose out big time if it goes fugazi,'' he continued, forestalling the complaints from the collected barons, "but who loses most? Not only do I lose my dream, but I owe all you guys enough jack for you to move in and take over Salvation.''

"A fair point, Silas, I'll grant you that,'' Lord mused. "But the fact remains that work is running behind, and taking up more time and jack than it should. So why? And, more importantly, who?''

Silas shrugged. "Beats the hell out of me.''

"Well, it shouldn't,'' Lord continued. "After all, it's your sec boys who are patrolling the work areas, and who are guarding the well and refinery, as well as patrolling the camps. So why don't they spot anything?''

"Because whoever it is manages to make their attacks and plant their bombs between patrols, and I've only got so many men to patrol a big area and a hell of a lot of people.''

"So bring in some of our sec,'' Red Cloud countered.

Silas leaned forward, eyes blazing. "You think

I'm some kind of fool? Let some of your sec in and before long you oust me.''

"You don't and we do it anyway," Red Cloud said calmly. "This can't continue.''

Baron Eddison had been silent throughout the exchange, but now spoke up. "There's one thing that bothers me about all this, though.''

Silas raised an eyebrow, unable to hide the contempt he still felt for his old ville. "And that is, pray tell?''

Eddison leaned forward, looking down at the table, marshaling his thoughts before speaking. "Okay, let's look at it this way. We all have our villes near the old blacktop, which is how come we all are in this, right?'' He waited for a general agreement before continuing. "Yeah, so that means that the only way there could be any sabotage other than us is if it came from some ville that was from outside the area. 'Cause it'd have to be a big ville to have resources. Now apart from a few small scavenger tribes, there ain't jackshit like that around. Certainly not with the firepower to cause this much damage. We all agree on that?''

There was a muted agreement from around the table before Eddison continued.

"'Kay. So if it was some bunch of desperadoes from outside the area, ain't no way they could have slipped past every post on the way, or past every outlying sec guard for every ville on the way without getting' some kind of interest. That right?''

There was a silence while the assembled barons pondered the words of the quiet man.

"Guess that's right," Baron Silas agreed eventually, on behalf of all of them.

Eddison nodded. "That's what I figure. In which case, it's an inside job. Now we all ain't that stupid to want to shaft each other—" he took a long hard look at the barons gathered around the table "—leastways, not so that we shaft ourselves, as well. So it wouldn't make sense it if it was us."

There was an uncomfortable pause. Silas looked at the puzzled faces of the barons around the table…puzzled apart from Eddison, who was looking deep in thought.

Cay eventually spoke, his deep voice exploding into the silence. "But if it ain't outsiders, and it ain't us, then who the fuck is it?"

Eddison shook his head. "I dunno, but I could guess."

Silas had an uncomfortable feeling that he knew what the quiet man would say, so decided to get his view in first.

The baron coughed before speaking. "You wouldn't happen to be thinking along the same lines as I am right now, would you?"

"Depends what they are," Eddison said.

"It occurs to me that if we aren't responsible ourselves, it could be that our people are."

"You triple stupe!" Silveen roared, bringing his fist down on the table with a thump that made the wood shake. "If we're not responsible, then how could we be if…if…'' He spluttered into a red-faced silence, shrugging.

Silas allowed himself a smile. It was obvious that Silveen hadn't used his brain to get the baron's position in Mandrake.

Baron Abraham, who had been listening in silence as the argument unfolded, leaned forward and spoke, directing his comments generally although he looked at Silveen as he spoke.

"We might not be directing it, but our people could still be fighting among themselves, right?"

"I suppose it's possible, but why are they attacking the project and not each other?" Silas asked with a shrug.

"Does it matter?" John the Gaunt asked with soft menace. "The only thing that matters is that they're stopped. And the buck for that stops with you." He emphasized the last word with a jabbing, bony finger that was directed at Baron Silas.

The baron looked from the pointing John the Gaunt to the other barons, all of whom were now staring at him.

He had to do something. The success of the oil well and his continuing reign as baron of Salvation would depend on some kind of action…and a visible action at that.

AFTER RECALLING this exchange to the companions, Baron Silas sat back and held up his hands, gesturing to the hall around him.

"So this is all at stake. This and the dream."

Ryan said nothing for a moment. He looked around at his companions. J.B. had an impassive expression, still contemplating the baron's words. Mildred looked unimpressed, as did Krysty. Jak was, if anything, more impassive than the Armorer. Dean caught his father's eye, and Ryan saw his own cynicism at the baron's words reflected back at him. As for Doc, well, Doc was off in a land that only Doc knew.

"I don't buy the dream bit," Ryan said eventually. "I never met a baron yet who didn't place jack, good trade and his own skin below a dream. But I'll grant you need some action. Question is, what."

Baron Silas rose to his feet and walked over to one of the ironwork-covered windows and looked out on Salvation with his hands clasped behind his back.

"You have any idea why the people from the villes would put all this at risk?"

"Because it isn't theirs," J.B. answered. "Salvation isn't theirs, no matter where any baron sends them. And no matter what they're supposed to be doing, there's no way they're going to be happy living and working close to those who've been their enemy for so long, not without the chance to hit back."

"So why not just fight each other?" Silas questioned. "Yeah, we've had a few bar and gaudy brawls between different ville folk, but that's all. Why attack the project?"

Doc smiled, allowed himself a throat clearing, then spoke. "I suspect, my dear sir, that you already have an answer for that, but wish to see if we are smart enough to work that out. I would assume from what you have said that the camps with the workers are located in close proximity to each other at the site of the well and resurrected refinery.'' When Baron Silas assented with the briefest of nods, Doc continued. ''Then it would be reasonable to assume that they have—if not so originally placed—then certainly gravitated into groups concomitant with their place of origin.''

The baron turned and gave Doc a quizzical look.

''They are in groups like miniature versions of their villes,'' Doc clarified. ''And indeed, they are working on their own tasks in these groups.''

Baron Silas nodded. ''It made more sense to keep them like that.''

Dean exploded. ''Hot pipe! I got it, Doc! Crow said something about big jack bonuses for getting work done on time. Mebbe the different villes are trying to screw up each other's chances.''

''Stupe behavior,'' Jak said simply. ''Longer work take, less jack all round.''

''Maybe, but maybe they wouldn't think that far ahead,'' said Mildred. ''People don't when they're faced with their own prejudices.''

''Some things haven't changed through history, no matter what,'' Krysty added.

Baron Silas returned to his position at the head of the table, but remained standing, leaning on the table with his knuckles and looking them over.

''I needed something different, and quick. Then

you came out of the desert like the answer to a man's prayers. Make no mistake, I would have had you chilled at any other time, 'cause you would have got in the way. But Crow had a feeling you could come good, and so we let the workers rag you, see what you did without any weapons. You got chilled, then too bad. But you didn't. You did good, real good. And you're just what I need.''

"So what's the deal?" Ryan said simply.

"The deal is this—you get your blasters and other weapons back, and you become my elite sec, patrolling the camp, well and refinery until the project is complete. I figure you could whip those bastards into line without too many problems. All you have to do is stop them blowing each other and the project to hell. Shouldn't be too hard.''

"And then?"

"Then you leave with a jack bonus. You do me right, I do you right.''

Ryan looked at the man. His every instinct told him that Baron Silas Hunter was a ruthless, single-minded baron. And yet his coldness was such that he would be the worst liar Ryan had ever met.

"Why don't you trust your own sec?" he asked.

"I trust them, but I know from experience they can't handle it. Too many other duties. Besides, they've been too involved. You're harder, and you come from outside, with a fresh eye—no offense," he added with a mirthless smile.

Ryan ignored the crack. Either heavy humor or an insult to establish superiority, it wasn't worth the trouble either way. He said simply, "We'll discuss it."

Silas walked the length of the hall to the door in silence. It was only when he was about to close the doors and leave them alone that he tossed over his shoulder, "Not much to discuss, but I'll give you some time."

When he had closed the door, Mildred sat back and blew out her cheeks, tossing her plaits around her head.

"Shit, what have we got ourselves into?"

"What have I got you into, you mean," Ryan said wryly.

"No, you just did what was right at the time," Mildred replied. "I just don't like the look of it."

"Yeah, mebbe you've got a point there," Ryan said, stroking his chin. "It's not a good position, but we've been in worse."

"There's no immediate danger," Krysty said. "But it's going to be hard to get through this. We're walking into what amounts to a ville war where everyone's really within hitting distance."

"And on top of that, we're going to be sitting on top of a fuel dump that could literally blow beneath us," Dean added.

"Thanks for reminding me," Mildred said.

"Problem is, we needed to give up our blasters to get food and water, and the chances of us getting better supplies depended on us going along with Crow. Mebbe we could come out of this with some jack to trade with," Ryan said.

"That's if we can trust Silas," Krysty said softly.

"I think we can," Ryan said firmly. "He's hard and mean, all right, but that type can't lie. He'd enjoy telling you what he was going to do to you too much. He's put us in a shitty position as it is—there's no need for him to be hiding anything. Besides which, if we don't play ball, we don't get our weapons back."

"That's his winning hand," J.B. mused. The Armorer pushed his fedora back on his forehead and scratched. "Way I see it is this—if we agree, then Baron Silas Hunter gets his extra sec force. If we fuck up, then he blames us and chills us. If we come good, he gets credit and glory in front of the other barons. In return we get our weapons back, put ourselves on the line and mebbe come out of it to the good. But he knows we've got no option. After all, here we are in the middle of his house, surrounded by his sec people and in the middle of his ville, which is heavily walled. He knows we've got no option. We could mebbe get so far, but get right out of here in one piece, unarmed?" The Armorer shook his head and pushed his spectacles up his nose.

There was a moment's silence. For J. B. Dix to make such a long speech was rare, but in the circumstances he had articulated the thoughts of everyone on the subject.

"Shit, I ain't happy about this, but I guess J.B.'s right," Mildred said eventually.

Ryan nodded. "Then we do it."

They all assented, albeit reluctantly in some cases.

Ryan strode to the double doors and flung them open. Baron Silas was waiting outside, leaning against the wall with his Stetson hat pulled down over his eyes.

"I knew you'd agree," he said before Ryan had a chance to speak.

Chapter Ten

Baron Silas Hunter led the companions down through the levels of the building until they reached the basement. Each floor, from what they could glimpse on their way down, was stuffed full of predark treasures, both in terms of furniture and art. Certainly, Doc and Mildred, whose existence in the days before skydark gave them a better knowledge of such things, got the impression that Silas Hunter, for all his seeming bluff approach, had a side that relished the finer things of the predark age. And even though these items had little value in the new age compared to essentials like fuel, food and water, those whose business was to trade still knew of select markets that would pay good jack for such things.

All of which added up to an expensive habit that Baron Silas had to feed. It was no wonder that he was keen to stamp out the sabotage to his well and refinery.

"Notice how all the sec men here are kept out of the way," J.B. muttered to Ryan as they descended the staircase from the ground floor to the lower level, and then through a less ostentatious room to a smaller, plainer stair that led to the basement.

"Yeah," the one-eyed man grunted, "unless I'd

seen those sec men earlier, I'd wonder if he had any at all.''

''So where does he keep them, and how do they know when they're wanted?'' the Armorer queried.

No sooner had the question died on his lips than the answer became apparent. The baron opened a small door that sat at the foot of the staircase, which wasn't entirely lit by artificial light as they had descended below ground level. The old light fittings of the house down here were powered by a generator that ran through the light ring circuit with a gentle pulse, causing the slightest flicker of the light. It cast a sinister shadow over the baron's features as he turned and smiled his peculiarly humorless grimace at them.

''Welcome to my nerve center,'' he said before opening the door and ushering them in.

They entered with Ryan and J.B. in front, followed by Krysty, Jak, Mildred, Doc and Dean bringing up the rear. As Dean entered the room, with Baron Silas behind him, closing the door, he let out a whistle that was long and low.

''Hot pipe! This is some setup!''

For the room, with two doors leading off at the far end, seemed to run the length of the building, and housed the sec for the baronial palace. Twelve armed sec men, all heavily muscled, milled about the room. Some were talking among themselves, two were ready at each door to move on command and the rest were either stationed at, or observing casually, the bank of monitors that ran along the wall.

"Like most of these old predark places, this must've been used as some kind of local sec building," Baron Silas began, "and I picked this as my dwelling and nerve center because of that. It's built to be almost impregnable, and once I got the metalwork in place, it was virtually impossible to get in without being seen. Which brings me to this..." He moved in front of the monitor systems, the screens of which all had a slight shimmer that ran in sync with the pulsing light and, presumably, the pulsing of the generator. "This," he continued, "is my secret weapon when I'm here. This makes the place about as safe as you can get. All of this was in place when I took over the building. Lord alone knows what they did here before the nukecaust, but it must have been pretty damn important, and they must've liked to spy on whoever was here, 'cause when I first saw this I wondered where the hell the cameras for these were. Shit, some of them are so well hidden in the rooms that it took me hours to find them, even trying to work it out from what I could see. 'Cause first thing I did was get a generator fired up and get some good ol' boys in here to take a look at what we had. It's a good system, and we're fucked if it ever breaks down 'cause no one hereabouts has ever come across one like it. But it works...."

Baron Silas moved away from the monitors and stood in the middle of the dimly lit hall that stretched under the building's length. "It means that I can keep my eye on anything that goes on in here, and listen in to anything, 'cause those cameras've got microphones on them, too.'' He paused, to allow the import of this to sink in, then continued. ''So I know that you're none too keen on this job, but you know you ain't got a choice. And that's true. You either do it or you don't leave…and believe me,'' he added, addressing J.B. directly, ''you were right about how hard it'd be to get out.''

''So if you know how we feel, why all this?'' Ryan said, indicating the room and the sec men, who were listening curiously.

''Just to let you know, and to say that I know how you feel. And that's okay. But don't try and slack on me, 'cause I'll come down hard. You're outnumbered here, remember that.''

Ryan allowed himself a wry smile. Of course, that was why they were getting the warning and the view of the palace's full sec force and facilities.

''Point taken, so just give us back our weapons,'' he said simply.

Baron Silas nodded, and two of the sec men left the room by one of the far-flung doors, returning a few moments later with a collection of weaponry that they placed carefully on the floor in front of their baron. Silas stepped back and indicated that the companions retrieve their individual weapons.

Ryan picked out his SIG-Sauer, his Steyr and his trusty panga, as well as the ammo for his blasters. Jak followed, collecting his .357 Magnum Colt Python and his leaf-bladed knives. They were secreted in his jacket so swiftly that no naked eye could follow where he hid them. Krysty retained her .38-

caliber Smith & Wesson Model 640, while Dean went for his Browning Hi-Power and Mildred her Czech-made ZKR. Doc reholstered his LeMat pistol, and was pleased to see his silver lion's-head swordstick once more, with its blade made of the finest Toledo steel. Which left a pile of weaponry that belonged to J.B. alone. As he sheathed his Tekna knife and took up his Uzi and Smith & Wesson M-4000 before pocketing the supplies of ammo, the grens and plas-ex in the capacious pockets of his jacket, it was easy to see why he was called the Armorer.

For almost the first time since they had encountered him, Baron Silas Hunter showed some genuine emotion as he whistled long and low. "Shit," he said softly as he watched J.B., "you're a one-man army, boy. No wonder Crow figured you people'd be useful."

As the companions settled themselves back into their weapons, adjusting once more to the weight and balance of the hardware about their bodies so they became as one with the weapons, Baron Silas moved toward the far door, beckoning them to follow.

Falling into the regular line with Ryan in lead and J.B. behind him, they left the sec room and the sec force who were still openmouthed in amazement and admiration at the load carried by the Armorer, and joined Baron Silas in a large underground garage space that housed two wags. Both were open-topped trucks of the type used for the transportation of men and goods, similar to the one used for taking the construction materials to and from the cinder-block site where they had first encountered the people of Salvation. The garage space stank of fuel, and had tools and engine parts scattered on a workbench. It was lit by a single low bulb, with an old spotlight lying idle unless needed for repairs.

"Not much like a Baron's wag," Krysty said, indicating the two vehicles with a toss of her red mane.

"I like good things, but it don't do to show too much," Baron Silas said. "If I need to travel far, then I use one of the armored wags from the depot we have—like the one you came back in. Otherwise, these do fine for getting out to the well, seeing as every time I go I have to take men or supplies. I seen some of them old wags come through our hands that other barons might use, but they just look pretty and don't have no purpose. First thing I learned about wags and fuel when I came here is that they ain't jackshit good unless they do something. Otherwise they're just a waste. Besides which, one of those fancy wags wouldn't fit all of you in, and since we're headed out for the well right now..." He let the sentence hang in the air with a slight shrug.

"Mebbe you're right and we can trust him," Krysty whispered to Ryan, "but, lover, he sure as hell is a complex man for a baron. Can we actually second-guess him?"

"Just have to try," Ryan answered as the companions climbed into the back of one of the wags and settled on the dusty bench seats that ran on either side of the low wag, the frame over the top standing bare, its canvas covering long since perished or lost.

Baron Silas climbed into the front, taking the driver's position, and was joined by a sec man who came from the other room to ride shotgun on the journey out.

"I trust you people can ride your own shotgun," Silas shouted over the noise of the old wag engine as it fired up.

"Trust no one better," Jak answered. The baron wouldn't have heard him over the engine noise, but his companions did. It was something with which they all agreed.

THE WAG ROARED out of the underground garage and into the hard, harsh light of a day in Salvation. The sudden glare made them all squint, particularly Jak, whose red albino eyes were particularly sensitive to light.

Sitting on the bench seat and holding on to one of the otherwise useless metal covering supports, Ryan shifted his weight so that he could see where they had emerged. His good eye adjusting to the light, he could see that the entrance to the garage was down a steep slope at the rear of the building, and as he looked back down that slope he could see a pair of sec men pushing heavy ironwork gates back into position before closing the double doors behind. It was difficult to tell at such a distance, but the doors seemed to be of iron themselves.

Baron Silas was obviously a firm believer in keeping his ass covered.

The wag slowed suddenly as it came around the

front of the building and ran into the crush of people that they had noticed on their entrance to the ville. All around them was a heaving mass of people, jammed too close together within the confines of the ville. The street surfaces were of stone and tarmac, but some areas had been stripped where old buildings had fallen and been cleared, and the dry earth beneath had been revealed. These sections of the roads and walkways threw up clouds of dust that mingled with the sweat and odor of the too densely packed population, forming an almost visible cloud that choked the atmosphere, making breath hard to grasp.

There was an immense noise that hit them as they rounded the corner, like walking into a wall of speech and song, the sounds of people trading, conversing and arguing as they went about their daily business. People hung from windows, shouting at those below while the subjects of their attention returned the favor with an equal volume. There was the clash of metal on metal as barrows and bicycles collided, while workmen hammered and sawed, and the sound of brick, stone and wood being beaten down by everyday life. And to complete the overload to the senses, there was a riot of color as people from Salvation and the villes who were part of the alliance collided in the street with an array of hair and skin tone, clothes in an assortment of wildly colored rags and fabrics.

If there was an order to what was occurring, if there was any reason to the tasks and any purpose to the actions, then all of this seemed lost in the general melee.

"Makes the desert seem kind of attractive," J.B. muttered, observing it.

"You may not be saying that if where we're headed is anything like this, John," Mildred pointed out.

Doc stroked his chin and smiled mirthlessly. "Like a maze fit for rats, and possibly populated by them. Ah, if the encampments at the well and refinery bear even the most passing of resemblances to this Byzantium, then proverbs involving needles and haystacks spring readily to the mind."

Dean looked at the seemingly old man, a puzzled expression on his face. "I keep trying to tell you, Doc—less words, more meaning," he said wearily.

"Second that," Jak agreed.

Krysty decided to interpret. "It's an old predark phrase. Doc just means it'll be a triple-stupe task, like looking for an honest man in a gaudy house."

The wag made its torturous way through the streets of Salvation until it came to the ville walls, following the roadway around until it reached the gateway. Whether this was the same one they had come through, or one of the other compass points of the ville it was impossible to say, as they weren't as yet familiar enough with the ville of Salvation.

The fact that they were with the baron of the ville meant that the gates were opened and they were allowed to pass with the maximum of speed and the minimum of good-natured banter. Another point

Ryan noted was that the sec men were almost in awe of Baron Silas, suggesting that he ran a hard regime among his sec forces.

Looking back as they drove away down the road from Salvation, they could see the gates being closed on them, and the teeming life beyond, which was in stark contrast to the desert that stretched out around them. The road they traveled was made of concrete, the long slabs being joined together by tar that had worn away in places, making the ride less than smooth. From this, and from the fact that the sun had moved in the sky, they could tell that they were leaving from a different road, and that their destination— the well and refinery—were to the east of the ville.

The desert sun beat down on them, unprotected in the rear of the wag. It was a different kind of heat from that in the ville: drier, more directly intense as they traveled under the sun with nothing to break up the orange-red orb's rays.

It wasn't long before they were sweltering. Even the breeze created by the speed of the wag, which had picked up under Baron Silas's hand since they left the confines of the walled ville, wasn't enough to dull the heat.

Ryan stood up and made his way to the front of the wag, clinging to the iron bars that lifted naked into the desert air and swinging the top half of his body around so that he could put his head in through the open window on the driver's side.

As he swung around, he found himself staring a blaster full in the muzzle.

"Fireblast!" the one-eyed warrior yelled involuntarily as he switched the weight of his swing, using the momentum to carry him out of the range of the blaster as the muzzle exploded with a deafening roar, a brief burst, seemingly of flame, and the stink of cordite as the slug ripped past the space where his good eye had been a fraction of a second before.

The wag swerved and screeched to a halt, and Ryan was thrown from his tenuous position, hitting the ground in a roll at a force that took the breath from his body. It was just fortunate that in swerving, the wag had turned so that he was thrown onto sand rather than the concrete road surface that would have pulped his shoulder and ribs.

As he straightened painfully, he saw his friends leap from the back of the wag, and the driver's door open to disgorge Baron Silas.

"You triple-stupe bastard!" yelled the baron, coming over to Ryan. "Why the fuck did you do that? Instinct made me draw and fire before I could think."

"Guess I should be impressed," Ryan hissed painfully through gritted teeth as he rose to his feet. A look to his companions told them to withdraw hands that were poised to unholster blasters.

Baron Silas stopped in front of the one-eyed man and offered him his hand. Ryan took it, and as the baron helped him to his feet, Silas said, "You shouldn't have done that. I've been jumpier than a stallion with fleas and a mare in season since this shit started to go down. Anyone comes up on me like that is likely to end up chilled.''

"I'll remember that," Ryan said with feeling. "All I was going to do was ask how long till we reached our destination.''

"'Bout as long as it takes to get over there," Baron Silas replied, casting his arm out and pointing to the horizon.

There, shimmering in the heat haze, an oil derrick and a cluster of buildings were visible. To one side was a motley collection of shacks and shelters.

And in the middle of it all was an oily cloud of smoke bespeaking a fire.

"Looks like we're riding right into trouble without being able to draw breath," the one-eyed man remarked.

"They not know what hit them," Jak replied, shielding his eyes to stare into the distance.

"That's what I'm relying on," Baron Silas countered.

"What we're all relying on," Doc added.

They remounted the wag and the baron fired it up, turning and heading toward the oil well…and toward a firefight in more ways than one.

Chapter Eleven

As they approached the well and refinery, they could see more clearly that the thick, oily black cloud was coming not from the area of the well or the refinery buildings, but from the encampment where the workers had their shacks and settlements.

"Looks like they're trying to chill each other this time, not fire the well," Krysty remarked, the wind from the speeding wag making her hair whip in its wake.

"Yeah, and if we're headed for action we'd better be ready for it," Ryan replied, wincing as he flexed his battered shoulder. As he rotated the ball in its socket, it grated and sent a wave of pain down his arm as far as the elbow. He could think of better times for this injury than when he had a firefight in view, but what choice did he have now?

As the wag jerked and bumped at high speed over the derelict concrete road, the companions checked their weapons, making sure that they were in working order after their brief sojourn with Baron Silas's sec men. All weapons were loaded with cartridge, shot or shell, and rounds were chambered ready for action, which was getting closer with every twist and turn of the road.

There was no indication of where the well and refinery area actually began or ended. Ryan remembered the baron saying that the sec force he had on-site was stretched thin, but how thin was nonexistent? For, as far as his eye could see, there was little sign of any sec force actually standing guard over whatever passed for the perimeters of the area. Maybe they'd all had to hightail it over to the area where the smoke originated from. That would leave the area wide open if that was a decoy. Right at that moment he wished he could ask Baron Silas about the sec setup, but at this speed and with the baron in the driving seat, that was an impossibility.

The one-eyed warrior turned to his people, all of whom had completed their weapons check and were now perched on the bench seats, riding the twists, turns and bucking motion of the old wag.

"Okay, we don't really know what we're riding into here, but it's going to be a tough one. We don't know how many sec men Silas has in there, or whether they'll recognize us. And if there's some kind of firefight going on between the different workers, then it'll be a free-for-all."

"Won't be the first time, won't be the last," J.B. remarked. "Anyway, where are these sec men of Silas's anyway? I haven't seen jackshit as we've got near. Anyone could move about and screw up the well."

"Anyone could if they could get across this desert," Mildred said thoughtfully. "But what if the trouble in the camp is a diversion, because maybe there's some sabotage at the well or refinery.''

Ryan nodded. ''If the sec force is that thinly stretched, that'd be the way to do it during daylight. Mebbe we should take a little diversion and have a recce, just because…''

The one-eyed man strode to the front of the wag and rapped hard several times on the roof of the cab with the butt of his Steyr. The finely shaped and molded stock made a sharp cracking sound on the battered metal of the wag that cut through the full-throated roar of the wag's engine. At first, Baron Silas ignored the constant rapping, but Ryan kept hitting the roof, cursing to himself at the stubbornness of the baron in ignoring him.

Eventually, the wag slowed, almost to a halt, and Ryan yelled, ''I'm coming around!'' before swinging himself around, wincing at the pain forced down his arm from his shoulder, to face the baron through the window.

''What the hell is it?'' Baron Silas asked, keeping the engine ticking over and the wag moving at a walking pace.

''Your sec force—they'd move to sort out trouble at the camp, yeah?''

The baron assented. ''That's their job. What else would—?''

Ryan cut him off. ''Then if they're as thinly stretched as you say, it could be that they've left the well and refinery open to attack.''

"The workers on there have blasters, they could hold off until—"

"Until what? If you're right, then they might be the ones out to wreck the well. They could be fighting among themselves even now."

Baron Silas's jaw dropped. It was an obvious assumption, but one that had momentarily escaped him in his determination to reach the camp. "Shit," he muttered quietly, "then we'd better—"

"Yeah, take the long way around and check out the well first. Now go!" Ryan swung himself back into the main body of the truck.

Needing no second bidding, Baron Silas Hunter gunned the engine into life once more, slamming his foot down and putting the gears through torturous changes in his eagerness to get the vehicle up to its maximum speed. He slewed off the road and took the short route across the dusty but hard-packed earth of the Texas desert, driving the wag over terrain that wasn't meant to take an ancient vehicle with poor suspension.

"Assuming that we arrive in one piece, will we be able to see straight enough to aim and fire at any particular enemies?" Doc asked grimly as he was thrown across the width of the wag.

"That'll be nothing if we can do this without breaking any bones," Dean retorted as he, too, was flung to the floor of the wag.

J.B. joined Ryan at the front of the wag, both men standing firm against the back of the cab, using the metal stanchions to support themselves as they fixed their gaze on the well and refinery buildings, which were approaching at rapid speed.

"Seems quiet enough," the Armorer remarked. "Too quiet. I can't see anyone moving...or is that just these damn spectacles?"

Ryan allowed himself a smile. "You need glasses, and I've got just the one eye, but between us we should be able to see if there's some fireblasted activity, and I sure as hell can't see anything, either."

As they came even closer to the derrick and outbuildings, it became obvious that there was little sign of any work taking place, or of any workmen on-site. The wag came up close to the derrick, and from their position on the back both Ryan and J.B. could see that the workers had left the site in a hurry. There were tools and partially completed works everywhere, discarded and left where they had been dropped.

"What do you reckon?" Ryan asked his oldest friend.

"Figure they saw the smoke, ran for the camp," J.B. mused. "It'd work as a diversion."

"You mean they all run for the camp except those who know that trouble's coming, and then they get a clear run to do whatever they want."

J.B. nodded. "Yep, that's just about the size of it."

The wag came to a halt, and Baron Silas and his sec guard scrambled out. Ryan and his group stayed in the rear of the wag. Silas looked back toward them.

"Y'all not doing anything?" he asked, his voice half anger and half bemusement.

"Not just yet," Ryan replied calmly. "First of all, I want to know a few things. How many work on the site?"

Baron Silas furrowed his brow and gave Ryan a searching glance before framing an answer. He couldn't see why the one-eyed man wanted to know, and to him it just seemed that they were wasting time. Finally he said, "Guess there's about two hundred all told, most of them on the refinery works. On the derrick, I'd say about fifty, mebbe sixty when there's some heavy construction."

Ryan nodded absently as he took the figure in, then asked, "So how many people all told in the camps?"

Baron Silas answered heatedly. "Most of them have got womenfolk with them, some with kids... mebbe double that, a little over. But what the hell has this got to do with—?"

Ryan cut him off. "It's got to do with playing numbers. That's a shit load of people for anyone to sec, let alone a few of your people and just us. And that's also a real easy number to get lost in. Any saboteurs in there are really going to be able to hide easily—too damn easily."

"So why the fuck are you standing there pissing in the wind when there could be some sabotage going on right now?" Baron Silas yelled angrily.

"Because anyone who's up to anything would have heard us arrive, and they'd as sure as shit hear you now. The camp is how far?'' Ryan added, appearing to go off on a tangent as he looked around to locate the camp. It was easy to find by searching out the column of smoke that was rising above it. It seemed about a mile off to the southwest. "How long does it take to reach there?'' he added before Baron Silas had a chance to answer the first question.

"Not long by wag,'' Silas replied.

"But how do the workers do it?'' Ryan quizzed.

"By foot. I guess it takes about fifteen minutes,'' Silas said after a little thought.

J.B. was staring into the distance toward the camp. "Fire must've been going longer than that, because there's no one in sight. So they're either in the camp, or still here.''

"They?'' Silas asked.

"Whoever's sabotaging the refinery—if that's what's going on,'' Mildred replied, climbing down from the wag, where she was joined by Jak and Dean. "Because they aren't in sight, and they aren't here at the derrick. So, if anyone's still around to do a little quick sabotage, then they're at the refinery buildings. It's simple when you think about it,'' she added with a touch of sarcasm that didn't escape the baron.

"Then shouldn't y'all be doing something?'' he retorted.

"That's just what we're about to,'' Ryan answered in a cool tone as he dismounted the wag. J.B., Doc and Krysty joined the others, until they were all standing on the side of the wag that faced away from the derrick and toward the refinery, which was a couple of hundred yards distant. The one-eyed man faced his people after a searching glance at the refinery buildings, and the maze of pipework that connected the two.

"Okay," he began, "we don't know the layout and we don't know what we might be facing, so let's go triple red and stay frosty. J.B., you and Dean take the first two buildings, while Mildred and Jak take the other two. Krysty and Doc, come with me. We'll split into three and take the pipe sections one at a time. Be real careful. That's a real maze in there, and there's a shit load of places for any coldhearts to hide and chill us. We're looking for more than just people. Keep a sharp lookout for any plas-ex that may be around, and careful of booby traps." He looked at his companions. They had taken in every word, and were ready. He nodded, as much to himself as to anyone else. "Okay, let's go."

They separated into the three groups and headed off—J.B. and Dean toward the blocks nearest, and Mildred and Jak circling to take in the more distant of the two refinery buildings.

The buildings were all alike—old red brick constructions surfaced in concrete, with old wire reinforcements over window openings that had lost their glass many decades ago. J.B. and Dean arrived at theirs first, flattening themselves on either side of the open doorway.

J.B. held the Uzi, set to single shot, which he figured was his best option in an enclosed space. Dean had his Browning Hi-Power ready. The two fighters exchanged glances, and J.B. signaled with a brief, almost imperceptible nod.

The Armorer went first. Turning swiftly, he flung himself into the open doorway, Dean behind covering him. Crouching, J.B. sought cover and found it behind a large metallic pump, coming up with the barrel of the Uzi resting on top of the metallic structure. His eyes adjusted quickly to the gloom, noting that the running strips of neon that took the length of the ceiling hadn't been repaired, and that the light that existed within the building came from low-level oil lamps that were used to spotlight the actual work sites in progress. They had been left burning, suggesting that the evacuation to the camp had been swift and sudden.

Dean had reached the same conclusion as he sought cover behind a console that controlled that range of pumps and filters in the building. He listened intently, and like the Armorer was sure that the building was empty. He looked across to where J.B. was reconning the area, and their eyes met in the gloom. Dean picked up a piece of metal tubing and held it so that J.B. could see it. The Armorer knew what the boy intended to do. With an overarm throw the young Cawdor tossed the metal tube into the air, following an arc that took in most of the length of the building before clattering on a workbench and piece of machinery, then rolling noisily across the floor before coming to a halt against the far wall.

It was followed by total silence. There was no

sound, no sudden reaction of blasterfire, nothing to suggest that anyone else was in the building.

J.B. looked across at Dean and made a motion with his arm, indicating that they take the sides of the building, staying close to the walls to give themselves protection. At the drop of J.B.'s hand, they ran down the sides of the building, taking each aisle and indented position where an enemy could hide with a combat stance, ready to fire first and ask questions after.

They reached the end of the building in less than thirty seconds. It was empty. The second building was connected by a corridor and then a covered walkway. J.B. and Dean stopped by the doorway.

"I'll take it first. You cover me," Dean said breathlessly. J.B. nodded, and the boy weaved his way down the narrow walkway to the far door while J.B. covered him with the Uzi, set to rapid fire.

Again it was silence. Dean assumed a secure position at the far end and took guard as J.B. ran down the walkway to join him.

"Same as before?" Dean said shortly. J.B. nodded, and they repeated their procedure for the second building.

It, too, was empty.

As they walked back through the buildings—still on triple red, in case a hidden intruder should have evaded them—J.B. remarked, "I wonder if there is anyone here?"

IT WAS A QUESTION that Mildred and Jak were also asking themselves. It took them a little longer to get to the far buildings, which were of a different shape. Where the ones that J.B. and Dean investigated were rectangular, these were square buildings, and were the two main pump houses for the whole refinery site.

Which meant that there was little cover inside. The open doorways showed once more that the only lighting was supplied by oil lamps, and the interior was deathly quiet and Mildred and Jak stood on either side of the first door.

"Me first—cover," Jak whispered, his .357 Magnum Colt Python seemingly too large in his small hands. Mildred nodded, her ZKR ready to provide cover as the albino sprang into action.

Jak was through the door in a blur, his red eyes adapting to the gloom with ease, in fact preferring the lower level of light to the desert sun outside. There was little cover afforded by the inside of the building, as large piston-driven pumps took up the majority of the space. The good thing about this was that if it afforded little cover for Jak, then it would also afford scant cover for anyone else who was still in the pump house. Jak found himself a niche in a space between two piston housings, and took up a covering position. Mildred saw him settle in, then followed into the building, flattening herself to the wall and crouching as she sought cover.

It was obvious that the pump house was empty, but they double-checked, with Mildred covering Jak while the wiry albino hunter combed every crevice within the walls. He drew a blank and returned to her shaking his head.

"Next one," Mildred said quietly, to which he nodded.

Unlike the buildings that J.B. and Dean had investigated, the two pump house buildings weren't connected by a walkway or corridor, and there was only the one door in and out. So Mildred and Jak had to leave and traverse the side of the building they had just investigated before reaching the other. They took it in relay turns, one covering the other and using any cover available until they had moved across the short distance between the two pump houses.

"Same as before?" Mildred asked quietly as they reached the doorway. Jak gave her a brief nod, his stringy white hair snaking across his scarred face, red eyes glinting through, before disappearing through the doorway as Mildred swung around to provide cover with her ZKR.

They repeated the same procedure and found this building also empty.

"If planting plas-ex, then in Ryan's place," Jak commented as they exited the blockhouse.

BACK AT THE SYSTEM of pipes that traveled the distance between the well and the refinery, Ryan, Krysty and Doc were dividing up the territory. It wasn't easy, as the pipes took in both the well and refinery areas, and also the storage tanks for the final product, which stood some distance apart. There was nowhere to hide within them, as they weren't housed in buildings, standing open in the sun. But they could provide cover for anyone who wanted to stand surveillance on whoever may come along the pipe system. So the open nature of the ground left Ryan, Krysty and Doc with a problem—recce it without being an open target. The only good thing was that, by the same token, anyone who may be opposing them would have the same problem.

"Doc, you take the route from the outbuildings to the tanks," Ryan said as he sized up the problem, and the trio stood by the wag. As he spoke, the one-eyed man used his SIG-Sauer to indicate the nearest set of buildings, which were just about to be scoured by J.B. and Dean. Doc nodded briefly at that, understanding that Ryan had given him the nearest point to begin as he was the least swift of them.

Ryan switched the point of the SIG-Sauer barrel to the far buildings, and indicated the point where Jak and Mildred were about to enter their recce position. "Krysty, you take the pipe system from that point. We work our way toward the tanks. I'll take it from there," he continued, indicating a third position out to the farthest side from the refinery buildings, where the pipes came from the derrick. It was the greatest distance, and also the most open.

"Okay, lover," Krysty said softly, "we meet at the storage tanks, and stay calm. In that tangle of metal we don't want to make any mistakes, right?"

"Yeah, that would be kind of embarrassing, at the very least," Ryan said with the hint of a smile. "One more thing—let's just try and hold back on the blasterfire unless necessary. These pipes'll ricochet, and I don't think Baron Silas here will thank us for ripping holes in his system when that's what we're supposed to be stopping.''

He looked over at the baron, who, with his sec man, was standing against the wag, allowing the one-eyed man to take control. Just as though it were a test, which, in a sense, it was. Their first real test for Baron Silas Hunter.

Ryan glanced back to Doc, who was cradling his LeMat percussion pistol ruefully. ''I shall endeavor, my dear Ryan, to refrain—if necessary, then I shall use the ball alone,'' Doc said. ''After all, the shot would cause more damage—although that is, of course, its primary intent.''

''Fair point,'' Ryan said. ''Just stay triple alert, triple red, and keep moving as fast as possible, just in case there are any fuckers hiding among all that metal.''

The trio parted to begin their search.

Doc moved toward the nearest buildings, half running to conserve energy under the hot sun but also keep up speed. He could hear the movement of Dean and J.B. within the building, but as attuned as they all were to the sounds of one another, he could tell that they had so far found nothing, and so could devote all of his attention to traversing the pipes.

The metal was dull and dusty, but still acted as a conductor to the heat, and as soon as Doc moved into the snaking maze of pipes, he could tell that the heat had increased. It was an oppressive, dull and heavy heat that seemed to weigh down upon his brow, making him sweat harder and forcing a band of pressure around his forehead, making his skull ache and his eyes seem heavy and unfocused.

Pausing to shake his head to try to clear it, Doc began his recce of the pipes. Treading softly, and with his eyes darting glances to each side, he moved slowly along the middle of the narrow dirt path that had been formed between the pipes, presumably for the purposes of maintenance access. The pipes ran in stories of two or three, and were supported by large metal brackets that held them together. Between the pipes there was a little space with which to see on either side. They twisted and turned rather than running straight. Doc could only presume that this was to give them a greater overall running distance and so allow whatever processes were taking place in the refinery to settle in the precious liquid before it reached the storage tanks.

Right now, all it did was make life harder for Doc. There were a few blind bends on the way, and he slowed as he came to them, straining his eyes and ears for the slightest sign of movement. But there was nothing. In some ways, he would gladly have welcomed some action: it would have been a relief to nerves stretched almost to the breaking point.

The heat and the unending vista of dull and dust-encrusted metal began to get oppressive, and Doc found himself getting unaccountably angry. Why was he doing this? Why were they in thrall to an idiot cowboy who wanted to rebuild a technology that had taken him from his home and placed him in two futures that had prematurely aged him and taken his sanity? Why—?

Doc stopped suddenly, frozen to an almost uncanny stillness by a sound. It was getting nearer... Soft footsteps, but in a familiar rhythm. Very familiar...

Doc looked up instead of around. The towers of the storage tanks stood almost before him. He allowed himself a small smile. The footsteps were those of Krysty.

Like Doc, the woman had found the heat within the reflective surfaces of the pipes to be oppressive. Her hair coiled close to her neck with a combination of sweat and mutie sense—not exactly danger, but more an acute awareness that she was not at her best in this kind of atmosphere, so she had to exercise more caution.

Which she did, her flashing green eyes rapidly scanning the area around, taking in as Doc had the gaps between the brackets and stories of pipes. She moved fastidiously, her silver-tipped boots making little noise on the densely packed, dry earth, throwing up little clouds of dust around her ankles. She held her Smith & Wesson Model 640 blaster, its .38-caliber shells capable of blowing away anyone who would try to jump her. But she was unwilling to use it in such a confined area, and would rather rely on her strength and suppleness in hand-to-hand combat if it came to it—which it might, she reflected, as the enclosed space would make it hard for any attacker to use a blaster without endangering themselves.

She just wished it weren't so claustrophobic, an impression increased by the heat that seemed to beat off the metal pipes in waves and hit her around the head, making her eyes swim with a shimmering haze that she couldn't be sure wasn't external rather than just in her head.

And that tapping and shuffling... Was it for real or was it her imagination?

It was real. Krysty snapped from the fuzzy haze of her head into a hyper-real consciousness where pure instinct took over. She was still moving forward, but now everything was clearer than it had ever been, her instincts switched on to alert her to the slightest move. Looking ahead, she could see that she had almost arrived at the end of the pipe maze and was now within sight of the giant storage tanks. Her heightened senses also identified the only sounds other than her own: Doc. She relaxed slightly as she realized that they had both arrived at their destination simultaneously. There was a point ahead where they would both emerge into view: a point where the pipes finally began to feed into the tanks.

She slowed, and noticed that Doc's pace had also slowed.

"Doc," she said in a firm and clear voice, "it's me. I haven't found a damn thing."

"I know it is you, dear lady. I would recognize that most delicate of steps anywhere. I fear that I have also found nothing. Could it be that the site truly has been deserted, and we're not going to strike lucky with a saboteur?''

"That's a funny way of looking at things, wanting to find trouble," Krysty replied with a smile as they came into view of each other. "Though I guess if we did find someone messing with the site we could get a whole lot of answers out of them.''

"It would simplify our task somewhat," Doc mused. "But sometimes things don't run as smoothly as—''

He was cut off by the sound of voices and blasterfire. Without even looking at each other, both he and Krysty immediately set off to assist Ryan, who evidently had stumbled on something.

THE ONE-EYED MAN had been making similar progress to that of his companions. He jogged out to a point where the single pipeline from the oil well hit a series of wheels and junctions that carried the raw product off to the refinery buildings and then ferried it back before diverting it to the tanks. The knot of pipes, some piled four stories high with heavy metal brackets between, was a denser maze than the points he had sent his two companions to recce: but Ryan believed without question that, as leader, he had to take the most difficult tasks. Otherwise, what right had he to call himself leader and make decisions for others? Although his upbringing in Front Royal had ended in deceit and treachery, his father, Baron Titus, had certain ideas of what a baron or leader should be. His son had learned lessons that he carried with him always.

So Ryan took the hardest route to anything. There were always things to learn from that route. Although sometimes you could regret such ideas—such as now, when you were jogging across open ground toward an area where someone in concealment could pick you off as easily as shooting crows.

But this was a fortunate day for Ryan Cawdor, as he reached his destination with nothing in the way of danger. Squinting down the single pipeline to the well, he could see no sign of any activity or habitation. So anything that was going on would be within the knot of pipes that now stood to his left.

The one-eyed warrior didn't hesitate before plunging into the morass of metalwork, taking it in with a single glance. Although there was a complex maze, there was little room within for maneuver, and so it would be difficult for any enemy to conceal himself. But there was still that chance.

Ryan soon found the conditions as troublesome as Doc and Krysty had on their own recces. The reflected heat and the dust made his head pound, forcing him to concentrate even harder…which, in turn, made his head begin to ache even more. But he grimly set his jaw, ignoring the sting of salt sweat that ran into his one clear blue eye, and trickled beneath the patch, tracing the line of his scar and settling in the empty socket.

It was because he could be so focused that he heard the slightest of movements to the left of him, about ten yards ahead. A snuffle of breath, a shuffle of foot...it was enough for him to seek a cover position.

In the maze of twisted pipes, there was little to be found, but he had just turned a corner, and a quick step back took him to the cusp of the turn, allowing him a slight angle in which to seek cover.

"I got you," he yelled, "get into view with your blaster butt first and I won't rip you to shit."

"Big words when I've got the cover," returned a voice with a slight lilting brogue to it. It then said something in a language that Ryan couldn't understand. He had a feeling that it was something Krysty and Mildred had spoken about after their mat-trans jump to what remained of the United Kingdom. A language called Gaelic. But it was impossible to think—

This had run through the one-eyed man's head in the space of a few moments, during which time he had taken that step into cover and flicked the safety on the SIG-Sauer so that it was ready to fire. At the same time, his free hand snaked to the panga strapped to his thigh, the finely honed blade glinting even in this dull light when he slipped it free.

"Show yourself," Ryan yelled.

"Show myself and get chilled by some bastard that wants our jack bonuses? You think I'm as thick as you say we all are?"

Ryan's brow furrowed at the man's words. What the hell was he talking about? "You mean you're not here to wreck the pipeline?" he asked.

The hidden man laughed. "You think I'm going to fall for that? Go 'Oh no, of course not,' step out and get myself blown to hell? Mister, I knew that the fire downtown was caused by you people, and when everyone else went like a herd across the plain I was damned if I was going to let that happen again. That's why I'm waiting for you."

"I think you've got the wrong man, friend, but there's no way you'll believe that unless I make a gesture. If I throw down my blaster—"

"You'll have another behind your back," the hidden man retorted. "You think I'm some kind of simpleminded stickie or something?"

With which he decided to stop talking and start firing. Stepping out from his cover, he fired two rapid shots from a blaster that looked like a small but powerful handblaster—maybe a Smith & Wesson remake. But Ryan didn't intend to investigate too closely. Right now it didn't matter what the blaster was, only that it could rip holes on him and buy the farm.

The one-eyed man slammed himself up against the pipes on the angle of the turn, sideways on so that he made a smaller target. The ricochets from the two shells cannoned around him, but he ignored them, steeling himself. If they hit him, there was nothing he could do about that, as there was no point giving into his reactions there. Instead, he focused his entire attention on the man who was now standing out in the open.

Stupe. He was an open target, his fury and desire

to chill Ryan making him forget the most basic ideas of keeping cover. That was always assuming that he had ever known them in the first place.

It would have been good to have just wounded him, perhaps keep him alive so that they could question him about what had been going on. It was highly unlikely that he had anything to do with the sabotage, especially as his avowed aim had been the same as that for which Ryan and his companions had been hired. But that was immaterial. Right now he was an enemy, a danger, and like a mad dog on the loose. There was only one thing to do with him.

The one-eyed man raised his blaster and leveled it, aiming at the man's head. While the stupe stood in full view, trying to sight the partially concealed Ryan for another shot, the one-eyed warrior squeezed the trigger, loosing a 9 mm shell from the P-226, the blast muffled through the built-in baffle silencer.

There was a sudden silence, the muffled blast fading quickly and leaving no ricochet as the bullet hit home. The man stood for a moment, an expression of surprise crossing his face and then fixing there as life drained from him, freezing his features. The entry hole was small, but the exit wound at the back of his head was larger, part of the skull detaching and splattering on the earth behind, blood and brain bringing a small measure of moisture to the dry soil.

The blaster dropped from nerveless fingers, followed shortly after by the crumbling figure of the blaster's owner, now a lifeless husk.

Ryan holstered his SIG-Sauer and sheathed the

panga before stepping out of the scant cover and taking the few strides covering the short distance between him and the corpse. One thing for sure—the man was no fighter, as he had left himself open to attack and had missed a man in little cover from a short range.

Kneeling in front of the corpse, Ryan checked for any other weapons, or any plas-ex or grens. There was nothing that could suggest that this man was a saboteur. He moved away from the chilled body and checked the area where the man had been hiding. Again, there was no sign of anything that could remotely have been used to damage the pipeline. Adding this to what the man had said, Ryan could only assume that he had been taken for a saboteur himself.

He was still checking the area when Krysty and Doc arrived. He explained to them what had occurred, and was in the middle of this explanation when the others arrived. He filled them in briefly, and after he had finished, Mildred spoke.

"The Molly Maguires," she said simply.

"Which means?" J.B. asked, scratching his head beneath his fedora.

"It was something I remember from history lessons—the Gaelic Ryan mentioned triggered off a memory. It dates back to the end of the nineteenth, turn of the twentieth century. A group of migrant workers, from Ireland originally. Only I think it was coal rather than oil...maybe near Kansas. Anyway, they formed themselves into a secret society called the Molly Maguires, and set to a campaign of sabotage where they were working. It was designed to win them better working conditions, better pay. Maybe that's what's happening here. We should ask Baron Silas if he ups the jack bonuses every time there's trouble and the work falls behind schedule.''

"Ask me now,'' the baron drawled as he and his sec man came up to where the companions were gathered. "I see you got one of the bastards,'' he added, pushing through and prodding the chilled corpse with the toe of his boot. "From the look of him, I'd say he was one of Silveen's people, from Mandrake. They dress that way,'' he added, remarking on the vest and open undershirt the man wore, along with his heavily patched denims, thick leather belt and heavy boots. "So they're behind it, eh?''

"Don't jump to any conclusions,'' Mildred answered. "You heard what I was saying, right? Well, the Maguires used sabotage to up their pay and conditions, and maybe an equivalent group is doing this to up their bonuses. But maybe it's really just an interville fight that's spilled over onto your well. Just because the Maguires were Irish, and this man spoke Gaelic so I assume that Mandrake has a heavy Irish-descended population... Well, just because of that it doesn't mean to say that the Mandrake people are behind the sabotage. After all, Ryan found no evidence.''

"Mildred's right,'' the one-eyed man added. "This man had no plas-ex or grens on him, and there's none hereabouts. And from what he said to me, he thought I was the one who was going to plant them. So I reckon this poor stupe was trying to stop any sabotage, but wouldn't calm down enough to listen to me. It's not going to be that simple.''

Baron Silas Hunter fixed Ryan with a steely glare. ''It better be some easy, or else you may find that you don't get your easy passage out. Remember why I hired you.'' He turned on his heel and stormed off toward the wag, followed by his sec guard.

''Touchy, is he not?'' Doc remarked quietly.

''Guess you'd be if you had a whole heap of barons on your back and a big project like this that was screwing up on you,'' Dean replied.

''That is a fair point,'' Doc agreed before turning to face the camp, where the oily plumes of black smoke had decreased in intensity. ''It looks as though whatever happened back there is under control, so perhaps our friendly baron may wish to show us the forces he expects us to marshal.''

''You mean people he want us sec?'' Jak questioned, then shook his head sadly when Doc assented. ''Breath you waste on words chill me,'' the albino remarked.

''C'mon, let's go,'' Ryan said, leading them back to where the baron's wag was waiting, leaving the chilled corpse behind to be dealt with by another sec party, when the workers returned to their posts.

Baron Silas was waiting behind the wheel of the wag, the engine ticking over, staring impassively ahead. The sec man sat next to him, as blank a cipher as any living being could be. The companions climbed into the back of the wag, and Ryan leaned around the side of the wag again to talk to the baron.

"Looks like the trouble in the camp has died down, but now seems as good a time as any to see what was going on. So how about you take us there? And one more thing," he added as the baron put the wag into gear. "Getting pissed at us is no answer to your problem. We can't do jackshit until we've actually looked the area over and got to see the people in their own shit. Don't get heavy on us, because that isn't going to help anyone."

The baron's cold eyes met Ryan's ice-blue orb. He said nothing for a second, as though assessing the one-eyed man once more, then grunted. "Okay, but I need results bad."

"Fair enough. You'll get them, but it doesn't mean to say you'll like them," Ryan commented as he swung himself back into the rear of the wag and the vehicle lurched into motion.

The wag careered across the harsh desert surface, raising clouds of dust in its wake as it followed a track beaten into the earth by the constant tramping back and forth of the workforce. As they neared the camp, the companions could see the workers coming toward them in ragged lines, policed by a group of sec outriders who were mounted on unruly, flea-bitten horses that they could barely control.

"Horses?" Mildred yelled.

"I guess they save on fuel for the sec men and Baron Silas," J.B. said, "and until he gets that well and refinery running, every drop of fuel is like burning jack. Especially if he's into the other barons for a lot of that jack.''

Dean laughed. ''Hot pipe! If those are the best horses they can get, then we really are gonna be up to our necks in horse shit.''

Ryan said nothing. He was too busy watching the faces of the workers as they went by. A mix of different peoples, even in procession they had segregated themselves into groups that bespoke of their villes. From the state of some it was obvious that whatever had caused the fire in the camp had been precursor to a fight. There were abrasions and contusions on many of the workers' faces and exposed arms that showed a pitched battle had taken place. And from the small size of the sec force, it was also clear that the number of people involved had been hard to control.

The one-eyed man already knew that their task was to be difficult. This was brought home even harder when the wag entered the camp, and he could see the almost visible dividing lines between the different peoples. It was visible from the way the huts and tents were constructed, from the ways that the children, running ragged, played and stuck to lines that were so clearly demarcated that they could almost have been drawn, and from the appearance and dress of the womenfolk tending to the camp.

They all had one thing in common, though: the hostile glares with which they greeted the wag as it passed.

This was going to be harder than Ryan had thought.

Chapter Twelve

Baron Silas took the opportunity to give Ryan and the companions a tour around the camp. With the workers on their way back to the refinery and well, and the fire and interville fight quelled, it was the right moment to show them what they would provide sec for with the minimum of interference.

The fire that had emptied the work site was in the part of the camp that housed the migrant workers from Water Valley. As they entered this quarter, the companions noted that the dwelling switched from the blanket, material and wooden pole constructions of the Running Water people into the much harder lines of huts constructed from scrap wood and sheets of corrugated iron, the wood gouged deep with running joints for the metal to slide into, securing it against the vagaries of the weather.

"Those Crow's people," Jak said to Dean, pointing out the Running Water women, who were dark-skinned with dark hair, and dark-eyed children at their feet.

"Yeah," the younger Cawdor replied, "and I'd guess they get less trouble with the elements than these guys—" he indicated the run of huts "—but they must be near to each other, their villes, because they seem to at least tolerate each other.''

"Which makes one wonder," Doc added thoughtfully, ''who started the fire…''

They had taken a circuitous route through the camp in order to get to that point, taking a counterclockwise path that had led them from the remnants of the fire at first, taking in the other areas, before landing them back to their point of origin.

A couple of sec men, their horses tied to a post supporting one of the Running Water dwellings and attracting the attention of children from both Running Water and Water Valley, were helping the womenfolk from both villes to clear the scorched debris of the fire.

As they dismounted from the wag, it was easy to see why the folks of Water Valley and Running Water stuck together. Whereas the vast majority of the camp was Caucasian, albeit from different areas and with different tribal and predark origins, the two villes whose homes were water based were of a different stock. The Running Water people were, as the companions had guessed from what both Baron Silas and the Crow had told them, a Native American people, which made them stand out. And the Water Valley dwellers displayed a much wider mix than anything they had seen in the camp. The women and children who were clustered around the huts showed Native American, black and Hispanic blood among them, the children having a glorious array of skin tone and features that made them a truly eclectic tribe.

Mildred looked at them, taking in the multiplicity of human types, and turned to J.B. ''John, this is the sort of thing they could still only dream about before skydark. When I was young, my daddy used to tell me that one day the people of the earth would be one. Shit, he didn't think it'd take a holocaust to do it.'' And for a moment she stopped being Dr. Mildred Wyeth and became once more the little girl at her daddy's knee, listening to him tell her tales of the marches with another Dr.—Martin Luther King. Then she looked at the remnants of the fire, and her heart burned with a fire of anger. ''One thing, John,'' she continued, ''if that's why this is happening, and it's not the oil well, then some bastard's going to pay.''

''Dark night, keep calm,'' the Armorer replied softly. ''I don't know why it's gotten to you—how can I? But I do know we're gonna need to keep frosty or get chilled.''

Mildred looked at him. ''I know you're right, but it might be a little hard.''

Baron Silas and Ryan walked from the wag over to the site of the fire, where the sec men were kicking over the ashes to kill any last smoldering sparks. They deferred to the baron as he reached them, and he said, ''What happened?''

''Hard to say for sure,'' replied the taller man, who had a finely honed musculature and a long gray beard. Ryan reckoned him to be past fifty, but still a match for any fighter. And from the way the stockier, younger sec man let him answer, he obviously had some kind of authority. The sec man continued. "Trouble is, as always, they waited till a patrol was past these parts before firing up. Asked a few questions, but answers are garbled. Sounds like kids—too old to be around the women, but not yet old enough to work on the well. Guess they got bored, listen to their fathers talk shot about each other, and decided to have a little fun and make a little trouble. Lord alone knows we ain't likely to catch them—not from the descriptions. Could be anyone, from almost any ville, though some do stand out," he added with a glance at the women and children around.

"You don't think it was intended to cause a diversion and bring the workers back?" Ryan asked.

The sec man sized up the one-eyed man before answering, and his reply was slow and considered. "Figure it could be to do with fucking up the well, eh? Mebbe I'd agree if there'd been any damage at the well, which I guess there hasn't 'cause you're here not there, Baron," he added to Baron Silas. "And mebbe I'd agree more if it'd been at night. But this ain't right for that. There were too many people about to see who fired it up, and it's too early in the day—even if you could pull everyone off-site, there's still the chance of being seen." He shook his head firmly. "No, this is villes hating each other, but it ain't the well."

Ryan nodded. "Okay, sounds good," he said simply. Everything the sec man had told him made sense, and the one-eyed man needed to let him know that he would trust his judgment. If this sec man was in charge of camp sec, then it was important Ryan establish friendly relations.

Baron Silas introduced him as Myall, the head of camp sec, as Ryan had deduced, then explained who Ryan and his companions were. The one-eyed man wasn't surprised to see the distrust cross Myall's face when the baron revealed their reason for being there. If Ryan had been in Myall's position, he knew that he would have felt slighted and snubbed by the introduction of an outside force. It implied that Myall couldn't do his job, and that he was lesser in the view of both the baron and—ultimately—his own men and the people he was policing. In which case, how could he carry on? So it was important they establish a rapport and that Ryan and his people were careful not to step on any existing sec toes...unless, of course, it became an imperative.

When Silas had finished explaining, Ryan stepped forward and proffered his hand. "Fireblast, this is a difficult situation for us all. We'll need you if we're to do anything. We're extra firepower, and we need you as a guide. Are you with that?"

The tall, gray-bearded sec man paused for a few seconds, then took the proffered hand. Although he was wirier than Ryan, he was a couple of inches taller, being almost the same height as Crow, and his grip was iron strong.

"We've got some interesting times ahead," Myall said with a grin. "Welcome aboard."

THE SEC BASE for the work camp was on the northern edge, fenced off from the camp itself by a barbed-wire fence that ran ten feet high and was designed as much to keep the horses in as to keep the workers and their dependents out. The sec men slept in a bunkhouse made of wood and sheet metal, and ate in a tented shelter. Baron Silas drove the companions to the bunkhouse, followed by Myall and McVie—the name of the second sec man—on their horses. Baron Silas discharged the companions and left them in the care of Myall, who showed them the scant facilities and directed two of his men to build a tented shelter for them to sleep. He and McVie then led them to a small shack on the far side of the compound, away from the sleeping quarters and the mess tent.

"Guess you should stay outside," Myall said as he opened the door, stooping in the low doorway, "'cause there ain't enough room to swing a rat, let alone anything bigger, in here."

Looking over his shoulder, they could all agree. The shack had room enough for one table with a large radio receiver on it, and a chair, currently occupied by a fat sec man who looked up bleary-eyed when Myall entered.

"This my change of shift?" he said in a monotone. "Feels like I've been in this bastard oven forever."

"Then it's gonna seem that way some more, Todd," Myall said good-naturedly. "It ain't time yet.

Harv's still out on patrol. But hang in there, boy, won't be long.

"See, it gets so hot and boring in here," he continued to the companions, "that the poor boys in here damn near go mad with heat and nothing to do. But they know their shit, and that's all that matters.

"Todd," he said, turning back to the fat sec man, "these here people are new sec that the baron has brought in. So you all tell them about these." He gestured to a rack that hung behind the bleary-eyed sec man.

"Okay, if that's what you want," Todd said without enthusiasm. "Y'all familiar with old tech like this?" he asked, and when they assented he added, "Not that I'm being funny with y'all, but you'd be surprised. Some of the people out there, when I'm on patrol, look like they've seen weird mutie shit when they hear a voice come out of this, you know?" he explained, tapping a handset that he had taken from the rack.

He went on to explain in great detail how the radio worked and how to pump the batteries, and it soon became apparent why he was one of the few who were detailed to the radio shack, for despite the drone of his monotonal voice, he couldn't help but enthuse over the way the old tech worked. To the companions, who had encountered much more in their travels, it was a case of waiting for him to cut to the chase. However, it soon became apparent that this salvaged tech was used by the sec patrols to keep in touch with one another and with their base camp while they were out, and report any trouble that may arise.

"Yeah, but it don't have to work, does it?" Dean whispered to Doc.

"Of course not, young Dean—I assume you are thinking, as I am, that if the saboteurs have a set, as well, they can track their opposing numbers with ease." Doc commented, to which Dean readily agreed.

Todd finished his lecture and handed out handsets to the companions, making sure that they knew how to use them to an almost pedantic degree. When he had finished, and Myall had dispatched him back to his post, closing the shack door, McVie allowed himself a chuckle.

"You'll have to excuse the boy, but I reckon all that heat does something to the brain," he said, making a screwball motion against his head with his index finger. "But what the hell," he continued, "it ain't your brains that are gonna get shaken up now…am I right?" he asked Myall.

The head sec man laughed, throwing back his head. "Last thing, boy. Last thing…"

Chapter Thirteen

It took a few days for the companions to break and to completely master the horses Mydall assigned to them. None of the friends had done as much horseback riding in such a short space of time in their lives, and the rough riding combined with the ability of some of the beasts to throw them to the ground meant that the companions had more than a few contusions and cuts. Most of all, they had aching muscles in places that hadn't been tested in such a manner before. The most common complaint was a stretching of the muscles in the small of the back. Krysty and Jak were able to counter this with massage techniques that differed slightly but had a similar result, and had been learned in their own villes.

"Easy strain muscle while hunting. This help you get out again quick," Jak commented while pummeling J.B.'s back.

"You sure you got that right?" the Armorer winced as the pain seemed to increase instead of decrease.

Krysty's technique was subtler. Learned in Harmony, it involved a manipulation of the sore muscle with the balls of her thumbs, softly at first in circles but digging ever harder and ever deeper until it became like a burning needle into the flesh. Her "victim," Ryan, bit hard into his lip as the pain reached a pitch that he hadn't known for a long time.

"Hurts whatever way it goes, so don't think I'm getting off lightly," he said through gritted teeth at his friend.

It was Doc and Dean, however, who gave the greatest cause for concern. Doc had been thrown four times, and although his body was prematurely aged by his experiences, and he was little older in truth than any of the others. Still that premature aging had given him some physical aspects of a more elderly man. He had landed heavily on his back, and Mildred was worried that he might have damaged his spine.

"Trouble is, osteopathy was never my strong point, especially among geriatrics," she explained to Doc as she probed along his backbone with her finger and thumb, manipulating the flesh and muscle to feel for the vertebrae.

"Despite that, and despite your insistence on calling me a geriatric," Doc said somewhat peevishly, " I still find myself—perhaps to my utter amazement—trusting your judgment." He winced as she hit a sore spot. "Even though it quite literally pains me," he added.

Mildred finished her examination, and Doc rolled over onto his back before sitting up. He could see that, despite their apparent antagonism, there was a look of relief on her face.

"I take it from your apparent relief that you found nothing seriously amiss?" he asked.

"Unfortunately, no," she replied with a wicked grin. "I think you might just outlast us all, you old buzzard. Although," she added, "I'm concerned that, if there's a hairline fracture to one of the vertebrae, I can't find it just by feel, and it would make you extremely vulnerable to another fall."

Doc nodded slowly. "I appreciate what you are saying, but it does occur to me that the same could be true of any of us. After all, we've all taken at least one tumble…not to mention what we've been through before this."

"So stop worrying about you, right?" Mildred queried. And when Doc nodded, she added, "As if I could be bothered about an old fool like you."

"Madam, I would expect nothing less," he countered.

Which just left Dean. Mildred had found some steroid and antihistamine cream in the medical supplies she had looted from the redoubt, and there was also a steroid solution in one of the sealed hypodermics that she had secreted in her coat. The injection had calmed the boy's raging immune system, and the cream, sparingly used, had soothed the itching hives that had erupted on his skin.

But there was only one other steroid injection, and even though the cream was being used sparingly, there was only the one tube, so Mildred was a little concerned about what would happen if the cream ran out, and the effects of a possible second injection subsided, before they had completed their mission.

"I don't understand it," Dean complained as Mildred checked his skin. "I've ridden horses before, and we're always out in the wild among shit like this, but I've never had anything like this."

"Well, for a start we hardly ever get close enough to get bitten," Mildred pondered. "Animal fleas need to jump on, bite, then jump the hell off. And we aren't stupid enough to get close to most of the mutie critters we come across for the fleas to make that jump. And as for riding horses before... I'd guess that the problem lies in the fact that animals and insects across this pesthole land are all mutated in different ways. Those horses aren't like any we've seen before, so mebbe the fleas aren't, either. So you just lucked out, Dean."

"Great," Dean replied sardonically. "So what do I do if the cream doesn't last, and we don't nail these saboteurs first?"

Mildred stayed silent for a second. "Not much any of us can do," she said. "Krysty's looked for the right plants to make you something, but we haven't had much luck. So I guess we've got to hope that the luck comes in nailing the bastards who are causing the trouble."

She exchanged a glance with Dean. It wasn't a satisfactory answer, but it was the only one. Just one more factor to be added to their race against time.

Just another pressure to be added. Like the others.

FOUR DAYS into their stay at the sec camp, Myall arrived. The companions had completed their riding training under the watchful and amused eye of

McVie, and had found that the sec man was, despite his apparent humor at their mishaps, keen to assist and teach. He watched them all carefully and, after using them as the butt of his jokes, had given insights into their riding techniques that helped them master the animals quicker. They saw less of Myall, as the sec chief was called away to marshal his meager forces in the camp and workplace. There hadn't been any more instances of sabotage, but the ville groups were at one another's throats constantly, each accusing the other of wanting to destroy the project.

And Baron Silas was getting restless. Each day Myall had to go to the sweatbox radio shack and talk to the baron about the progress of the new sec force; Ryan always asked him on his return what the baron's view was, and the sec chief had confided that the baron was less than pleased.

"Hell, I think you're doing good 'cause I know just how awkward those bastard creatures are to master, and a fresh face and more of them is gonna help no end when we get out there," the sec chief had told the one-eyed man, "but the baron wants results yesterday, and there doesn't seem to be anything I can tell him to make him see otherwise."

"Yeah, if you'd sent us out straight away it would have been impossible to control those beasts, and the workers would have branded us as easy," Ryan said. "But there haven't been any more attempts to stop progress on the project?"

Myall shook his head. "It comes and goes in waves. Right now, I'd say that whoever is doing it is either lying low to see just what you're like, or they're too busy fighting other battles in the camp.''

The sec man took a long drink from a canteen and offered it to Ryan, who took it and found his throat assailed by a raw-vegetable distilled spirit. He had been expecting water, and it was all he could do to stop from choking at the bite of the bitter alcohol.

''It's the only way we've been getting through this,'' Myall said, noting Ryan's surprise. ''Helps you sleep—that's for sure.''

''As long as it doesn't stop you from being triple red when you're out there,'' Ryan added.

Myall grinned. ''Hell, I sometimes think that'd be better. Y'know, if I died tonight I think hell would be like this…stuck in the middle of nowhere with a whole bunch of misfits who want to blast the fuck out of each other, and no idea who's really doing shit to who.''

''Sounds like everyday life to me, not just here,'' Ryan commented.

''Yeah, well, mebbe that's why it stinks worse than those bastard horses,'' Myall said, taking back the canteen and sinking some more of the spirit. ''I'll bid you good-night, my friend. And one more thing,'' he suddenly added as he rose to leave.

''Yeah?'' Ryan queried.

''Crow arrives tomorrow.''

''What's he been sent here for?''

Myall allowed himself a grin that was entirely devoid of humor. ''To get you out there. Baron Silas is a hard man, and he demands payment for everything he does. It's your time to pay, I guess.''

"We're ready," Ryan said evenly.

"I know that," Myall said simply before leaving the one-eyed man alone with his thoughts.

THE NEXT MORNING Ryan rose to find the giant Native American breakfasting with the sec force in the mess tent.

"So we meet again," Crow said with a glimmer of good humor in his low, quiet voice. "Under more pleasant circumstances this time, however," he added.

"That rather depends on what you mean by 'pleasant,'" Doc returned with an equal tone as he seated himself beside Crow and Ryan.

"It's a relative term," mused the Native American, "but at least you're not half-dead from heat exhaustion and lack of food and water. And at least you get to keep your weapons this time. Let's just hope you get a chance to use them."

"Wouldn't it be better to say that we don't get a chance to use them?" Ryan countered. "If us just being here stops any more sabotage, then the well and refinery can open, the workers get their jack, the barons get their power, and everyone's happy."

"In a perfect world, mebbe," Crow said at length. "But you're no fool, Ryan Cawdor—you know it won't be that way. Whoever is behind this will crawl out of their little hole again, regardless of if you're there or not. Mebbe even because, if they feel it's a challenge. So what happens then?''

"Okay, you make the point well," Ryan conceded. ''But we won't know for sure until we actually get out there.''

"Which will be when?''

"Today," the one-eyed man replied. ''That's why you're here, after all.''

Crow allowed a smile to crack his impassive, leathery features. Under the shadow cast by the brim of his hat, his eyes glittered.

"To say that's very perceptive would be an insult in your case," he said softly. ''Are you ready to go?''

"As ready as we'll ever be," Ryan said. ''Right, Doc?''

Doc winced slightly as he thought of his sore back. "I think it is safe to say that, my dear boy.''

As the sec force went about its daily tasks, the rest of the companions joined Ryan, Doc and Crow in the tent. And when they were replete, they walked out to the paddock, where McVie was waiting for them.

"Hey, the big day, right?" he said as they approached, sparing a nod of greeting for Crow. "You're on second watch, and your route will be through the camp rather than the work sites. Myall reckoned it would be better for you to check that out tonight, as that's when most of the sabotage has occurred anyway. He figures it's better for you to get a night view from the start—besides which, if you're seen today it might stir some action."

"Seems a reasonable course of action," Ryan mused. "So when do we head off?"

"'Bout two hours," McVie replied, "so I guess you've got plenty of time to get your blasters stripped and ready."

Ryan nodded. "So who's giving us the lowdown on the camp as we patrol?"

"I am," Crow said before McVie had a chance to reply. "I know all of these peoples. I traveled a lot before coming to work for Baron Silas, and they all know of me. I can fill you in on any background you need."

"And report back on us to the baron, right?" Ryan added.

Crow shrugged. "I'd be a fool to deny that," he said simply.

Ryan nodded and led his people away from the paddock and back to the tent they had made their base in the sec camp. Crow stayed with McVie, knowing that it was right to give them space.

When they were in the tent, and had begun to clean and check their blasters—a task that was made easy by J.B.'s continuing insistence on blaster maintenance that made each clean and check an almost perfunctory matter—the Armorer asked Ryan, "Do you think we can trust Crow?"

"Everything we say and do will go back to the baron. But other than that, I think he'll be straight with us. Hell, he has been so far. He didn't have to tell us he would report it all back.''

"Open man,'' Jak commented as he checked his .357 Magnum Colt Python, chambering a round. "No bullshit.''

"Yeah, I don't get a bad feeling about him,'' Krysty said. "He's just got his job to do and a line to walk. Same as all of us to different degrees, right?''

They finished checking their weapons, and J.B. went through his stock of grens and plas-ex. "Won't need these in the camp,'' he commented. "Far too closed in to risk it. More likely to chill ourselves than anyone else. But mebbe later, when we get to the work sites.''

Ryan checked his wrist chron. "Time to go. Let's stay hard out there, and triple red for everything.''

THEY MOUNTED their horses and rode from the sec camp across the short distance to the outskirts of the workers' camp, passing the incoming patrol on the way. They had nothing to report apart from the usual complaints and insults among the different ville tribes. There had been no fighting and no sign of any real trouble.

"Looks like you may get broken in easy,'' Crow commented as they rode on, "which'll at least give you a chance to learn about these people before you have to start chilling them.''

None of the companions were sure if the deadpan

Native American was joking, and refrained from comment.

The first nest of huts and tents belonged to the people of Haigh, whose baron was John the Gaunt. A severe name for a severe baron, and that was reflected in the dour and downbeat appearance of their encampment. The material that comprised the tents was of dull, stained colors, and the women and children were quiet, going about their chores and play with a deadened demeanor, as though just going through the motions. They hardly looked up as the patrol passed through.

"Can't see these being much trouble," Mildred said. "What are the men like?"

"Like this," Crow replied. "They work hard and keep themselves to themselves. Haigh's not a rich ville, and they've had to work their land hard and drive hard bargains based on work rather than jack. They like to keep their energy for work, because that's all they had to keep them alive for a long time. The road and the well will bring them more than they could ever dream, but John the Gaunt won't let them get soft on it. I'd figure they were part of some old religion before skydark, and that harshness has stayed with them. They're the last ones I'd bet on to be sabotaging the works. One thing, though—don't be fooled by how quiet and peaceful they seem. You cross these people, and they're the hardest fighters you'll ever come across. Even the bastards from Mandrake avoid them, and they'll fight anyone."

As Crow finished speaking, a woman holding a

roughly made broom walked toward them, unflinching of the animals as they twitched at her approach.

"Good day to you," she said in a monotone. "There is no need," she added as she noticed hands ready to unholster blasters. "I have no quarrel with you. I merely wish to ask a question."

"Well, that's fine," Crow said in an even and friendly tone. "Ask your question, my friend."

"I know of you," she said, looking directly at Crow. "You are from the Baron Silas. I would be thinking that these are outsider mercies brought in to stop the sabotage."

When Crow answered her with a nod, she continued, now addressing the companions. "Do you be thinking that you can stop an entire army? For that is what this camp be. I have no love for any others, and they not for me. But if they wish to cause war, then are you enough?"

"I don't know," Ryan said simply. "It depends on who is causing the trouble."

"Are you so naive that you do not realize that all cause trouble for all? We fight each other, because it is not right for us all to be so close."

"But mebbe the sabotage isn't from you all," Ryan said. "Mebbe your fights only give cover to those who want to stop the well."

The woman said nothing, but assessed the one-eyed man shrewdly before finally saying, "I think you may be capable." With which she turned and returned to her hut, sweeping as though they were no longer there.

The patrol moved on, and when they had reached the obvious demarcation point between one ville and another, Dean whispered, "Are they all that weird?"

Crow allowed himself a wry grin. "Start with the strangest and everything else is easy to take in," he answered cryptically. "You'll see, son, you'll see."

The lines marking the boundaries between the different groups within the camp were clear. Within a few yards of the spot where they had stopped to speak with the woman, they turned a corner and entered somewhere that seemed entirely different.

The huts, shacks and tents were constructed in a different matter, seeming to veer over and be ready to collapse. It was obvious that little effort had gone into their construction, although they were garishly decorated in paints and dyed fabrics in a collision of orange, white and green. The women talked, the area was dirty and the children ran riot. There had been some indication of this in the distant noise as they had rode through the quiet of the Haigh sector, but nothing could have prepared them for the sudden contrast.

The children whirled in and out of the horses' hooves, disturbing the animals and causing all the companions to tighten their grips on the manes. The women ignored their children and carried on conversing in loud voices, not caring what was occurring and seeming not to notice the riders among them.

"Bedlam," Doc whispered.

This part of the camp smelled strongly of distilled spirit, and there were signs of smoke from some of the huts that suggested the inhabitants were either brewing spirit or else had forgotten to extinguish fires and were about to lose their homes. Not that it seemed that they cared.

"So who are these?" Ryan asked, trying to keep his voice level.

"This, my friend, is the Mandrake sector. Putting these people next to those from Haigh wasn't the best piece of foresight anyone ever had," Crow remarked sardonically. "To say they loathe each other would be an understatement."

"So this is a source of trouble?"

Crow shook his head. "Baron Silveen is a rich man, and he wants to be richer. He's sunk a lot of jack into this, and he won't be too keen on it going west because of some squabbling. These are fierce, short-tempered people, but they fear their baron more than anyone else."

"Enough to stick to his word when they're this far away?" Ryan queried, looking at the groups of women who were eyeing them suspiciously, the children who were throwing stones at one another—and at the horses' forelocks when they thought no one was looking—and at the few older men who lurked in the doorways of the huts, eyeing the patrol suspiciously.

Crow laughed. "If you'd ever met Baron Silveen, you wouldn't be asking that question. Take it from me, no one would want to cross him. That's not to say that some, fired up by the spirits, may not."

"And they're the ones to watch out for," Ryan muttered.

"Yeah, but how do you tell?" added J.B., who had ridden up to join them. "Ryan," he continued, "don't be fooled by the way they look—take a look at some of the blasters, then sniff the air."

Ryan frowned, and tried to get a look at the blasters carried by the women without being spotted. The Armorer was right. Although the women seemed unkempt, and their clothes were colorful, tight fitting and sluttish, the handblasters that all of them seemed to pack were, as far as he could tell from what was visible, highly polished. If they kept the visible part of the blaster in that good a condition, then chances were that the mechanisms were also well maintained. And the air? The one-eyed man was about to comment to J.B. that he could smell the chemical aroma of plas-ex being broken down and reconstituted, and possibly homemade explosives, too, when a sudden flurry of violent activity distracted him.

A fight had broken out among one group of women. Ryan hadn't heard the argument that led to it, but Krysty and Mildred had. Two women were arguing about an old man who lurked in the doorway of one of the huts, and did nothing to stop the argument. In point of fact, he seemed to revel in the sudden chaos he had caused.

"I tell you he wouldn't go with you if you was the last woman on the face of the world, which you'd have to be to get any attention from a man," the younger of the women added to drive her point home.

The older woman—who was about a hundred pounds heavier and had dark red hair shot through with silver—replied angrily, "Shit, he must hate being the father of such a gaudy slut. How many of these kids are his?"

This was too much for the younger woman. Despite her inferior weight, she yelled in incoherent fury and threw a haymaker punch that caught the older woman on the side of the head, making her stagger backward with a startled yelp.

She recovered quickly, however, and charged back at her opponent with a snarl, catching her under the chin with a roundhouse blow that would have rendered her unconscious had it properly connected. It didn't, but it was still hard enough to knock her backward into the rest of the women, who were now beginning to draw up sides for the fight.

It looked as if it could get out of hand quickly, and Krysty and Mildred knew they had to act. They also knew that it would stamp the companions authority hard if they were the ones to quell the disturbance, rather than the men.

The two Mandrake women were locked together now, wrestling in a small circle, the better to try to gain the upper hand. The other women were closing in, swapping insults with each other depending on the sides they had chosen. There were some blows being flung, but so far it hadn't escalated into a full-scale fight.

And it wouldn't if Mildred and Krysty had anything to do with it.

Both women were off their horses and into the midst of the fledgling fight before anyone had a chance to react. A glance between them determined that Krysty would take the older woman and Mildred the younger. Krysty was slightly taller than Mildred, and would have the height and leverage advantage to overcome the weight of the older woman, whereas Mildred's lesser height would enable her to fight face-to-face with the younger woman.

But first they had to get them apart.

The speed and unexpectedness of their attack gave them an advantage in breaking through the crowd, both women using their elbows and heavy boots to crack shins and cause the crowd to part as their ribs became the object of a series of blows. It didn't take a second for Mildred and Krysty to reach the center of the action.

The two Mandrake women were still locked together, neither giving ground, all their attention focused on each other. This made it simple for the outsiders to part them. Mildred jabbed her opponent beneath the rib cage with a straight-finger blow that sent a searing pain through the woman's kidneys and took her breath away. She folded onto one side and tried to throw her balance over to compensate.

Her opponent could have used this to her advantage if she, too, hadn't also come under attack. Because of her weight and stance, there was no option for Krysty to do anything but take a handful of the woman's hair and pull back. She had to hope that her opponent was sensitive to having her scalp pulled, and didn't have the kind of bull-like neck muscles that would preclude it working. In this she was lucky. With a gasp of surprise and sudden pain, the older woman jerked her head back, leaving her throat and neck open to attack.

Krysty wasn't slow in following this up. Still grasping the older woman's hair firmly, she chopped at the exposed throat, hitting hard on the windpipe and cutting off the woman's breath. It was all she could do to stop herself from blacking out at the sudden shock, slumping against Krysty and almost throwing her off balance. But Krysty yielded to the slump and then pushed back, reversing the momentum so that her opponent was thrust away from her. As the older woman careened away, Krysty still kept hold of her hair, using it to twist the woman's head and deliver a punch to her temple that caused her to fall the rest of the way into unconsciousness. She dropped like a stone as Krysty let go of her hair.

Mildred was also in the process of finishing off her opponent. Doubled with agony, and with no breath in her body, the younger of the two Mandrake women turned to face Mildred, her face contorted by pain and rage. She made to grab at the black woman's swinging plaits, but Mildred was too quick, dodging her grasping hands and swinging up her leg in the same movement, catching her opponent in the abdomen with the toe cap of her heavy boot. As the woman pitched forward, Mildred finished her off with a blow to the back of her neck, delivered with the straight edge of her right hand.

Before both Mandrake women had settled in the dust, Krysty and Mildred were back-to-back, ready for the rest of the pack to attack.

It didn't come. Instead there was a sudden hush, and the other women stood around, not knowing what to do or who would be the first to break forward.

Mildred stalled them. "Listen to me. I don't know what that was about, and I don't care. I just know that we're here to keep the peace, and if it means beating the shit out of every last one of you, then that's what we'll do. But you don't give us crap and everything'll be fine. You understand me?"

There was a silence, followed by a low rumble that could have been a grudging assent, but was certainly not dissent.

"That's okay, then," Mildred said as she and Krysty relaxed slightly, then made their way back to their mounts. "Just remember that, and we'll have no argument with the people of Mandrake."

As soon as Krysty and Mildred were on horseback, Crow kicked his steed into motion, and they left the narrow street in the Mandrake sector of the camp, with a grudging respect and possibly resentment behind them.

When they were out of earshot, Crow murmured, "That was impressive. They'll be looking out for you now. Mebbe need to watch your backs from some, but you'll get less shit from others."

"That," Mildred replied, "is the general idea."

THE REST of their journey around the camp was less eventful. The sectors that housed the people from Water Valley and Running Water they had already encountered on their journey into the camp with Baron Silas. There was nothing new for them to learn from there as of yet.

Moving on, they came to the sector where the people from Salvation itself were housed. It came as no surprise to anyone that they had the best-constructed home site. The huts and shacks were put together from a better quality of salvaged material, and the manner in which they had been constructed suggested that a ville of engineers had been at work. Even the tents were of a stronger fabric, which looked as though it had been chosen with care from that available to make a series of moveable homes that could be transported and reerected with ease. Ryan, and J.B. in particular, had to admire the way in which the host ville had managed its section of the camp. Crow was well-known here, and it soon became apparent from the comments they met with that word of this new sec force had spread among the natives of Salvation. The companions were told that it was up to them to stop the sabotage and keep the jack bonuses going up for the workers and their families.

"One thing I do notice, though," Ryan commented as they left the Salvation sector. "They all blame different villes for the damage, just as the woman from Haigh blamed someone else."

"Could be bluff," Crow replied. "Could be that they want to blame someone else to cover themselves. Could be they want to blame someone else just because they're different."

"Yeah, and it could be that no one there actually knows anything about it," J.B. countered.

Crow looked at him shrewdly. "Ideas?" he asked simply.

J.B. shrugged. "Not yet."

But the Armorer continued to think about it as they traveled around the rest of the camp. They had already seen the work sites, and knew the layout. It was hard for anyone to hide there, and so the sabotage had to be perpetrated at a time when everyone not involved on the task would be safely out of the way. There was too much risk of anyone being seen during daylight and working hours, as not only were there sec patrols but also it was highly unlikely that any of the individuals involved would want to sabotage their own areas of work and so put their own jack bonuses at risk. Other areas and other workers' bonuses, maybe, but only a stupe would do that to himself. And J.B. was sure that this was not the work of a stupe.

So if the sabotage couldn't be done by day, then it had to be done by night. By necessity, the sec patrols at night were concentrated on the camp, to stop any fights that may break out inside. This left the work site relatively open to attack. But the problem any saboteurs would then have was in getting out of the camp, going about their tasks, and getting back into the camp without being seen—if not by the sec, then by someone from a rival ville. The fact that no one seemed to have any definite facts, within such a closed hothouse atmosphere, made J.B. wonder if Baron Silas and his sec men were looking in the wrong direction.

As this passed through his mind, he wondered if he should talk to Ryan about it, so they could begin asking questions. But one look at the one-eyed man riding next to Crow dissuaded him. It wasn't that the Armorer didn't trust the Native American, it was more that he didn't want anything of his notion getting out—particularly to Baron Silas—until such time as they had a chance to investigate its validity.

Besides, there were still four sectors of the camp with which to become familiar.

Crow led them into the sector that housed the workers and their families from the ville of Dallas. It was immediately obvious to all that Baron Silas had deliberately planned the camp so that the poor folks of his original home ville would have their noses rubbed in the dirt by being placed next door to the richer constructions of his new ville. For the Dallas camp was dirty and disheveled, and the women and children who were on view seemed downtrodden. They had no life or energy and appeared to be almost completely disinterested in the mounted party as they rode down the small streets of the camp. Their huts and tents were hovels that

hung loosely together, constructed of materials that
the other villes would have thrown away, and completely devoid of color under a mantle of dust.

"I fear these are least likely to be our culprits,"
Doc murmured as they passed by almost unnoticed.

"Could be that they want revenge," Dean argued.

Doc shook his head sadly. "No, my dear child.
These are people with the fight knocked out of them.
They just want the scraps from the table—though
they do appear to be the kind of whipping boys who
would be singled out for blame, should it need to be
apportioned."

"No one believe it," Jak interjected. "Smell of
fear, being chilled. Quarry," he added dismissively.

"I'd agree with you there," Crow said, listening
intently. "Thing is, for a variety of reasons everyone
I've shown you so far would be too obvious. Dallas
is too downtrodden. The people of Water Valley and
Running Water look too different to hide easily.
Haigh is too strictly run, and Mandrake is too damn
loud to do anything except out front."

"And Salvation?" Ryan queried.

Crow allowed himself a smile. "The enemy inside? Mebbe, but there's too much for everyone to
lose. These last three villes, though… They don't
look 'different,' so they could blend in easy. And
they've all got reason to hate the other villes, and
each other."

"Yeah?" Ryan stopped his horse. "Fill us in some
background before we look them over."

Crow also stopped, and when the horses had clustered, he said, "Carter, Baker and Hush are basically parts of the same old predark stock. They have common stories relating to oil jack from before the nukecaust. Like a lot of areas that were old well places, they're very white, which means they hate the villes that aren't, and even Mandrake they hate because of it's predark allegiances. They're also pissed because they aren't rich. And because Salvation will be. Never mind that their barons have done this to get a share of the jack. They don't think like that. And they're close to those they hate, and the place that represents their being under the hammer to Salvation. So if they get some spirit, or some jolt..." He shrugged.

Ryan nodded. "That's worth bearing in mind." And he indicated that Crow should lead them on.

Considering the differences they had seen between the other villes and their sectors of the camp, the differences between the last three sectors were remarkable for their lack: the huts, shacks and tents were constructed in a similar manner, and the materials used betrayed a home ville that was scraping around for trade and salvageable merchandise. The people seemed to be from the same stock, and the way in which they dressed and colored their environment with their clothes and the decorations in their camp sector was almost exactly the same. As was their attitude of sullen and mute hostility to the companions and Crow. The burble of conversation and activity died to silence as they passed, and they were watched closely, even though no one spoke directly to them.

It was an uncomfortable ride, the focus of hostility seeming to be Crow and Mildred.

"That was fun," Mildred said sardonically when they emerged from the camp and made their way back to the sec camp.

"Wasn't it," Crow replied. "So what do you reckon?"

"Mebbe this isn't going to be as easy as Baron Silas hopes," Ryan said.

Crow shook his head. "He won't want to hear that."

"I don't give a shit what he wants to hear," Ryan answered. "The fact is that the camp covers a lot of ground, and so does the work site. There's only a dozen sec, and only seven of us. And a shit load of possible trouble. We may be able to stop attacks, but I figure it'd be better to get to the root of it. And we've got a lot of options to cover with no time to do it."

"So?" Crow said softly.

"So Baron Silas has to decide whether he wants us to get to the bottom of this or just blast everyone. I know which I'd rather do, and which is better for us," the one-eyed man stated, dismounting his steed. "And it's not acting like a triple stupe and blasting your workforce out of existence. So tell Baron Silas he may get results, but not necessarily the ones he wants."

Chapter Fourteen

Trouble came looking for the companions with a rapidity that surprised them all.

After Crow bade them farewell and returned to Salvation, they rested for a short while, ate and waited for Myall to return from his patrol out at the work site.

"Figure we'd better get some kind of routine established, and triple fast," Ryan said to the others. "The women and kids have seen us, and the workers saw us when we arrived. So now we need—"

"To let them know we're here and here to stay," Mildred interjected.

"Exactly. And the only way to do that is to keep visible."

"Yeah, that's okay," J.B. said thoughtfully, "but I really think we should concentrate on the well and refinery next. That's the root of the trouble."

Ryan gave his friend a sideways glance. "There something you're not saying, J.B.? Because you sound like you've got a few ideas. Mebbe you should share them."

"Sure." The Armorer nodded. And he outlined his theory that perhaps a force outside the camp was responsible before explaining that he didn't want his notion to get back to Baron Silas via Crow. "So I figure that our best shot is to hit the well and refinery tonight, see what happens. Besides, it'll be good to recce it in the dark and get used to it."

That was something with which they could all agree, and when Myall returned from patrol Ryan was able to agree on a patrol roster. They would take the first watch at the work site and would travel to it via a roundabout route through the camp.

"I STILL DON'T GET why we have to go this way," Dean whispered as the procession of horses made its way through the Haigh section of the camp and cut across to go past the Mandrake section.

"Because, my dear boy, it is a show of strength, a display, if you will, of our presence," Doc returned in a low voice. He was riding directly in front of Dean, with Mildred and J.B. at the rear behind the younger Cawdor, and Jak and Krysty in front of Doc, with Ryan in the lead.

"But they know we're here, especially in this place," Dean added, taking in the glares they were receiving from the men and women of Mandrake, accompanied by low muttering.

"Yes, but they also have to know that we are— right now—on our way out to the work site. Word will spread, and then we will see if they have the nerve to attack. Or, indeed, if it is anyone from here."

"Guess you're right," Dean said uneasily, "but I

can see us getting into a firefight here and leaving the work site unprotected.''

"A first-night risk,'' Doc returned. "I suspect Ryan has weighed the odds.''

But what about the odds on stumbling onto an interville fight? The one-eyed man had expected an attack on themselves, but what happened next hadn't occurred to him.

As they left the Mandrake sector and were about to cross into the Salvation sector, all hell broke loose.

At the crossroads that marked the clear delineation between the villes, a bunch of men were standing on the Salvation side. They were drunk on home brew, and Jak's keen night vision could detect that their eyes, in the flickering lamplight of the camp, were dark with the effects of jolt. They watched the seven horses cross, and also the posse of Mandrake workers that had followed at a distance, a tactic that had failed to spook the companions or their mounts, but set up the Mandrake men for what followed.

"Hey, assholes,'' yelled one of the Salvation men, "I hear your women got beaten by the new sec women.'' When there was no answer from the sullen Mandrake men, he continued, "I guess the women could take you as well, right? You are a bunch of shit, right?''

As one, the companions stopped their horses, Ryan wheeling his around to face his people. He didn't have to speak. One look at them told him that they could all sniff the danger in the air and the trouble that was about to break.

Behind them, the Mandrake men were muttering among themselves. They weren't replying to the taunts of the Salvation drunk, but were obviously contemplating a response.

And in the middle were the seven horses and their riders, waiting for the storm to break. It didn't take more than a second.

"Yeah, bunch of shit." The Salvation man laughed, turning to his friends. It was as he turned away that the knife skimmed past his ear, nicking the skin enough for blood to flow like a stream down his neck, before embedding itself in the arm of a man behind him. Caught unawares, with the sharp blade embedding itself in the muscle and sinew of his biceps as he stood there, the shock and pain made the man scream in a frantic, high-pitched tone.

"Fireblast! Get them," Ryan yelled, swinging himself off his mount.

With a chorus of yells and whoops, the Mandrake men charged across the space between themselves and the startled and temporarily wrong-footed Salvation men. In the middle were the companions, who were prepared to make this a fight without blasters unless necessary. Mildred, Krysty and Dean would have to fight unarmed, while Jak palmed a leaf-bladed knife into each hand. Doc's silver lion's-head stick revealed the blade of finely honed Toledo steel that was hidden within. J.B. and Ryan, at each end of the line, were prepared with their blades, J.B. his Tekna and Ryan his trusty panga. Each of the companions picked a direction in which to face the oncoming mob, knowing that the adjacent companion covered his or her back.

Recovering from the shock that had temporarily frozen them, the Salvation men rushed forward to meet the Mandrake men. It wouldn't be a fight of skill and savagery, but rather a drunken brawl where those who get hurt usually end up being hurt by accident.

A Salvation worker threw himself past Doc and landed on an oncoming Mandrake man, throwing him backward onto the dirt where they wrestled aimlessly, neither able to get a satisfactory grip. Doc earmarked them for attention in a moment. His more immediate problem was being sandwiched between two more men, both of whom had blades in hand.

As one dived, Doc sidestepped and brought up the swordstick, the upward thrust catching the diving man's blade and diverting it skyward. Doc followed through in an arc and brought the sword down, slicing at the wrist of the opposing fighter, drawing blood and making him drop his knife. From there, it was simple for Doc—who wasn't befuddled by spirit or jolt—to take the LeMat from his belt and use the heavy butt to render one of his opponents unconscious while kicking the other in the groin and making him collapse. From there, he turned elegantly to deliver another kick that separated the two wrestlers. The hand of one snaked toward his blaster, but a sudden slice from Doc's sword split open the flesh of his arm and caused him to cease, and his opponent to scuttle away in the dirt.

Three Mandrake men, incensed by the earlier incident and forgetting their Salvation opponents, headed directly for Ryan, who took out one with a backhand slash of the panga, and attended to another with a kick from his heavy combat boots that caught the man in the chest, making him collapse. That left one man, and Ryan was left partially vulnerable. Although he left no area of attack open, he was still distracted enough by the two opponents to be unable to fully counter a full-on attack by the third man, who flung himself at the one-eyed man. There were no vulnerable areas that he could attack, but the force of his onslaught did drive Ryan onto the ground. But experience taught him to go with the fall, letting his body go limp so that the impact and any possible damage were lessened. His opponent hit him hard, but rolled off the one-eyed man with the force of his impact, enabling Ryan to turn swiftly so that he was on top of him. One swing with the handle of the panga caught the man under the jaw, snapping him instantly into unconsciousness.

All around, the companions laid waste to their foes. Jak was a whirling blur of white hair and flashing knives, the cuts slashing at the faces and hands of his opponents, rendering them useless through pain and defenseless as their own weapons dropped. Dean, Mildred and Krysty had more than held their own without blades, while the Armorer had found it unnecessary to use his as a few maneuvers in unarmed combat rendered his opponents defeated.

Within a few minutes, the area was a scene of

carnage, as blood soaked into the earth and dyed it dark beneath the semiconscious and unconscious bodies that lay around, with only the companions still standing. An audience of women and other men had gathered on each side of the divide, but neither showed any willingness to come forward and either collect their wounded or carry on the fight.

At a signal from Ryan, they mounted their steeds and made ready to head off to the work site. But before they left, Ryan paused and spoke out.

"They're alive because Baron Silas needs them to work. But I warn you all now—anyone else tries to attack us, or any of the sec patrols like this, then we'll chill the bastards."

"Weren't attacking you, were attacking the others," came a voice from the Mandrake side.

Ryan turned to face it, unable in the dim lamplight to single out who had spoken.

"Doesn't matter. This shit stops the work being done, and that's what we're here to see. You do that, then that's attacking us. Understood?"

And before anyone had a chance to answer, he charged his horse and led the line out of the area of the fight, and through the rest of the camp toward the expanse of desert that separated the work site from the workers' dwellings.

No one spoke as they traversed the sandy earth, each lost in his or her own thoughts, until Ryan spoke up, spotting the incoming four-man sec patrol and hailing them when they were a few hundred yards from the storage tanks.

"Hey, how's it going?" asked the leader of the sec patrol as they came within recognizable distance under the light of the crescent moon. The returning patrol was lit by the lamps they carried and was led by McVie. "Hell, you look like you've been in a fight," he added when he could see the companions more clearly. And when Ryan explained what had happened, he whistled low. "Shit, that's gonna make a few people drop their load. And that kind of shit will flush out any troublemakers triple fast, 'cause they're gonna be way pissed with you."

"That is partly the idea." Ryan grinned. "If we're going to fight, then I want to know who."

McVie acknowledged this with an inclination of his head. "Fair point, big guy. So you're covering the site now?" And when Ryan assented, he continued. "Well, it was all clear up to half hour past. Trouble is with only four of us, by the time we've covered one sector, then anything could be happening back where we started. And you ain't got any lamps, either," he added.

J.B. answered, "Don't want them. With more of us we can cover more ground and mebbe catch anyone unawares. So having no lamps would be a real bonus."

"Fair point," McVie conceded. "You take it easy out there. It's quiet so far, so mebbe you've had all your action for one night."

"Let's hope so," Ryan said. Although it crossed his mind that at least a sabotage attempt may give them some clues as to the perpetrators.

WHEN THEY REACHED the work site, it was deathly quiet, but Jak seemed to be concerned about something.

"Ryan, something happening," he whispered as they brought their horses to a halt by the storage tanks. The one-eyed man had intended to split them into three groups at this point, and cover the whole site in a staggered, circular route so that anyone trying to avoid one part of the patrol was likely to be picked up by the following group. His plans were stayed by the sudden reaction of the albino hunter.

"No noise, but smell," Jak continued. "Not sure...like gas."

"We're at an oil well. I'd be surprised if you couldn't smell fuel of some kind," Dean uttered, perplexed.

Jak shook his head. "Not like this," he said shortly, indicating the tanks behind them. "Like gas used on a wag...like shit belching out behind."

"You can smell wag exhaust?" J.B. asked. "But how come the last party missed it? Dark night, it wouldn't be like you couldn't hear a wag out here!"

"Mebbe enough time between them leaving and us arriving to sneak in," Krysty answered, "especially if it was someone who was familiar with the patrol schedule."

"Which makes your idea ever more likely, my dear John Barrymore," Doc mused. "An outside saboteur. Intriguing."

"Mystifying more like," Mildred snapped. "Let's

get the bastard and find out just what is going on here.''

Ryan nodded. ''We need to move fast and silent. Leave the horses here and go on foot. Mildred, you and Dean take the pipeline with Doc. He's familiar with it. J.B., you and Jak cover the refinery buildings. Krysty and me'll take the wellhead. Jak, any idea where the smell comes from.''

The albino shook his head. ''Not get direction. Just know here.''

''Okay. Let's go. Triple red, people,'' Ryan added before setting off for the wellhead.

Mildred, Doc and Dean took the route along the pipeline, dividing into three in order to cover every inch thoroughly. In a hoarse whisper, Doc described the manner in which the pipes were laid out, and warned that there was little cover, both for any saboteur and also for themselves. The three companions took a different pipe route, knowing that they would all end up at the refinery buildings.

Which was exactly where Jak and J.B. were headed, the albino and the Armorer moving across the desert floor at a run, crouched low lest they be seen against the horizon. They stayed silent, saving their breath for the run, and their concentration for any signs of activity ahead of them, ignoring what lay behind as that was in the capable hands of their companions.

Krysty and Ryan headed toward the derrick, which stood out starkly against the night sky, illuminated even by the dim light of the crescent moon. It was obvious from the sight of it that any attempt to damage higher up the derrick would be seen, the scaffolding and gantry of the construction providing no cover.

"Think they're here, lover?" Krysty asked.

"Mebbe. What do you reckon?"

"I can't feel it. I don't think it's here."

"Okay, but we keep triple red in case," he replied.

At the base of the derrick, there were enough piles of construction material, and a small brick blockhouse containing the derrick valves, to provide cover. The duo split up and covered each side of the derrick, finding it clear, until there was only the brick valve housing. It was a large enough building to hide someone, and blowing the valves would cause major damage to the wellhead.

Ryan and Krysty exchanged glances. Without a word, the one-eyed man went to the door, crouching, while Krysty took a covering position. He opened the unlocked door and flung himself to one side of the wall. There was silence. Counting to three, he entered the blockhouse, ready to fire at the slightest sight or sound.

There was nothing. It was then that the sound of a wag firing up, and blasterfire, distracted him.

Mildred, Dean and Doc were also brought up short by the firing and the explosions of the wag engine. They cut short their search and headed toward the source of the sound—the refinery.

Jak and J.B. had reached the refinery in triple-fast time, and each man knew the layout of one of the refinery buildings, as they had each searched one before. Using eye contact only to signal, they had opted to take the double building, joined by a covered walkway, as their first target. It had proved to be empty, and it was as they covered the ground to the second block that Jak suddenly stretched out a hand to stay the Armorer.

In reply to J.B.'s quizzical look, Jak pointed to the open doorway of the block. A shadow darker than the others was moving out of the interior.

J.B. swung his Uzi off his shoulder and clicked to rapid fire. He pointed to the block, indicating that Jak take the building while he followed the shadow.

It was as he did this that the shot whistled over their heads, the shadow suddenly bolting for the rear of the building. J.B. didn't hesitate. He took off at a full run, knowing that he was too far away to waste ammo on blasting at his target. It also registered somewhere in his mind that the shot over their heads sounded to him like a fairly heavy caliber handblaster—a .44 or .45, but not a .357 Magnum like Jak's. That could be information worth storing for later.

But right now, he had quarry to pursue.

Jak was also in pursuit of prey. Moving swiftly and close to the ground, the albino approached the open front of the building, using any darker patches of shadow cast by the moon's feeble light to hide himself. His dark camou pants and the patched jacket provided some degree of disguise, but his white mane and pale skin still gave him away. Coming around to the open door, he held his Colt Python blaster in his hand, gripping the butt tightly with his index finger looped loosely around the trigger.

Flattening himself to the outside wall, he ignored the sounds of J.B.'s pursuit and concentrated on what he could smell or hear from within the building.

It was almost silent: one sound could be heard— a light ticking noise that was barely audible. But he was sure that the building was empty. The warm smell of danger and fear was absent.

Jak entered the building, still cautious of any booby traps.

Meanwhile, J.B. was chasing the lone saboteur across the dry earth. The man was tall and rangy, and his long strides carried him faster than J.B., despite the Armorer's strength and speed. J.B. cursed under his breath and lifted the Uzi. The movement disturbed his momentum and he lost more ground. But it didn't worry him. There was no way he could catch up to the saboteur before he gained his wag, which had been parked to the rear of the buildings, leading off into desert and the ribbon of old road that lay beyond. It was an old jeep, and would be swift across the desert, far swifter than their horses, even presuming they could have brought them nearer.

There was only one course of action that the Armorer could take. Dropping to one knee, he steadied the Uzi, using his knee to prop one elbow and take good aim. In the time it took him to do this, the saboteur had clambered into the jeep and fired the engine. J.B. could hear the grinding of gears loud across the empty desert sand as he took aim. He squeezed the trigger as the vehicle leaped into life and began to move across the land, a stream of bullets spitting from the muzzle of the blaster.

The jeep was moving away fast, but not so fast that the shells didn't at least strike home. In the dark, the Armorer had been trying to take out the rear tires of the vehicle, as he wanted to disable it and question the saboteur if possible. But in this light, at this distance, there was also a chance that he could just take out the fuel tank and blow the wag off the sandy earth. It was a chance he was willing to take, and in the event it proved that neither option came to anything. There were flickers of sparks and light in the darkness as bullets struck the rear of the wag and ricocheted harmlessly into the air. But neither tires nor tank was touched as the wag roared off into the night.

"Dark night, Jak!" J.B. muttered as he let the Uzi drop. One man may have gotten away, but did Jak need assistance?

IN THE DARK and still of the building, it took the remarkably honed senses of the albino little time to locate the ticking that he could hear. It was muted because the source was a small chron attached to a package of plas-ex that was hidden beneath a valve leading from one part of the system to another. Take out that valve and the piping system supplying the entire building would collapse from the shock wave, the delicate balance of the still not fully restored refining system being upset beyond repair.

The light was too dim to see the device fully, so Jak lit one of the lamps that had been left in the building when the day's work had concluded. Turning up the light and positioning it so that no shadow was cast over the immediate area, Jak could see that the device had no booby attached, and had been hidden only to maximize its impact on the intended target. It was a simple timing device, and had been set for ten minutes to allow the saboteur enough time to make good his escape.

"Jak? You okay in here?" came J.B.'s voice from the doorway. "Bastard got away," he added in a rueful tone.

"Left gift," Jak replied. "Timer, plas-ex…only few minutes."

"Want me to take a look?" the Armorer asked as he came up to where Jak was crouched.

The albino nodded, and J.B. knelt in front of the device while Jak drew back to allow the Armorer room to work. He also turned to stop the others from entering, as he could hear them approach. Having met up as they all made their way to the sound of the disturbance, they were clustered just outside the refinery block.

"Take cover. Bomb," Jak said simply.

Outside, glances were exchanged. Ryan nodded briefly at Jak and motioned the others to move back a little.

Inside, the Armorer was studying the bomb. He knew more than enough about the construction of timers and bombs to know that this was a crude but effective device. In truth, there was more than enough plas-ex to do the job, and more worryingly there were signs from an initial study that the wiring was crudely connected to the chron. There was every chance that the device may not go off on time. More alarmingly, it could be that the wires would short when he disconnected them because of the way they were fitted. Actually disarming a bomb like this was simple—if it was well made. It was the crudity that made it dangerous.

"Jak, get out and get the others to take cover," he said levelly.

"Sure?" Jak asked simply.

"Uh-huh. And hurry," the Armorer replied.

Without taking his eyes from the bomb, dissecting every part of it to see if there were some flaw he could detect, J.B. listened while Jak left the building and told the others to take cover. He heard them move back in the otherwise silent night, and only when their footfalls told of a sufficient distance did he move.

His hands steady in the lamplight, J.B. took one of the wires joining the chron and the plas-ex, and straightened it out so that he could see how much slack he had to play with. The wire stretched for six inches, and he could lay it on the flat metal surface of a valve plate. He then took his Tekna knife and steadied the wire as it lay flat. This was something he had to do quickly and cleanly. He had no wire cutters, so he had to use the whetted blade of the Tekna to slice through the wire in one swift cut.

There could be no second chance, no opportunity to take a second cut.

J.B. was suddenly aware of the quiet around him, and the sweat that was gathering on his forehead and running toward his eyes. It was now or never, before the slightest glimmer of nerves or doubt caused his rock steady hand to waver.

With his jaw set so tight that he could feel his teeth grind together, J.B. sliced with the Tekna. The wire cut clean through in one move, and the blade scored on the metal valve plate.

He could hear the ticking of the chron, could hear the in-time pounding of his heart and the blood that coursed through his veins, could hear the silence around and running through these as he was aware of one thing and one thing alone.

The bomb hadn't gone off, and he was still alive.

The Armorer slumped slightly, and then, drawing a deep breath, he sliced the other wire and threw the chron across the room. He examined the plas-ex, thinking that it would come in useful after he had ascertained whether or not it had been stolen from the site's stocks. And only then did he call the others.

THEY COLLECTED the horses and rode back to sec camp after checking for any traces that could be found. Jak retrieved the chron from where the relieved Armorer had thrown it, and it told them nothing, being just part of an old wrist chron that was battered and dust gritted. The plas-ex didn't come from the work site, as they immediately checked the types of plas-ex in the store area. Not only was it of a different type, but also the store showed no signs of breaking and entering. The tracks of the wag could have been from any vehicle, and headed off to the road where they would be lost. There were also no signs that the fuel tank of the wag had been hit. At least a trail of lost fuel would suggest a chance of catching up with the saboteur.

Ryan reported the matter to Myall, who checked it in with Baron Silas via the radio. When he asked why they hadn't used their handsets to call for assistance, Ryan told him simply that no one could have arrived in time to help, a point the sec chief had to concede.

Their patrol ended in the knowledge that they had stamped their authority on part of the camp and had thwarted another attempt to sabotage the refinery, but were still no nearer finding out who was responsible.

Although the odds were getting better on it being an outside job, as J.B. had suspected. If so, it was then a matter of who or why.

Something it would be hard to answer as long as trouble continued to distract them within the camp.

THEIR NEXT PATROL was the following evening, and they had spent the day resting and maintaining their arms before getting in a little more practice on the horses. Mildred was still worried about Dean's allergy, and after he had spent some time on horseback during the afternoon she had him in their sleeping quarters, stripped and laid out on one of their make-shift beds.

"How's it been feeling?" she asked, examining the hives that littered his upper body and thighs.

"Could be better," Dean replied, wincing as she probed at a small cluster on his ribs. "At least I don't have any on my balls, which would drive me crazy, or too many on my face. If they were near my eyes…"

"Yeah, that could be tricky," Mildred replied in a distracted tone. "Tell me—and be honest—how have you been feeling?"

"Like I said, they don't itch too much, and they're manageable—"

"I didn't mean the hives," Mildred cut in, with her voice showing an underlying concern. "Tell me if you've been feeling unclear or drowsy."

Dean propped himself up on one elbow, meeting her steady gaze. "I haven't had anything like that. What's this about?"

Mildred paused for a moment before replying. "It could be that I'm worrying unnecessarily, but the injections I've had to give you for this allergy can lead to symptoms that would affect your concentration. And—"

"And the last thing we need right now is me letting anyone down because I'm not triple alert at the right time," Dean interjected. When Mildred assented, he continued. "Honestly, I haven't had anything like that. If I had, I would have come straight to you because I was worried. The last thing I want to do is set myself or anyone up for a chilling because of a bunch of horse fleas.''

Mildred nodded. "Okay, I believe you on that. But I had to check. Still, you won't have to worry about that anymore, because we've just run out of injections. All we can do now is eke out the cream and hope for the best. There may be enough residual of the drug in your system to keep the irritation to a minimum, but it may get unpleasant from here.''

Dean shrugged. "This place is already a pesthole, so I guess I can live with it—as long as we can clear this up quickly.''

"Lord, don't we all want that." Mildred sighed.

Sentiments that were echoed not just by the rest of the companions. Shortly before they were due to begin their patrol, they were joined by Crow, who had ridden in on the sec camp supply wag, bringing food from Salvation.

"What brings you here?" Ryan asked the Native American as he walked across the compound to them. Despite his apparently friendly greeting, there was an undertone to the one-eyed man's voice that suggested he was less than pleased to see Baron Silas's right-hand man.

Crow smiled, slow and easy, and replied in a manner that suggested he was only too well aware of Ryan's attitude. "Well, I was just heading out this way to catch me some sun, and I thought it might be good to drop in and see how you're all doing. No, you know why I'm here. Baron Silas got Myall's report and wants to know more.''

"There's little more to tell," Ryan replied. "Mebbe we'll find out more tonight. Mebbe whoever it is will come back and try to finish the task."

"Mebbe," Crow replied with a thoughtful nod. "I figured that was how it was. But the baron's more nervous than a virgin first time around. Mind if I ride with you? Mebbe I can report back then and let you guys get on with it."

Ryan glanced at his fellow riders. There seemed to be no dissent, so he replied, "Okay, get a horse. We're about to leave."

Joined by the Native American, the sec party rode toward the workers' camp. In answer to Crow's unasked but obvious question, Ryan told him of their fight the previous night.

"If they want trouble, they can have it. Mebbe it'll give us some clues. But as far as I can tell, all they want to do is beat shit from each other and blame each other for the trouble at the well. We'll see."

They didn't have to wait long. The Haigh sector was quiet as usual, the dour ville men keeping themselves to themselves, but as they entered the sectors where Running Water and Water Valley crossed with Hush, they found that they were riding into a full-scale battle.

"Fireblast!" Ryan swore in lead as he heard the sound of blasterfire in among the clashes. "Someone'll get chilled, and that'll fire up the whole camp."

Crow assented. "Better get in. Hush men are hard fighters, and the water villes aren't in the same league. Even outnumbered, I'd back the white-meal boys." The Native American kicked his horse, spurring it to greater speed.

"Watch him," J.B. yelled to the others. "Running Water is his ville. This is one time we can't trust him."

The horses clattered through the streets, turning into crowds massed around the area where the three sectors met. The outlying edges of the crowds were more people rubbernecking, trying to see the fighting rather than join in, and it was relatively simple for the companions to push their way through, scattering those reluctant to actually fight. The core of the action was centered on one street, and Crow was already in the thick of it, trying to break up the fighting men and women from the three villes. He had opted to stay on horseback, and was kicking at the fighters, figuring that he stood a greater chance of hitting a larger number and not being brought down himself if he stayed mounted. But he was making little impression alone.

Ryan turned to his people. "Off the horses, we'll make better progress on the ground," he yelled.

And that was true. Where Crow was hemmed in by the fighters, the companions were able to dismount and attack at a ground level. Although some blasterfire had been heard, the majority of the fighting was still hand-to-hand, with knives, sticks and pieces of glass and metal used as weapons. Dean, Mildred and Krysty were quick to pick up such pieces and put them to good use, while Jak once

more palmed two of his leaf-bladed knives and used
them to slash at the crowd of fighters, moving swiftly
through to the center of the conflict with his flying
feet causing as much damage through his heavy combat boots.

Ryan and J.B. had their own blades to hand, and
both men had learned to fight hand-to-hand the hard
way over many a year. They took the flanks of the
fighting crowd, picking off the pairs and groups of
fighters in the mass brawl, their fists and feet doing
most of the work to be followed by incisive blows
from the panga and the Tekna when necessary. While
this was going on, Doc made a path for himself down
the center, heading straight for the Native American,
his unsheathed blade of honed Toledo steel doing its
utmost to assist his passage, none of the fighters expecting such a seemingly frail old man to be so tough
and fight so strongly.

Within a few moments, the companions had
cleared a path to Crow, and left in their wake a
bloody and defeated crowd of Native Americans,
blacks, Hispanics and whites, united in their defeat.

"So will anyone tell me what the fuck this is
about?" Crow yelled over the sudden silence, encircled by the companions, backs to him, ready to fight
more if necessary.

"We know these scum are responsible for holding
up the project," one of the Hush men said, rising to
his feet.

"Bullshit, it's you people and your hate of anyone
not white," replied a Hispanic woman. "And those

fuckers are just as bad,'' she added to Crow, indicating the companions. ''You're a traitor to your people, Crow.''

''I have no people,'' he replied. ''And they—'' he indicated the companions ''—are on all our sides.''

''Yeah?' With a black and a mutie?'' the Hush man shouted. ''Like hell. They'll only help their own.''

''We don't belong to any of you,'' Krysty said heatedly. ''We just want to do our job and leave.''

There was a general mutter of disbelief as the crowds began to disperse, leaving the companions and Crow almost entirely alone in the center of the roadway.

''Great,'' Mildred said. ''One side thinks we're prejudiced against whites, the other that we hate all other colors…and none of them are going to help us to get at who's really causing the damage.''

''Stupe bastards,'' Ryan muttered, surveying the emptying street. ''They don't deserve anyone's help. Shit,'' he spit in disgust, ''let's get mounted up and get out to the work site. At least it doesn't smell so bad out there.''

Chapter Fifteen

Over breakfast the next morning, Crow and the companions sat in an uneasy silence. Around them the midmorning sun beat down on the sec compound. The heat was dry but still heavy, flies buzzing in the sun, drawn to the paddock by the horses.

The meal seemed slow and as heavy as the heat, the silence almost oppressive, until finally the Native American spoke.

"Guess you feel like this is a hopeless task after last night," he said softly. "If everyone feels you're against them, not only are you not going to get any breaks, but you're risking being under attack, which will only cloud the issue of the sabotage."

Ryan considered that, then nodded. "That's about right," he said simply.

"So what do I tell Baron Silas?" Crow asked blandly.

Ryan cast his good eye over his gathered troops. J.B. stared back with his impassive, stoic expression. Ryan knew he could count on the Armorer to back him all the way, and also knew that his old friend hated not seeing things through. And then there was Mildred. Her dark eyes stared across at Ryan, her face set. She had faced challenges all her life, both before skydark and in the world she had awoken in as a freezie. Mildred hated stepping down, and wouldn't start now.

Krysty would back him all the way. A strong sense of natural justice ran through her, cultivated by the influential Uncle Tyas McCann from her days in Harmony, and her anger at injustice could run as red as her hair. Next to her sat Dean. Looking at him was like looking into a mirror for the one-eyed man, and he saw himself as a youngster, with fire in his veins. The only thing Dean lacked was experience, and traveling with his father was giving him plenty of that. Dean had Cawdor stubbornness. He wouldn't back down from anything.

That just left Doc and Jak. The old man was mentally unstable at times because of the things he had experienced in his bizarre and unique life. But the bottom line was that Doc's determination and fire kept him mostly sane, and was what had caused the prenukecaust whitecoats to push him further forward in time after plucking him from the past. Doc wouldn't like the idea of walking away from a job half-done. And Jak was another matter altogether. He was a born fighter and hunter who had lived through seeing his wife and child killed before tracking down the killers and exacting revenge. The albino was the last person to leave anything undone.

It seemed to Ryan like forever since he had last spoken, and he was aware of Crow watching him intently. If the Native American reported back to Baron Silas that Ryan and his people couldn't or wouldn't do the job, then would the baron decide that they had a price to pay for opting out?

The attitudes he knew his friends to hold, and the possible repercussions of leaving, were two factors that combined to make only one answer possible.

"Tell him we're going to get the fireblasted shitters behind this, and to hell with what those stupes think. We don't run away from a fight if we can win it, and this one we can win."

Crow allowed a rare smile to crack on his heavily tanned and lined face. "I kind of figured you'd say that. So is there any plan of action that you want to tell me, or would you rather keep it to yourselves?"

"I don't see any harm in sharing it with you or Baron Silas except for one thing—we don't really have a plan," Ryan replied. "That's what we need to get together before we patrol tonight."

J.B. sat back, pushing his fedora up on his forehead and scratching at his head as he spoke thoughtfully, "I guess what we really need is to get an overall idea of the layout. We've ridden it, but we need to quarter it up so that we can plan a series of watches."

"Exactly," agreed the one-eyed man.

He turned to Crow. "Are there any plans of the sites that are down on paper and that we can use? I'd guess there should be."

The Native American agreed. "Myall must use something to plan his patrols. I guess the best thing is to ask him."

"Let me," Jak said, rising to his feet.

The albino walked out into the sun, screwing up his eyes as the harsh and brilliant light hit him. He walked over to the paddock, where he could see McVie coaching some of the sec riders.

"Hey, Whitey, how's things?" McVie greeted Jak as he approached. "Hear you and Crow had some trouble last night."

"Stupe fighting," Jak said offhandedly. "Myall around?"

"Sleeping. He was on late patrol out at the well," McVie replied. "Unless it's real necessary I wouldn't like to disturb him, so is there anything I can do?"

"Mebbe. Got paper for this?" Jak asked, indicating the immediate area with a sweep of his arm.

"What, the sec camp or the workers' camp?"

"Both. And well and refinery," Jak added.

McVie scratched at his chin, screwing up his eyes as he thought. "Guess there must be, 'cause we must have planned the patrols somehow. But it's been such a while that I can't...just used to doing it from memory," he added.

Jak said nothing, but it crossed his mind that the sec patrols had been taking the same routes for so long that they had grown stale, maybe not so attentive to change. That would make them soft, and easy prey for the saboteurs.

"Tell you what," McVie said finally, "come with me."

Jak followed the sec man across the camp, past the area where the radio shack was erected, and to the back of the blockhouse where the food for the camp was prepared and served.

"In here," McVie said, beckoning Jak to follow him through a door that led past the kitchens and into a small office area. It was a room barely big enough for the table and chair that stood in it, and the table was bare on top, with two drawers beneath. "Myall keeps our patrol schedules and routes in here," he said as he opened one of the drawers. "I don't know what's what, seeing as how I don't read, but I guess there must be a map of some kind here as we had to know where we were going in the first place, right?"

The stocky sec man took a bundle of papers from the table drawer and placed them on the top. He spread some of them out, looking for something that was a drawing rather than covered in—to him—incomprehensible writing. There were several drawn maps, and although all of them were labeled, he was unable to work out which ones mapped out which areas.

"Hell, I sure hope you can make something out of all this." He shrugged, stepping back to let Jak come near. The albino had limited reading skills, but he knew enough and had enough intelligence to work out which of the maps were of the camp area, and which of the well and refinery. He picked out two maps that folded out to nearly the area of the table, and put the rest of the papers back in the drawer, closing it.

"Tell Myall have these," he remarked to McVie.

"Yeah, sure," the stocky sec man replied. "Wanna tell me why you got them, just so I can tell him?"

Jak studied the sec man's face, his red eyes piercing over his thin, hawklike nose. McVie felt a shiver of fear pass over him at the cold way Jak regarded him, like an eagle about to stoop on its prey. For his part, Jak was trying to decide whether McVie was asking the question from anything other than an idle curiosity.

Finally, he replied, "Just say Ryan need."

He walked past McVie and out of the office, leaving the stocky sec man with the feeling that he had come close to buying the farm, without being able to explain why he had that feeling.

When Jak arrived back at the companions' quarters with the maps, Ryan and J.B. spread them out across the long dining table. The two maps joined together to form a long diagram of the work camp, the refinery, the well and the area in between.

"Look at this," J.B. said as he indicated the area between. "In the dark night there are blind spots where even the most alert of sec patrols could be avoided."

"Even if the saboteurs used wags like the one we saw the other night? Surely the sound would carry across the desert and alert us," Dean said.

"Yeah, but any wag could outrun those horses, so the speed would beat the noise factor hands down," Mildred pointed out.

"That's true," Ryan agreed. "If we leave the

work camp to Myall and his men, to keep it sealed at night, that still leaves us a lot of ground to cover with just the seven of us.''

"Then may I suggest, my dear Ryan," Doc said as he removed one of the maps and let it fall to the floor with a gentle flutter, "that we completely forget about the area between there and here, and concentrate instead on the work sites themselves.''

"Problem there is that we've got the pipeline between to cover," Krysty said, running her index finger along the line on the map that represented the pipe system linking the well to the refinery and the storage tanks.

Ryan examined the map closely. It was a relatively large area, and an extremely awkward shape to cover from all angles.

"J.B., what do you reckon?" Ryan asked his old friend. The Armorer had a mind like a steel trap when it came to sec matters.

"My opinion?" J.B. pushed his spectacles up the bridge of his nose. "I don't think we can actually cover the whole area completely with just the seven of us. And I don't think we can trust the sec here to help us. Not," he added hurriedly as he saw Crow's expression, "because they aren't any good, or might be behind this, but because they're not used to being with us, and it'd be more difficult to manage if they were just running around out there trying to second-guess what we were doing.''

"You'd have the radios," Crow said simply.

"Yeah, but we know how to fight together. They'd

get in the way and make it hard. They could end up getting hurt. More important, they could stop us getting at whoever is behind this," Ryan interjected.

Returning his attention to J.B. he asked, "So how do we quarter this up?"

The Armorer felt in one of his pockets and produced a stub of pencil with which he drew a series of lines swift and straight across the map. "Way I see it, there are twelve points on here where they could stage an attack that would take out the site and cause a lot of damage." He marked twelve points: two at the storage tanks, three along the pipeline, two at the well and five at the refinery buildings, including the pipes that ran between them. "We need to keep a constant watch on those twelve."

"Except there are only seven of us," Krysty added.

Ryan nodded. "So the best thing we can do is take seven of those points on each watch, keep on them for four hours, then move around to another seven points for the next four."

"That keeps the night watch busy, and covers all points, but leaves five points unprotected for half the night."

"Not much we can do about that," Ryan said, "except mebbe to keep those uncovered points staggered so that no two of them are close together, and to stagger them on each night so no one can work out a pattern."

"Sounds good." Crow spoke softly but firmly. "Baron Silas will approve."

"Baron Silas doesn't have any choice," Ryan answered shortly. "Now pass me that pencil, J.B., and let's get the first night's route planned right now."

BARON SILAS WAS SEATED at the head of the long dining table in his dining hall, surrounded by his predark antiques. He was brooding darkly on the situation regarding his well and refinery, getting slowly drunk on moonshine brewed on the far side of the walled ville, in a quarter that was allegedly under scrutiny from his sec force. In fact, it was the home of an illicit still that he kept from being closed down because it supplied the best moonshine in this or any other ville. He had a large pitcher in front of him, and it was almost empty.

"Girl!" he yelled, his voice echoing in the empty hall. The double doors at the far end opened, and one of the redheaded maids he kept as his personal fetish slid into the room.

"Yes, sir?" she asked in a honeyed drawl, her dark eyes and Hispanic coloring betraying the nature of her hair. "What can I do for you, Baron."

"Plenty, mebbe…mebbe later," he mumbled, before adding in a louder, clearer tone, "Get me more of this hooch, girl, and look lively about it." With which he drained the jug and sent it spinning down the table toward her. She took it smoothly and turned without a word, exiting the room silently.

"Gaudy slut," he mumbled under his breath. "Think I don't know what y'all say about me when I'm not around? Think I can't hear in this house?"

he added in a shout, knowing that the cameras would pick him up. "Shit, just give me a sign," he added inconsequentially.

He had just drained his glass when the door opened, and instead of the maid he was expecting, Crow entered with the jug of moonshine.

"Hellfire and damnation," Baron Silas breathed, "I do believe sometimes that my old daddy was right, and there truly is a greater force."

"That's as may be," Crow replied even though he knew it hadn't been directed at him, "but my people could have told you that a long time ago."

"There's a lot of things your people could tell me if I choose to listen," Silas snapped back. "But I'm only interested in listening to you right now. What's been going on?"

"Plenty. The usual fighting among the workers and their families—"

"Shit, what do we expect? They all hate each other from a distance, let alone when they're real uptight and close. It's a wonder they ain't all chilled each other already. Fuck 'em, as long as enough stay alive to open up the well."

Crow bit hard on his tongue. To see these people's hatred had a greater effect on him than on the cold-heart baron.

"Any of 'em tried to blow the well and got caught?" the baron asked.

"No, but there was an attempt to blow part of the refinery a few nights back."

"What?" Baron Silas sat forward, knocking a

dirty plate off the table as his feet clattered to the floor. "Why didn't Myall tell me of this?"

"'Cause he didn't know. Cawdor and his people stumbled on the attempt and chased off the saboteur. Didn't get him 'cause he was using a wag. Mean bastard of a bomb he left, too. But J.B. managed to defuse it. Brave man, smart with it. Ran a check on the plas-ex used, and it didn't come from works stocks. He reckons that mebbe it isn't any of the workers."

"So why didn't they bring Myall in?"

"Oh, they told him eventually, and he left it to me to report 'cause he knew I was headed here. But they had to check him and the rest of sec out first."

"Shit, they didn't trust him?"

"Isn't that why you hired them? To trust no one?"

Baron Silas thought about it, then nodded soberly. "Yeah, of course. So what do they plan to do about it?"

"It's an interesting kind of plan," Crow said, drawing a map from his vest pocket. "I stopped off downstairs and got this map of the site from your study. Got me a pencil, as well," he added as he produced a finely sharpened writing utensil. He spread the map out on the table and took an empty glass, then lifted the jug. "May I?" he asked. "This could take some time to explain."

"You take all the time you need," Baron Silas replied, indicating that Crow should pour some moonshine.

The Native American poured himself a glass and

took a sip, feeling the burning spirit coruscate down his throat before warming his chest and the pit of his belly.

He took a deep breath, then started to draw lines on the map, marking in the twelve points J.B. had identified as being weak spots, and explaining the way that Ryan intended to cover the ground with only seven people. It took him almost an hour and several glasses of moonshine to explain fully the way in which Ryan and his companions had been operating at the work site and camp, and the way in which they intended to operate.

Eventually, he stood back from the table, the marked up map in front of him.

"So that's it," Baron Silas said flatly. Crow nodded. "And they reckon that the sabotage isn't from the camp at all, but from an outside source?" Again the Native American merely nodded. Baron Silas whistled softly. "This is gonna be more difficult than I ever thought."

Chapter Sixteen

The night was still and silent. Dean exhaled, his breath misting on the cold air and mingling with the mist created by the breath of his horse, forming a cloud around them.

He looked at his wrist chron. It was only halfway through his watch, and he tugged gently on the mane of his mount to turn it slightly to the left, giving him a better view down the pipeline toward the storage tanks. There was nowhere for him to huddle, no recess to provide even the slightest touch of closed-in warmth. He shivered under his heavy coat. So far there had been nothing. If it stayed that way, then it would be a wasted night.

But it didn't stay that way. As he turned his horse the other way, to survey the opposite direction, he heard the distant rumble of a wag engine across the desert. It came from behind him...no, from the direction he was facing...but then again.

"Hot pipe!" Dean muttered to himself. "Three of the bastards."

JAK AND KRYSTY HAD BEEN the first to know they were coming. Krysty's mutie sense of danger and threat, and Jak's acute hearing, attuned through generations of hunters, had given them the indication before the others would have any clue. Jak was out by the derrick, and he could tell immediately that there were three wags. One was headed for the storage tanks, one for the refinery area and one toward him. He wheeled his horse around so that he could ride to the blind side of the derrick and see across the still and flat land beyond. His sense of direction told him that the wag nearest to him was circling around to come his way, the pitch of the engine changing as it moved behind dunes and hummocks of dry earth.

Krysty felt her hair tighten on her scalp before she had the opportunity to register the sound. The Titian-red curls drew in close to her skin, winding around her neck. She stilled her breathing so that she could hear better. Although not as sharp as Jak's, she had sensitive hearing, and could tell that one of the wags was headed for the refinery area, which was where she was stationed. Krysty had been assigned first watch on the two pump houses joined by the covered walkway, leaving the farthest refinery building unattended for the watch. It was also the building that faced out onto the desert, and although she had questioned Ryan as to whether it would be better to cover that and so keep the unprotected side of the entire refinery covered, she had accepted his reasoning that this way they could keep more of the actual machinery covered.

It had been a gamble where the cards were falling badly.

The wags were now approaching at speed, and were audible to every member of the party.

Dean spoke into his radio. "Three wags. Looks like one of them is headed for the storage tanks."

"Check. One is going for the outlying refinery block," Krysty's voice crackled over the handset.

"Fireblast!" Ryan yelled into his radio. "Anyone get a direction on the third?"

"Around back to wellhead," Jak snapped into his radio. "I take it."

"I'm nearest you," J.B. returned quickly. "I'll ride over. Doc, Mildred—you're nearest Krysty, so you head that way."

"Good," Ryan snapped back. "Dean, I'm nearest you, so I'll come to you. Head for the tanks. What I want to know is how the hell they knew those were unprotected points."

"Mebbe just luck," J.B. said.

"A whole shit load of luck if it is," Ryan said sourly. "Let's get moving."

THE QUESTION OF HOW the three wags knew to head for areas that weren't under watch was something that had crossed the minds of all of the companions, but right now there were more important matters to attend to. The wags were closing in fast, and although the distances involved weren't that great, the horses the companions were using weren't the fastest creatures any of them had ever seen. It was a race against time when there was no time.

Jak turned his mount and started to drum his heels

against the beast's flanks, spurring it into action and heading it toward the far side of the derrick. As he gripped the mane of the horse with one hand, his other drew the Colt Python and readied the blaster for action. Firing from a moving animal was harder than from a wag, but Jak had sure instincts and this should compensate if need be. Besides which, he knew the Armorer would be close behind.

J.B. was also whipping his mount to as much speed as it could muster, galloping it across the dry, sandy earth toward the derrick that stood upright against the clear night sky. The sound of the wag approaching from the blind side was now clearly distinguishable from the other wag noises. The Armorer reached behind him with his free hand and pulled the Smith & Wesson M-4000 checking that it was loaded and chambered. The blaster was loaded with its deadly cargo of barbed metal fléchettes that would spread across a wide area, the jagged metal inflicting a maximum amount of damage to whoever was in its path.

THE WAG ENGINE cut out, and over the pounding of his mount's hooves, Jak could hear two or three men moving out of the wag and around the derrick. One to the right, and two to the left. Shifting his balance to compensate, Jak held his blaster steady and also spoke into the handset.

"J.B., wag had three. Two on left side, one right. I take left."

"Okay," came the Armorer's cracked voice in return. "I have you in sight, about a minute behind. I'll veer right."

Jak didn't bother to respond. He knew what J.B. would be doing, and he could leave that in the man's capable hands.

Over the sound of his own speed, Jak could hear the faint voices of the two men. They were making no attempt to disguise their position or actions, which spoke to Jak of an overconfidence that would make them vulnerable.

One of the men was placing an explosive device in the small brick pump house that housed the valves to control the derrick's flow of raw oil. He bent over the timer, lighting his actions with a small lamp.

"Watch the lamp, stupe," his partner hissed nervously. "There's only one of the sec coming, all right, but why make it too easy for him? Shit, he looks like a real weirdie," he added with just a touch too much tension in his voice for the saboteur setting the bomb.

"Shut the fuck up, will ya? I just need to set it for enough time for us to get out of here, and then just chill the fucker, will ya?" he finished without looking up.

"Whatever you say," his partner returned with anger in his tone. He raised his blaster and took aim at Jak as he rode closer. He raised his rifle—a buttered Heckler & Koch G-12 caseless—and took a careful aim. He wanted to squeeze off one good shot and down the mutie bastard before he had a chance to return fire.

The only problem for the rifleman was that the lamp used by his partner cast enough ambient light around him to highlight him clearly against the darkness of the derrick. Jak could see that the man was taking aim at him, and bit into the horse's flanks alternately with his left and right boots. The movements made the horse respond by zigzagging, taking Jak on a suddenly erratic course.

"Jeez, the bastard's moving," the rifleman hissed to his partner, who was still absorbed in setting the bomb's timer.

"Just shoot, stupe," he responded angrily.

The rifleman tried to take aim, but Jak was moving too quickly and was outside of the light. He was a difficult target. The rifleman loosed a shot from the Heckler & Koch, but even with such a good blaster the shot whistled well wide of the onrushing albino.

If Jak presented a difficult target, then there was no such problem for the albino. The rifleman was static, only the upper part of his body swaying slightly as he attempted to follow the line of Jak's course. He was also standing in a pool of light that made him stand out clearly against the background. Jak was able to draw a bead on the rifleman with ease, and he squeezed the trigger of the Colt Python, a heavy .357 shell leaving the barrel of the blaster with deadly intent.

The round hit the rifleman in the chest, exploding beneath his raised arms as he tried to draw another bead on the rider. The entry wound was small, but had enough impact to lift him up onto his toes and fling him backward. He made no noise, any vocal exclamation of pain or shock being stilled by the waves of pain that swept through him as the soft lead of the slug expanded on its path through his body. It spread out, causing a ripple of damage that spread along his whole torso, ending only when the now distorted slug exited his body, taking half of his spine and ribs with it, the flesh exploding against his shirt, soaking it in his own blood. By the time that happened he had almost hit the ground, and the blood-soaked fabric started to spread its lethal load onto the dirt. The rifleman was chilled before he landed on the desert earth with a wet and obscene slapping sound.

"Shit, fuck, shit, shit," the bomber cursed loudly, setting the timer running and rising to his feet, drawing a long-barreled blaster of his own from the back of his belt.

The fact that it was stuffed down the back of his pants for convenience when setting the device, rather in a holster, was what chilled him. The extra fractions of a second it took to reach behind enabled Jak to jump from the horse while it was still in motion, landing with poise and dipping his shoulder to roll into the earth rather than onto it, absorbing the impact and letting it work as momentum to drive him closer to the scene of the sabotage. As Jak came upright, he fell into a combat shooting stance on one knee, bringing up the Colt Python and sighting on his opponent in one smooth motion. His finger tightened on the trigger, squeezing off another shot.

With one hand behind his back to pull the blaster from his pants, and the other instinctively flung out to balance himself, the bomber left his entire torso exposed. Jak's shot was swift and accurate, aimed for just above the chest area and beneath the throat, flying swift and true to between the bomber's collar bones, driving a bloody hole into the hollow beneath his Adam's apple and travelling on an upward path necessitated by the angle from which Jak fired.

Almost before the man had fallen to the ground, Jak was on his feet and running toward the small brick pump house, the two chilled saboteurs lit by the light of the lamp, their blood spreading darkly into the earth around them.

To THE OTHER SIDE of the derrick, by the edges that skirted the open expanse of the desert and protected from Jak's view by the pipes that ran from the well, the third man was rigging up his own explosive device. It was more complex, and was intended to take out the generator that powered the wellhead, and also the cabling from the generator that would power the pump house. It was a more time-consuming task, but the third man had that extra time because he knew he was farther away from the oncoming sec man.

To stop and consider it afterward would make it obvious that the saboteurs had a complete knowledge of the positioning of the companions. But there wasn't the time to ponder on that now. For J.B. there was only the knowledge that he was arriving when the party had already started, for as he circled out to the right to come around and tackle the saboteur, he heard the first exchange of shots on the other side of the derrick.

"Dark night," he swore to himself, knowing that he needed to attend to this triple fast in case Jak was hitting real trouble.

The saboteur had been concentrating hard on getting the wiring of the device right, linking up the charges of plas-ex to the trigger device. So hard that he didn't notice the Armorer until it was almost too late.

J.B. whipped his mount into a frenzy of speed, foam flecking from the creature's lips and spraying back onto its mane as it charged forward. With the M-4000 ready, the Armorer wheeled it around so that he was approaching the far side of the derrick from an acute angle. He could see the lamplight by which the saboteur was working, and could see the man outlined against the dark metal of the construction as he linked the plas-ex charges together.

J.B. swung his leg over the back of the horse until he had both feet on the same side, and slid from the horse and it charged forward, buckling to break his fall as the horse moved on toward the derrick. He fell a little awkwardly and hissed curses through his teeth as his body jarred on the closely packed earth. Picking himself up, he moved parallel to the horse's course, and then a little to one side, so that the saboteur would look away from him when the horse's approach attracted his attention.

The saboteur ignored the sound of the approaching

hooves for as long as he dared. He knew he would
have to face an attack, but was fighting against time
to get the multiple bomb wired up properly. So when
he did finally respond to the approaching hooves and
turn with his Uzi raised, he was taken aback to find
the horse coming toward him with no rider on its
back.

Standing, frozen in shock, by the light of the lamp
he was using to work, the saboteur presented J.B.
with an easy target. It crossed the Armorer's mind
that it would be good to take one of the saboteurs
alive and question them, to find out where they were
from, but to do that he would have to disable the
man enough to prevent him firing back or triggering
the device, and J.B. was too far away to take the
chance.

Too bad. The Armorer took aim and let fly with
the M-4000. The weapon boomed in the night air and
loosed its deadly load. The saboteur was turning at
the sound of the charge as the barbed metal fléchettes
hit him. He went down with a scream of agony as
the hot and jagged metal tore into his face and upper
body, some of the shot ricocheting off the derrick
behind. He died as he lay in agony, the last sound
he heard being the approaching footsteps of the Armorer.

J.B. checked the corpse, lest he be able to turn and
shoot when the Armorer's back was turned. Seeing
that his enemy had been successfully chilled, J.B.
turned his attention to the device, tracing the wires
from the charges of plas-ex back to the trigger de-

vice. The saboteur hadn't had time to finish wiring the bomb, and it was a simple task for J.B. to fully disarm and dismantle it.

On the other side of the derrick, Jak had cleared a path through the bodies and blood to where the small brick pump house stood, with its door open. It was lit by the lamp, and he could clearly see the bomb within, and hear the ticking of the timer. Moving across to it, he could see that it was set for fifteen minutes. Although he could risk calling J.B., there wasn't really enough time for him to do anything but disconnect it himself.

Jak had dismantled explosive devices before, but it was one of the few things that breached his iron nerves. There was always that chance that it had been wired incorrectly. He palmed one of his leaf-bladed knives and took the wire that should be the correct one to cut. He looped the wire around his finger, so that a small loop stood above his white fist, and cut swiftly and cleanly with one sweep of the razor-sharp blade.

The wire parted. There was no explosion. Taking a deep breath, Jak repeated the procedure with the second wire. Only then, when that was done, did he breathe easily.

He emerged from the pump house to find J.B. surveying the corpses.

"They don't look like anyone from the camp," the Armorer said simply.

"Outsiders," Jak agreed.

"Pity we had to chill them all. I wonder if the

others can get one alive,'' J.B. mused. "Then we might find out who's behind all this and stop it once and for all.''

DEAN AND RYAN HEADED for the storage tanks, where the squeal of tires and brakes announced that the wag had reached its destination. Both the one-eyed man and his son were some distance away, and were approaching from different angles. With the wag now silent, it was difficult to know where the saboteurs had come to rest, and both Ryan and Dean were only too well aware that they could ride full-tilt into the saboteurs before they had a chance to properly orient themselves.

"Dean, where are you?'' Ryan yelled into his handset.

"About three minutes away, the speed this dumb creature is going. I'm to the southwest of the tanks, and I'm taking a roundabout route to try and spot them,'' the youngster barked down the crackling connection.

"Okay. I'm in the northeast, and I'm bearing straight down. I haven't had a sign of them yet, and I'd guess they're at the back of the tanks.''

"Yeah, they might have left the wag there, but they'll have to come around to the other side to do whatever the hell they intend to do,'' Dean retorted.

"If they want to take out the pipes, yeah. But mebbe they just want to blow holes in the tanks. That'd really put them out of operation.''

"Take a shit load of plas-ex, as well," Dean replied.

"Exactly, so we need to be beyond triple red for these coldhearts until we see exactly what they're doing," Ryan ordered.

The horses were now approaching the tanks from their contrasting angles, and in the pale light of the moon reflecting on the old and battered metal, Ryan could see some movement at ground level, down in the shadows. It looked like a couple of men.

"Got two on my side," he snapped into the radio. "Check yours."

Hearing this, Dean narrowed his eyes and concentrated hard on the approaching shadows. There was no movement.

"Nothing," he returned shortly.

"Okay. You take the route around the back, try and find the wag. Mebbe they've left one on guard. Then work your way around to me. I'll take these fireblasted mercies."

Dean didn't even bother to reply. His father knew that he would follow this order without question. The younger Cawdor directed his mount toward the rear of the tanks, while Ryan homed straight in on the side where the two moving shadows were visible.

The one-eyed man could see them pause in their task, and he knew that they had spotted him. Hell, he was hard to miss, charging in on a horse from out of the desert. He pulled the Steyr SSG-70 from where it rested across his back, and readied the trusty rifle for action.

As he closed in on them, Ryan was acutely aware that the desert and dry ground behind him offered no shelter or cover, and that his silhouette had to be plainly visible from where the saboteurs stood; whereas they were little more than blobs of a different darkness, moving against the shelter of the storage tanks.

The first shot whistled past his ear, and a second kicked up some dust just in front of his charging mount. Obviously, the two men were using different blasters, one of which had a lesser range. Nonetheless, he was now coming into that range, and it would be better for him to adopt whatever evasive maneuvering he could. Which, he was too well aware, wasn't enough. Gripping the horse between his thighs, he raised the Steyr with both hands, resting the stock into his shoulder and sighting as best as he could. The weaving animal beneath him was making it hard to aim, as the target area moved both from side to side and up and down with the pounding of the frightened animal's hooves on the hard ground.

Shots were whistling around him with an alarming regularity now, and although the one-eyed warrior didn't flinch, he found himself hoping that a lucky strike wouldn't take him out before he had a chance to retaliate.

His finger tightened on the trigger, squeezing gently and with seemingly no hurry as he sighted— as best as possible—on his enemy.

DEAN HAD BROUGHT his mount to the back of the storage tanks. He could hear the shots from the other side, ringing out in the still air. From the sound of them, he knew that none of the blasters in action were his father's, and he figured that just maybe he could raise a little distraction.

He pulled his mount to a halt as he reached the tanks. The animal bucked and lifted its forelegs, Dean using the momentum of the movement to slide down its back and off, using the flanks of the animal as cover as he drew his Browning Hi-Power and checked that a round was chambered and the blaster was ready for use.

There was no response from the wag, which he could see sitting by the rear of one storage tank. Dean left his horse, which had calmed as suddenly as it had bucked, and was now wandering off, ignoring the noise from the other side of the tank, and made his way into the shadows.

Inching his way around, he blocked out the sounds of blasterfire from the other side of the tanks, and focused his attention on the wag and surrounding area. Although he stayed on triple red, every sense alert for the slightest sound or movement, he was soon aware that the wag was standing alone.

It was up to him to move quickly and provide the distraction. Moving over to the wag, which was a jeep like the wag he had seen driving away on their previous encounter, he could see that it was empty. There were no extra blasters or any plas-ex. They had obviously brought what they needed for the job and no more. That suited him fine, for what he had in mind would have entailed a whole lot more trouble if there had been plas-ex on board.

Dean took a piece of material from the wag. It may have been a shirt, or it may have been a piece of cloth that the plas-ex had been wrapped in. He neither knew nor cared. What was important was that it was there.

The youth unscrewed the cap on the wag's gas tank and prodded the piece of cloth down the hole, stretching it to make it as long as possible. The cloth touched the gas in the tank and began to soak it up. Dean pressed more of the cloth in, then pulled it out. One end was soaked in gas. He reversed the cloth and pressed the dry end down, repeating the action. When he pulled out the cloth, it was dripping gas, which he let drip down the side of the wag, from the open hole to the dusty earth.

He then stepped back, laying the rag out to give him a short fuse, and backed off a few paces before aiming his blaster and squeezing off one shot.

The rag sparked and flamed, the fire spreading up the side of the wag with a thin blue flame and down into the gas tank. Dean turned and flung himself to the ground, covering his head with his arms.

The wag exploded, and Dean felt the heat and shock of the blast sweep over him, rendering him temporarily deaf and scorching his back and legs. But as soon as it had passed over him, he forced himself to his feet, ears still ringing, and was ready to face the oncoming saboteurs.

Because he knew that they wouldn't be able to ignore this.

RYAN WAS RIDING into the blasterfire, moving from side to side and evading the bullets, although he did feel one tug at his shirt, just above the ribs. A hot pain, like a needle through his flesh, registered momentarily, but the one-eyed man had too much adrenaline coursing through his system, and was too focused on the action ahead, for it to stay his course.

He managed to squeeze off a couple of shots from the Steyr, the heavier ammo from the rifle resounding above the blasterfire from the two saboteurs. The shots hit the tank behind them, causing no harm to them but nonetheless deflecting them from their task. Their firing on the one-eyed man became more erratic, and they hadn't, so far, been able to leave their package of destruction.

And then the explosion came from behind the tank. For one moment, the area was illuminated by the light of the explosion, and in the strange shadows cast on the side of the tank he was approaching, Ryan was able to see the two saboteurs outlined against the tank. They were both stunned by the explosion, exchanging shocked glances. The ferocity of the explosion, and its appearance out of nowhere, had momentarily stopped then dead in their tracks.

Ryan was startled by the explosion, but he kept bearing down on them, taking the opportunity to straighten his mount's path for a second and take a proper aim at the two saboteurs. He had been expecting some diversionary action from Dean, although that wasn't quite what he had expected.

The one-eyed man squeezed off a shot from the Steyr, and it ate into the ground between the two saboteurs. Leave it to the others to maybe capture a saboteur and question them. Right now it was chill or be chilled.

The bullet from the Steyr hit the small package of plas-ex between the two saboteurs, and they disappeared from view in the middle of an explosion that knocked Ryan back and off his mount. The horse whinnied in fright and bolted off into the desert night.

The package had been heavier than Ryan could have supposed, and it scored heavily into the metal side of the tank, driving a huge crate into the ground and obliterating all traces of the two saboteurs.

As he pulled himself to his feet, he was aware that if he had caused some damage to be done to the storage tank, then it was a terrible error on his part. However, as he pulled himself to his feet and began to run, still deafened by the blast, toward the tanks, he could see that the side of the tank was scored and dented, but not ruptured. This was some kind of a relief, but it would be even more of a relief if he could find his son. He didn't bother to yell, as he figured that Dean would be as deafened by the blast as himself.

Dean ears felt as if they were bleeding, but when he put his fingers to one of them, there was no blood. He had just been heading around the tank when the second explosion had knocked him from his feet. As he scrambled up again, with the Browning Hi-Power ready to fire, he was thinking only of one thing—was his father okay?

Both the younger and older Cawdor had their blasters ready as they came into each other's view. But the razor-sharp reflexes passed from father to son prevented them from firing as each saw the other. Instead, there was a sense of relief. Both were alive, and knowing the other's capabilities, they knew that their enemies had been routed here.

But what of the third attack?

KRYSTY, MILDRED and Doc were approaching the refinery buildings from their different positions, and found themselves converging at the same point. But they still used the handsets to communicate, as it was difficult to be heard over the pounding of the horses'' hooves and the roar of the wag.

"How are we going to tackle this?" Mildred yelled over the static.

"I would suggest taking each building in turn," Doc replied. "I think we should stick together to avoid confusion."

Krysty shook her head as she shouted into her handset, her hair now tight to her scalp. "No, we can't risk them having spread out over the two buildings and caused damage. We'll have to split up."

"Yeah, I can see that," Mildred agreed. "There are three buildings, two of them linked by that walkway. I say we take one each."

"Very well," Doc yelled back, "I fear I am not the quickest among us, so I should take the nearest."

"Yeah, good idea," Mildred said. "I'll take the far one. You take the middle, Krysty."

"Okay," the woman agreed. "But stay alert, because this doesn't feel good."

Mildred nodded and spurred her horse, heading off to the far building, hoping that the saboteurs would be too busy to provide each other with covering fire. For she was sure the assumption that there would be at least one saboteur in each building would prove correct.

Krysty headed for the middle, taking her mount in a counterclockwise direction to achieve her goal, as opposed to Mildred's clockwise direction. If they had already been spotted, then at least they would divide enemy fire.

Which left Doc to take the straight course down the middle. Doc wasn't an easily frightened man, particularly not after the things he had seen and endured, but in his more lucid moments he was painfully aware of his shortcomings. And he knew that he was the weakest member, physically and in terms of sanity, of the companions. He also knew that he was the poorest horseman of them all. So he was glad that he had the shortest journey to the point of trouble, but also aware that even then it still made him an easy target.

The wag had long since ceased to roar, and in the darkness and shadow around the nearest refinery building, Doc couldn't tell if it was empty of if there lurked danger in the shape of a saboteur.

Knowing his limitations, Doc suddenly pulled up his horse and dismounted, going the rest of the way on foot. It would take longer, but he would feel more confident of taking evasive or offensive action without having to worry about staying on his mount. In fact, he could use the beast as a diversionary measure. A smile crept over Doc's face as he directed the animal toward the blockhouse refinery building and slapped its rump so hard that it made his palm sting. The pained and affronted creature ran toward the blockhouse, while Doc checked that his LeMat pistol was loaded. There were two charges.

Doc's use of the horse as a diversion was good judgment. Several shots rang out from the interior of the blockhouse—all from the one blaster by the sound of them, which suggested just the one enemy inside. Doc started to run toward the building, low to the ground.

The shots found their mark, and the horse screeched in pain, falling heavily to the ground as it was hit in several places. Doc followed behind, and used the chilled animal as cover. There was a moment of tense silence before Doc's opponent emerged from the blockhouse. A short, fat man with a handblaster clutched in his fist, he came out of a doorway in a crouch and, seeing the felled animal, took one tentative step toward it.

That was all Doc needed. It was a distance of just about 150 yards, and the man had stepped from complete darkness into a relative light from the pale moon. A light strong enough by contrast for Doc to sight him and pull the trigger on the LeMat. With a loud booming that seemed to resound in the sudden silence, the load of shot was expelled at high speed from the old blaster.

The red-hot grapeshot hit the fat saboteur full in the face and upper chest, the pellets of hot metal ripping his skin and flesh. His scream was gargled and stopped by the blood rising in his throat as he was propelled backward into the doorway.

He lay still, and Doc waited for return fire from inside. There was nothing. He waited a few seconds, then moved from around the chilled horse and made his way toward the blockhouse, moving close to the ground. He stepped over the chilled saboteur and looked inside, ready to discharge the ball charge at anything that moved.

But nothing did. One man down...

MILDRED HAD REACHED the far building and could see the empty wag. She crouched over the horse's neck, hoping that even if her mount was big enough to hit, she could make herself small enough to miss.

However, there was no fire directed against her. She swung herself over the horse, keeping her body on the blind side of the wag and refinery building. She slowed the horse so that she was able to touch the ground with her foot and hit the earth running, keeping pace with the creature in order to provide cover.

As she guided the horse nearer the wag, she could see that it was empty, and she slapped the horse's flank in order to drive it away. Keeping low, Mildred moved over to the wag. Using it as cover, she surveyed the refinery building. There was no sign of activity, but because the wag was empty of anything approaching arms and ammo, she was sure that someone had to be inside. They obviously hadn't seen her, so now she was faced with getting across from the wag to the building without being seen. And as it was an empty space with no cover, there was little she could do.

It was then fate played a hand. Fate in the shape of Krysty Wroth.

The Titian-haired beauty had made her way to the back of the refinery building that was part of the first complex, joined to its fellow building by the covered walkway. She knew that she was plainly visible, but felt there was little point worrying about that as it was inevitable. If it left her open to fire, the only thing she could do was take evasive action.

Which was exactly what happened. The shots came from the rear of the building and whistled about her head and body. She leaned low over her mount and pulled the animal around so that it was heading straight for the back of the building but head-on, so it presented a narrower target.

She had her blaster in her hand, and while she gripped the horse's mane tightly in one hand she took aim at the empty window in the back of the building...empty except for the occasional explosion and flash of light in the blackness as a blaster was discharged in her direction. She was dimly aware of the discharge of Doc's LeMat in the distance, a different quality of sound to the other blasters that were being fired in profusion, and somehow this spurred her on, reminding her that it was more than just her against whoever these saboteurs were.

Guiding the horse at a slight angle so that she could get a clear shot, she fired three times at the window. The first shot cannoned off the outside brickwork. The second shot went through and hit someone, as she heard a scream of pain. The third shot was the most deadly, as she heard it ricochet off the metal of the refinery pipes. A fraction of a second later she was thrown from her mount as the night erupted into light. The ricochet had hit the plas-ex that the saboteur was planting and had ignited it. The refinery building was ripped apart by the explosion, the wall nearest Krysty being blown out and scattering debris across the immediate area. She was thankful that her horse had thrown her, for the animal acted as a shield, taking hits from several chunks of brickwork that would otherwise have chilled her.

The explosion startled Mildred, but not as much as it startled the two saboteurs who were working inside the building just in front of her. Scared and thinking only of getting the hell out, the two men rushed from the doorway of the building, presenting Mildred with the easiest of moving targets.

She sighted with her Czech-made ZKR, the very model of target pistol she had used in competition.

She very rarely missed, and never at such a range as this.

The first shot caught her target between the eyes, puncturing his forehead with a neat, precise hole that dribbled blood as the slug pierced his frontal lobes. Before he had even begun to fall, she had sighted and fired on the second man, who took his bullet in the chest, shattering his breastbone and stopping his heart while bone shards ripped into his lungs. He hit the ground a fraction of a second after his companion, and Mildred waited a few seconds for anyone else to emerge from the building before leaving her cover to check it out. She then moved over to join Doc, who had run to Krysty's aid when the explosion sounded. Fortunately, her horse had taken the brunt of the blast, and the woman had only a few contusions to show for her part in the explosion.

And so it was over. The saboteurs were routed, and only one of the attempts to destroy parts of the well and refinery had succeeded—albeit by accident.

But still it gave no clue as to why or who.

Chapter Seventeen

It took several hours for Ryan and his people to gather their surviving horses and the chilled corpses of the saboteurs before they were ready to travel back to the sec camp. By that time it was daylight, and as the procession made its way across the empty desert between the camp and the works complex, it encountered the party of workers, tramping across the dusty earth to the well and refinery.

The sight of the companions, Mildred and Dean on foot, Doc and J.B. leading horses loaded with corpses, and Jak, Ryan and Krysty still on horseback, caused the line—and the sec men guarding them—to come to a straggling halt. Ryan's chest had been bandaged by Mildred, and although the bullet wound had been no more than a scratch, now that he was tired and the adrenaline had worn off, it felt sore and stiff beneath his arm. So the one-eyed man wasn't in the best of moods when one of the sec guards approached him.

"Heard the commotion last night," he said flatly.

Mildred grimaced. "Give that boy a medal for understatement."

"Reckon you could hear that all the way back to

Salvation,'' Ryan replied. ''Didn't get any backup,'' he added pointedly.

The sec man shook his head. ''Myall had us all out at the camp. All these fuckers thought each other was responsible and damn near tried to chill each other. If we get a decent day's work out of them it'll be a miracle.''

Ryan nodded. ''Well, let's see if we can get a reaction from them now,'' he said, moving his horse toward the crowd.

''Gather around,'' he yelled at the workers, beckoning them forth. As they started to move, he gestured for Doc and J.B. to unload the corpses from the backs of the horses. Dean and Mildred stepped forward to assist, and soon the chilled corpses of the six saboteurs—there being nothing left of two after the explosions—were laid out on the ground. Two of them were mangled and mutilated beyond any real recognition, but the others were still recognizable.

''Any of you know these?'' Ryan yelled over the top of the workers' startled conversation. He waited for the buzz of conversation to subside and some suggestions to come. But there was none. ''You sure you don't know them?'' he added.

There was a general silence. The companions exchanged glances. They would talk of this later, but from the looks they swapped they were all sure that they agreed on one thing: the workers weren't hiding anything here. At the very least, they would have expected them to try to blame men from another ville. But there was no such attempt. It was looking more and more likely that J.B.'s theory of an outside sabotage mission was correct.

"Okay, load them up," Ryan directed when he was sure there was to be no response. Doc, J.B., Mildred and Dean lifted the corpses back onto the horses, and they were ready to roll.

"By the way," the sec man said, staying Ryan with a hand on his arm, "there's something back at sec camp that Myall wants you to see."

"What?" Ryan queried with a furrowing brow.

The sec man grimaced uncomfortably. "I'd rather not say—" he made a motion toward the still stunned workers "—but I think you'll find it a hell of a lot more interesting than I can let on."

With this cryptic remark the sec man returned to his duty, and the procession of workers started again for the well and refinery, leaving Ryan and his companions to ponder on what they were about to find.

WHEN THEY REACHED the sec camp, they were greeted by Myall and McVie, who were both looking more solemn than any of the companions had seen in the short time that they had known them. The companions rode and led their horses into the compound and dumped the corpses on the ground.

"Take a look at them," Ryan said as the sec chief and his second in command approached. "Recognize any of them?"

Both men looked over the corpses.

"None of them look familiar to me," McVie murmured, "but then again I doubt if their own old ladies'd recognize these two," he added, indicating the mangled corpses.

"I didn't think you would," Ryan said softly. "They've been using wags—and good ones—to get to and from the well and the refinery. I don't reckon they come from the camp—"

"You could be right at that," Myall interrupted. "Come with me. Leave the chilled there," he added as he turned and led the companions to one of the sleeping tents dotted near the mess building.

"What's going on?" J.B. queried.

"Sure as hell what we'd like to know," McVie replied in a tone that encouraged no answer.

They walked the rest of the way in silence, and when they reached the tent, Myall drew the tent flap to one side. "He's mebbe starting to smell, so be careful," he said mysteriously.

The companions followed the sec chief into the tent.

"Dark night," J.B. whispered. "What happened to him?"

For on the ground, laid out in death, was Crow. The Native American was barely recognizable apart from his giant frame and teaklike skin, for he had been beaten to death. There were no stab wounds or bullet holes on his body, but his flesh was a puffy mass of contusions and welts. His skull was misshapen where it had been fractured, his cheekbones beaten out of shape and his jaw at an unnatural angle where it had been dislocated. His clothes were ripped and torn, covered in blood, and it looked as though he had been dragged behind a wag for some distance, as ragged strips of flesh had been torn from his arms and legs.

"The patrol out on the blacktop found him at first light," Myall stated simply. "Figure he's already been dead for some time. Probably happened some time during the night. Another thing—we found a shit load of plas-ex on him, a timing device and a heavy-duty handblaster. A Colt Python like yours, Jak."

"That's weird," Dean said, "I never saw him with a blaster before."

"Neither did I," Myall replied, "but that doesn't mean that he wouldn't have carried one when...when he was on a mission." The sec chief spit out the last phrase, as though he couldn't quite believe it himself.

"So you think he was with those?" Ryan asked, jerking a thumb behind him to indicate the chilled saboteurs who were lying in the morning sun.

Myall shrugged. "With all that stuff, on the black-top that leads to the well and refinery? What am I supposed to think?"

"Exactly what you are, my dear boy," Doc murmured. "A most carefully laid trail, but not without one glaring error."

"Eh?" Myall looked at Doc with a puzzled expression.

"So simple that it is obvious," Doc said slowly. "If he was one of the saboteurs out there, then how, pray tell, did he end up being chilled on the road…before they actually reached the well and re-finery?''

"Mebbe it happened on the way back, a falling-out of some kind 'cause it all went wrong," McVie began.

Krysty cut him short. "We chilled them all. Their wags are still at the site. If they chilled Crow, then it was on the way."

"And someone wanted him to look like a guilty man," Mildred added.

"Well, you'll have a chance to talk to the big man about it," Myall sighed. "I radioed Baron Silas straight away, and he's coming out here."

BARON SILAS ARRIVED about an hour later, during which time Ryan and his people had the chance to clean up and eat, if not to get any sleep. The baron drove into the camp in his large old truck wag, with the shotgun sec rider, and strode straight across to where the bodies of the saboteurs were still lying, rotting in the sun.

He nodded to himself, then turned to Myall, who had joined him. The sec chief showed the baron to where the corpse of Crow had been stashed, and when the two men emerged, they were greeted by the companions, who had left the mess building to meet the baron.

"Well, well, well," Baron Silas said as he greeted them, his eyes slits under the brim of his hat. "You caught some of them, but still managed to blow some of the compound."

"Nothing compared to what could have been done. Besides, you know we couldn't cover all the vulnerable points without extra cover," Ryan commented.

"You mean to say you didn't mount a full guard?" Baron Silas said with a startled tone.

Ryan examined the man closely with his single eye. "You know what our plan of action was. That's why you sent Crow out to ask us."

"I didn't send Crow," Baron Silas said flatly. "Your job was to protect the site and root out the saboteurs. Looks like you've done some of that, but not enough."

"What do you mean?" Ryan continued.

"I mean all the other barons are coming to Salvation in three days' time, and all I can tell them is that you've failed."

"You call that failure?" Mildred said angrily, pointing to the distant corpses of the saboteurs.

"Yeah, I do. There's still damage to the site, and you've no idea where they come from."

"And you have, from this evidence?" Doc queried gently, noting a certain tone to the baron's voice.

"Yeah, reckon I have," Baron Silas replied. "If Crow was involved, then it's got to be something to do with Running Water. And mebbe Water Valley. Could be that they've got an alliance going that has to do with their water-power mills. In which case, this'd be a problem for them."

"Then why would they come in with you?" Dean asked.

Baron Silas shrugged. "Because it looks good, and gives them a chance to hit me from within. I reckon it's pretty clear what's going on now. I'd suggest—" he put heavy emphasis on the word, making it clear he thought of it as an instruction "—that you search out the rest of the bastards behind this, and look in that quarter. All this crap about it being from outside is just that—crap." Finally, Baron Silas spit on Crow's corpse. "I trusted you, bastard."

"WE NEED TO TALK," J.B. whispered to Ryan as they, along with McVie and Myall, watched Baron Silas leave.

"With you on that," the one-eyed man agreed. "This stinks worse than those chilled mercies."

Myall, who appeared not to have heard the whispered conversation, turned to the companions. "I'll start operations in the camp, try and get to the bottom of it. You get some rest, ready for tonight," he told Ryan.

"You don't sound that happy about doing this," Ryan commented, noting a certain tone in the sec chief's voice.

Myall shook his head. "It doesn't make sense, Ryan. None of it. But I'm fucked if I can make head or tail of it. All I know is that if I don't follow through on the baron's orders, it'll be my head on a pole."

"It's a harsh life," Ryan commented. "But you're right. We should get some rest. Take it easy." He turned and led his people away to their sleeping tent, although sleep was the last thing on the minds of any of them.

"There's something really wrong with all this," Dean said as soon as they were alone. "No way was Crow one of the saboteurs. And what does Baron Silas think he's getting away with saying he knew nothing about our plans? That was why Crow was here yesterday."

"I think he reported to Baron Silas yesterday," Doc said quietly. "And I think he was killed in a deliberate attempt to make it look as though the sabotage comes from within the villes, and not from outside. I also think that we were perfect for the baron because we come from the outside, and to use us as his pawns would not endanger any of his sec forces."

"Meaning that we're in danger?" Krysty posed.

"I think we are," Doc replied, "in the manner of being what they used to call 'the fall guys.' Just as Crow was used in this way."

"You mean to tell me that you believe Crow was killed to provide a distraction?" Ryan asked. And when Doc nodded, so did the one-eyed man. "It'd make sense, I guess. Mebbe he knew something he shouldn't have done. After all, why the hell was he on that road at that time of night when he was supposed to be with Baron Silas?"

"Mebbe he was," J.B. mused. "Mebbe that's the whole problem. We've been looking for outside saboteurs when all the time it has been from inside. But not from the inside that everyone thought."

Jak gave J.B. a puzzled look. "Not make sense."

"Oh, but it does," said Doc slowly. "My dear John Barrymore, I think you may have cracked it. Supposing that Crow had reported to Baron Silas, and suppose that was why he died? To provide a decoy to the fact that all the points hit were ones that were not on the patrol rota at the times they were hit. After all, if he had not visited the baron, then only he would know the points that were vulnerable."

"Oh shit, I've just remembered," Dean whispered. "Baron Silas mentioned that the idea of the saboteurs being outsiders was crap."

Ryan furrowed his brow. "So?"

Dean turned to his father and fixed him with a stare. "So no one knew about that idea of J.B.'s except us and Crow. And the only reason Baron Silas would know—"

"—is if Crow told him," the Armorer concluded.

They sat in stunned silence for a moment. Finally, Krysty asked the obvious question. "But why would the baron want to sabotage his own project?"

"If, my sweet girl, there was something that would emerge and destroy his dream. Men have killed for less," Doc mused.

"Or just take all other barons' jack," Jak added more prosaically.

"Whatever, it leaves us in the middle," Ryan said grimly. "First thing to decide is this—what do we do about it?"

"Find evidence that we can present to the other

barons and get our necks saved,'' Mildred remarked. ''Because one thing is for sure—we're being set up to be next on the block after Crow.''

J.B. had been silent for longer than the others, looking pensive and lost in thought. Then he said, ''How long until the other barons come to Salvation?''

''Silas say three days,'' Jak replied. ''Two nights, guess…''

''Mebbe that's why the attacks have increased,'' J.B. said quietly. ''I've got to go and ask Myall something.''

''What?'' Ryan asked.

''If he has any record of the sabotage attacks on the well and refinery since work started,'' the Armorer returned over his shoulder as he left the tent.

MYALL WAS in his small office, drawing up new guard rotas in light of what Baron Silas had told him.

''J.B., what can I do for you?'' the sec chief asked wearily as the Armorer entered.

''Records—you keep notes on everything, it seems,'' the Armorer began, ''and I wanted to know if you had any records on the attacks on the well and refinery.''

''Such as?''

''Dates, sites that were attacked, anything that could give me a clue as to some sort of pattern.''

Myall scratched his head. ''Well, I don't keep any records of that as such, but I guess it all would be in the duty log I've got. Everything that happens on patrols I keep note of, just in case the baron asks me about something.'' The sec chief gave a wry grin. ''That way, at least I can tell the Baron something, even if I can't give him all the answers he wants.''

''Can I borrow the log?'' J.B. asked.

Myall shrugged and handed it over to the Armorer, wondering aloud what the hell good it could do. J.B. didn't answer, but took the collection of papers and notes back to the companions' tent, where the others were waiting.

''Now we'll see,'' J.B. said cryptically as he settled down with the papers.

After a few minutes, he looked up. ''Yep, it's just as I thought. The attacks increase in frequency to coincide with the visit of the other barons, which means the project is always in chaos when they're here and they never get to see the full picture.''

''Which means Baron Silas really does have something to hide,'' Mildred stated. ''And, if I'm not mistaken, means we're in for an interesting couple of nights. Especially as the baron knows our patrol schedule.''

''So we change it, catch him out,'' Dean said simply.

''No, not quite,'' Ryan added. ''We play along with him. We need to be able to prove all this to save our necks, because you can bet your last jack that when this comes out we'll be seen by the other barons as being part of it, unless we can prove otherwise. Tonight we stick to the schedule.''

''And if there are attacks?'' Doc asked.

"We see if they're on the undefended points,"
Ryan answered. "And if so, then the following night
we change the schedule and keep a triple red on those
points he thinks are unprotected. And then—and only
then—we've got the bastard."

"And kept hold of our skins," Mildred added.

THAT NIGHT BROUGHT exactly what the companions
had expected. They were positioned according to the
schedule Crow had relayed to Baron Silas when the
sound of wags became apparent across the silent desert earth.

Ryan spoke into his handset. "Which direction?"

Jak's voice came back over the crackling recciver.
"One headed for pipes to storage tank."

Doc's voice cut in. "Another is taking a second
shot at the refinery building they were foiled on last
night."

"Any others?" Ryan asked. There was a negative
response. So there were only the two wags sent on
this night. It was as if whoever was behind the plan
didn't want to risk too much. Ryan understood that.
His contention had been that the saboteurs would
want to marshal all their resources for the last night
before the meeting of the barons. This pair of attacks
would be to test the water. Had they worked out what
was going on? If so, would they havc changed their
rota?

Although he was almost a hundred percent sure
that Baron Silas was behind the attacks, the one-eyed

man didn't want to count on that fact and be caught out if it was someone else.

The following night would show for sure. In the meantime, they had to show themselves willing without risking too much.

"Okay, let's go after them." But not, he added to himself, too hard.

Ryan headed toward the wag that was trying to sabotage the piping that led between the refinery and the storage tanks. Along the way, he was joined by Jak and Mildred. All three of them were cantering with their horses, not wishing to charge into trouble. The following night would be the time to go hell for leather.

The sound of the wag had ceased. In the distance, they could see a dim light where the saboteurs were using a lamp to wire their device.

"They're not frightened of being seen," Mildred remarked.

"Need light. Mebbe one man on shotgun," Jak replied.

"So how do we tackle this?" Mildred asked Ryan.

"Circle wide. They'll have to put a timer on their bombs so they can get away. Take a few shots at them, then we'll let the bomb go off, make it look like we failed this time, and they caught us out."

"Sound good," Jak said.

"Hope it's enough to fool them," Mildred added.

Meanwhile, Doc had been joined by J.B., Dean and Krysty, headed toward the refinery block that hadn't been damaged the night before. They were adopting the same tactics as Ryan, Mildred and Jak, circling around the site and moving at a canter rather than a gallop. Like the other group, they wished to create the impression that they were out to stop the saboteurs while making them feel that they could succeed, and so open the way for the following night, when they would go all out against the saboteurs.

The wag standing outside the blockhouse was empty, and as they approached, it seemed that the building itself was empty.

"Must be inside," Krysty said. "We'll let them get out before we fire."

"Try and hit the wag, but don't chill any of them," J.B. muttered. "We want them to get away."

In both locations, the friends waited at a safe distance for the saboteurs to emerge from planting their bombs. It would be a delicate balance to appear to be fighting while in fact hanging back.

At the pipeline, the two saboteurs hurried back to their wag, to find themselves under fire from Ryan, Jak and Mildred, who had circled wide and were now homing in from three differing directions. The saboteurs fired up their wag and headed out into the desert with a squeal of brakes and a screech of tires. Bullets from the ZKR, the Colt Python and the Steyr bit the dirt around the wag, some hits scoring the sides of the wag. But none hit the saboteurs, who thought their luck was in. They didn't realize that the lack of visible success was deliberate.

Much the same happened to the saboteurs emerging from the blockhouse, who found themselves under fire from some distance. They ran to their wag, keeping close to the ground, clambering in and firing the engine. The wag bucked as the driver threw it into gear, and it roared off away from the blockhouse and toward the desert, under fire from J.B., Doc, Krysty and Dean. The shot from the LeMat splashed the side of the wag, pitting the metal.

As the wag pulled away, J.B. turned to the others. "Let's get the hell out before the bomb blows."

THE EXPLOSIONS from both bombs were visible from the workers' camp and the sec camp. The only people not to see them were the companions, who were headed back toward the sec camp with their backs to the work site.

When they reached the sec camp, Myall was waiting for them.

"Well? What the fuck was that?" he asked Ryan.

The one-eyed man fixed Myall with a stare. "Fireblasted saboteurs. We weren't able to stop them in time. They got into areas we weren't able to cover. Bastards got away this time, though I think we may have injured one of them. Didn't chill any, though."

"Shit! Baron Silas ain't gonna be pleased about this."

"Neither are we," Ryan snapped, leaving the sec chief standing as he headed toward their sleeping tent, followed by the companions.

"Think I sounded convincing?" he asked Krysty. "I'm a fireblasted terrible liar."

"I reckon you did okay," the woman replied. "I also think Myall's got more to worry about than us."

"Let's hope so," Ryan said thoughtfully, "because what we need is everyone to trust us until tomorrow night."

Chapter Eighteen

Evening came too soon. After the companions had rested, and then risen and eaten, Ryan had to discuss the previous evening's apparent debacle with Myall and seem to be irritated by his people's apparent inability to deal successfully with the sabotage attempts.

"I dunno what Baron Silas is going to make of this," Myall said softly as he sat back in the small room he used as an office, staring out of the window and not at Ryan, who stood uneasily opposite. The one-eyed man was too straight a person to be able to lie easily in such a situation, and he felt as though Myall would see through him at any moment.

"He can make what he wants," Ryan answered in an offhand manner, avoiding the sec chief's gaze any time it strayed from out of the window and back into the room.

"So easy for you to say, Ryan. You know the meeting of the barons is tomorrow, and they arrive in Salvation during the day, right?" When the one-eyed man nodded, Myall continued. "Thing is, if they'd arrived the other day when you'd chilled some of the fuckers, and we'd found Crow, that'd look good. Now, with another attack that's been successful, it don't look so good. And that's our asses on the line."

Why not state the fireblasted obvious? Ryan thought, but instead he said, "We're all doing our best here. Baron Silas knows that. The other barons will know that. And we have made progress."

Myall looked at Ryan as though he were stupe. "You think that'll cut any ice with these cold-hearts?"

Ryan resisted the temptation to grin, and answered, "No. But what the hell else can we do?" Adding to himself that they could nail Baron Silas Hunter to the wellhead and offer him up for the lying bastard he truly was.

Ryan left an unhappy Myall and returned to his people.

"So how's our happy sec chief today?" Mildred asked with more than a hint of sarcasm as Ryan entered.

"About as far from happy as he can possibly get, I'd say," Ryan returned. "Not that it's our problem, but the poor bastard has been given the shit end of the stick."

"There's always someone to get that," J.B. mused. "Main thing is to see that it's not you."

"Yeah, exactly," Ryan agreed. "Now, if we're going to get this matter nailed tonight and save our own asses, then we've really got to get to work before sundown."

BARON SILAS WAS a far from happy man. If the demeanor of his sec chief had betrayed strained nerves and apprehension about the forthcoming events to Ryan, then one look at the baron would only confirm to the one-eyed man everything that he and his people had suspected about the baron.

The man prowled the length of his dining room, the heels of his snakeskin boots clicking irritatedly against the polished flooring. He ignored the procession of maids that came in and out of the room in order to decorate it for the banquet with which he would greet his fellow barons that evening, before leaving them—hopefully drunk into insensibility—to complete his necessary tasks. If the drink didn't work, then he had some jolt to keep them amused and blasted. If not that, then there were always the women. One way or the other, he had to keep them occupied all the evening to enable his plan to take place. Already he had set up Crow as the ringleader of the saboteurs. Now he just needed to cause enough damage to the well to put it out of action permanently and set up Ryan and his people as fall guys. Oh, yeah—and, if possible, make sure that at least one of the other barons would find another of the barons to blame and so cause enough internal warring to deflect any attention from himself.

Shouldn't be too difficult.

"Shit!" he cursed loudly as a sudden explosion of sound in the otherwise quiet room caused some of the maids to start in their task around the table.

"Is there a problem, master?" one of them asked in honeyed tones.

Baron Silas Hunter had stopped pacing the room and was looking out of the iron-clad window at the people of Salvation going about their business. All of this, built with his own hands and with good faith, now in danger. Yeah, there was a problem.

But instead, he merely answered, "No, go about your business," in a curt and dismissive tone.

And he would go about his.

IT TOOK the companions all day to prepare themselves. Although they knew that this would in all probability be the culminative day of their time at Salvation, they also knew that they couldn't show this to anyone else in the sec camp. So after they had rested and eaten, they retired to their tent to prepare and clean their blasters for the night ahead, also taking the opportunity to work out and exercise, priming themselves for what was to come.

In the late afternoon, Ryan made his first move.

"Okay people, time to get this clear," he said simply, adding, "J.B., keep a lookout for anyone who could come near enough to hear."

"Think they may be on to something, lover?" Krysty asked.

"No," the one-eyed man grunted, "but I don't want to risk anything being overheard by accident and getting back to McVie and Myall. I'm sure they're not in on anything the baron has up his sleeve, but I don't want them blundering in on anyone's side, no matter how well-meaning they may be."

Doc nodded. "It will be hard enough to effect this action as it is, without any outside influence."

Mildred shook her head and laughed. "Always use too many words, Doc."

Doc smiled. "My dear good woman, a usage of arcane language could, in itself, be an effective cover. After all, if no one can grasp your meaning…"

"Yeah, well, it helps if we can, at least." Dean laughed.

"Okay," Ryan said good-naturedly, "let's cut the stupe stuff and get serious, though I guess us all being in a good mood is going to help."

"Not hurt," Jak commented.

"Right," Ryan began briskly. "I guess we all know the basic plan. There are five points on the patrol roster for tonight that will be left clear at the optimum time for attack. So what we do is quite simple. We reverse the roster and leave the other seven points uncovered, concentrating our efforts on those points that the baron and his mercies will think are vulnerable."

"Not much room hide," Jak commented. "How we keep in cover as bastards approach?"

"Yeah, I've been a little worried about that one," Ryan said. "There are some areas where we can take cover, but the horses could prove a problem. Some of the hideouts are only big enough for people."

"If we make good time, we could tether the horses at the points where we're supposed to be, and make it the rest of the way on foot," J.B. put in from his post by the tent's opening. "That way they can see our mounts if they try to check us out, mebbe figure whoever they're checking is taking a leak at that moment."

"Yeah, good idea." Ryan nodded. "That gives us some cover and mebbe buys a little more surprise."

"Sounds good," Krysty agreed. "So how do we divide up? Seven into five just doesn't go at all."

"We'll do a couple of pairs, and then the rest individually. I know the handsets are a risk to use because we might get overheard, and because the refinery works cause interference, but at least they'll give us some semblance of contact."

"Okay," Mildred said. "But who gets what?"

"Dean and Doc, you two pair up and take the double refinery building. That needs a pair to cover both, and it'll give you a chance to cover each other's back."

The younger Cawdor and Doc both agreed. In many ways, as the youngest and the least fit of the group, they would be able to compensate for each other's weak points.

Ryan continued. "Jak, you take the pipeline point C on the map. It's the most open spot, and I figure you'll be the best suited to finding a hiding place."

The albino hunter didn't speak, merely nodding briefly. His hunting prowess was such that he would be able to find the tiniest recess, the merest hint of darker shadow, and merge silently with it and remain still almost indefinitely. In such an open position, this was an invaluable gift.

Ryan turned to Mildred. "The far side of the storage tank, at point K. There's a lot of desert for them to come in from, so it could any angle. Keep triple sharp on it."

"You know it," Mildred said.

Ryan turned to J.B., who moved into the tent slightly so that Ryan wouldn't have to raise his voice. "As for you, J.B., you've got one of the shortest straws. I need you to cover the point that takes in the tip of the old blacktop. I guess that's the way they'll probably come, so you'll need to stay alert and mebbe let some past before picking up your target."

The Armorer scratched his head under the battered fedora. It was a difficult task, as he would need the patience and judgment to let some of the mercies through before taking action. But the Armorer was a man with a finely honed sense of combat, and could be relied on to kick into action at the right moment.

"Guess I can handle that," he drawled. "So that leaves...?"

"Leaves the wellhead itself," Ryan said grimly. "I figure that's the big target, because if that goes, then the whole thing is fucked over. And I guess because of that, Baron Silas will want to handle it himself. So that's where I want to face him down. And I'll take you with me," he added to Krysty, "as I'm figuring mebbe more firepower from the mercies there, and I'll need a backup."

The woman nodded slowly. "You can count on me, lover."

"Okay." Ryan looked at his wrist chron. "It's

about two hours till the sun starts to set. Let's get some rest.''

THE BANQUET in the baronial hall was in full swing. It was only John the Gaunt from Haigh who didn't seem to be succumbing to the flow of strong liquor and the lines of jolt, although the dour and severe baron was showing a glimmering of interest in the redheaded serving girls. Baron Silas whispered to one of his sec men, and it wasn't long before the Haigh baron found himself the center of attention from a couple of Salvation's finest gaudies, skilled in the art of seducing men.

The evening wore on rapidly, but not rapidly enough for Silas, who found it harder and harder to keep a slick smile on his face while the rest of the barons got more and more removed from reality.

''Boy, I'll say one thing for you,'' Baron Silveen slurred at one point, ''you can sure throw a party and a half.''

Baron Silas Hunter found it hard to smile in reply, just wanting them to pass out as quickly as possible. He had started the revelry as soon as the first baron had arrived, and had so managed to so far deflect away from himself any awkward questions. But unless they hit the tables in unconsciousness soon, he wouldn't be able to carry out his plan.

More jolt, more alcohol, more girls...

Eventually, he found that he was the only baron or sec man in the room able to focus.

Now was the time to slip away. By the time his task had been carried out, they'd all be comatose. And he'd be in the clear.

He hoped.

Chapter Nineteen

Myall watched the companions leave the sec camp as the sun began to sink and another night descended on the compound. McVie joined his chief at the doorway to the mess hall, where Myall had been completing new duty rosters and worrying about the meeting of barons that was taking place back in Salvation.

"You reckon they've got any chance of stopping this, Chief?" the stocky second in command asked.

Myall shrugged. "I dunno. I would have said so at one point, but after last night? I don't know if any of us have got a chance of stopping it, especially if we can't work out who the hell it is and how they get out of the camp at night."

"Mebbe they don't," mused McVie. "You know, J.B. has this idea—"

"Yeah, I know," Myall cut him short. "Trouble is, that just gives us a whole new set of problems rather than solving the old ones."

McVie laughed bitterly. "And how many more problems do we need, right?"

"Exactly," Myall answered as he turned back toward his poky office. "Anyway, I've got to get these rosters done. We'll need to look really on the ball when Baron Silas brings the other boys over tomorrow for a look around. Got to look on the ball—''

''Even if we ain't,'' McVie finished for him.

THE COMPANIONS RODE in silence away from the sec camp and across the desert to the work site. It was far enough, in the gloom, for them to change their positions without anyone being able to spy on them from either camp and give the game away, particularly as they shunned the use of lamps to light their way, unlike the regular sec patrols.

Before they parted to take their mounts to the expected positions, then change to the new points on foot, Ryan stopped and turned to his people.

''This is the big one,'' he said simply. ''If we're right, then we nail it down tonight. We need to get Silas, and the best way is to get one of these cold-heart mercies alive and get him to tell his story to the other barons. Otherwise, they'll figure we're in it with him and Silas, and chill us all without a second thought.''

There was a moment's silence while they considered that, then J.B. looked at the position of the rising crescent moon and muttered, ''Better get to it, before we miss them.''

THE SIMPLEST PART of the plan was to tether their mounts in the positions they were supposed to have taken and then make their way to their revised places. In the darkness that rapidly fell when the sun set, there was plenty of shadow for them to move silently. That wasn't their problem. For each, it would be a matter of finding a hiding place where they could observe what was going on and also keep out of sight until the moment of optimum surprise.

For Doc and Dean, there was also the matter of teaming up and making sure that they knew where the other was. If there was trouble, they didn't want to chill or endanger each other by accident. So it was that both the young Cawdor and the prematurely aged Doc Tanner found themselves approaching the refinery buildings from different angles, keeping a sharp lookout for each other.

Dean saw a shadow moving across between the two smaller buildings, keeping to the line of the covered walkway. He cut across from his position until he intersected the other figure's path…except that the other figure had vanished. Dean's finger tightened instinctively on the delicate trigger of the Browning Hi-Power as he scanned the darkness, straining for the slightest sound.

"By the Three Kennedys, you will have to do better than that," whispered a voice from the shadows.

Even though he knew it was Doc, Dean still dropped to one side, rolling as he hit the ground and coming up in a combat stance, only just stopping himself from firing.

"Hot pipe, Doc! Don't do that!"

Doc emerged from the shadows, LeMat in one hand and swordstick in the other. He was shaking his mane of white hair from side to side as he entered the dim light. "I could have taken you out right there and then. Please be careful when the enemy arrives, as I would not like to have to explain to your father how you were chilled.''

"Fair point, Doc,'' Dean replied, cursing himself for being caught. But, like a true Cawdor, he would learn from the experience. "So how are we going to take this?''

"I would suggest we cover a section each, and perhaps have some kind of signal to warn each other of our own approach during a tactical situation—to avoid any more confusion,'' he added wryly.

Dean ignored that, and replied, "I'll take these two buildings. You take the larger as it's less ground all around. And we'll just yell. In combat who the hell is going to hear a birdcall?''

"As you wish,'' Doc replied. He made to speak again, but his attention was snatched away by the sound of wags approaching.

"Let's do it—and now,'' Dean snapped, moving back into the shadows. Doc nodded his agreement, and with a surprising turn of speed for one seemingly so old, he, too, vanished into the darkness.

Although there were other wags audible in the distance, only one sped into the gap between the two refinery blocks, skidding to a halt. It had three occupants: a driver and two others, who jumped out as soon as the wag halted. On either side of the gap, Dean and Doc couldn't believe their luck as they were able to completely cover the wag and its occupants.

Mindful of Ryan's words, Doc chose to speak from the shadows.

"If you will kindly put down your weapons, we will desist from chilling you."

There was only a fraction of a second of stunned silence, although it seemed to be much longer, before the angry explosion of sound that was an Uzi on rapid fire. The driver rose from his seat to level the fire in Doc's direction.

It was short-lived, as Dean took him out with a single shot from the Browning that took away a chunk of the back of his skull and pulped his brain tissue.

"Fuck it, there's more than one," yelled one of the saboteurs to his companion. The two men, having already left the wag, had flung themselves into cover—or what they assumed was cover—against the side of the wag farthest from the direction of Doc's voice. Which made them perfect targets for Dean.

The man who hadn't spoken swung himself around in the dirt and rose to run for cover, expecting covering fire from his companion. When it failed to emerge, he swung his own blaster around and loosed a couple of rounds in Dean's direction.

Doc aimed from the shadows and fired the shot charge from the LeMat, the roar of the blaster being echoed only by the agonized yell of the saboteur as the shot ripped into his body, shredding his internal organs and splintering bone. But the yell itself was lost in the louder sound of an explosion. The saboteur had to have been carrying plas-ex on his body, ready to plant it within the confines of the refinery buildings. The shot from Doc's LeMat had hit the explosive and detonated it, causing the body of the saboteur to disintegrate in a ball of flame that lit the entire area between the buildings.

"Oh shit!" Dean yelled, throwing himself flat to escape the rain of debris that ensued as the force of the blast detonated plas-ex that was on the saboteur still taking cover by the wag, taking him out in a blaze of flame and causing the wag to explode as its fuel tank overheated and combusted. The triple explosions were so close that they sounded as one, deafening Dean and Doc as they took cover in their respective points and hoped that no stray piece of debris should, by chance, chill them.

It seemed like forever before the world returned to some semblance of normal, but it had to only have been a few moments. The light settled to a level set by the burning wag, and the only sound was the crackling of flames.

Dean and Doc, now both safe from any debris and certainly safe from any threat from the now chilled saboteurs, emerged from their respective covers and met in the middle, standing together to watch the fire begin to die as the fuel was used.

"So much for taking prisoners," Dean murmured.

JAK HAD ARRIVED at his position with little trouble. Moving silently and swiftly was a matter of instinct and nature for the born hunter, and so it presented him with no problem to find his way along the pipeline with little chance of any approaching agency spotting him.

The pipelines running from the refinery to the storage tanks were straight, with little or no cover provided, particularly at the vulnerable point that Jak was to guard. It was a series of valves and small pipe fittings that joined the two sections, and the shape of the construction meant that the whole piece jutted out into the desert, presenting a plain target with no recesses in which to take any kind of cover.

Within the maze of pipes at this point, there was a small gap that would provide scant opportunity for anyone to take cover. But Jak was small, lithe and supple, and used to keeping still for long periods of time. He forced himself into a tiny gap and settled down to wait, easing his cramped muscles with exercises taught to him by his hunter father that prevented him from either becoming stiff or from having to move out into the open to stretch. He slowed his breathing, making each breath deeper but spaced further and further apart. And he settled to watch and listen, his red eyes sharp in the darkness, his ears alert for the slightest sound out of the ordinary.

So it was that, as before, he was the first to hear the wags. He was aware of the handset sitting heavy on his hip, but he was unwilling to use it. Ryan had wanted them to maintain as much of a radio silence as possible, in case of eavesdropping. The others would hear the wags soon enough in the quiet of the desert night. The only thing that concerned Jak was being ready for the wag that would come his way—

for he had no doubts that Ryan and J.B. were correct, and that the five vulnerable points would be those that were hit.

So Jak stayed, patient and silent, keeping his senses alert. He could hear the wags roll from the blacktop and separate, the notes of their engines changing pitch with their directions, and forming a strange harmony on the dark desert air.

One of them was headed toward him. He increased his rate of breathing, keeping it deep to oxygenate his blood. He exercised his supple muscles, easing all signs of strain and cramp from them. He had to be ready for them when they arrived, which would be only a matter of seconds.

The wag rolled across the dark earth, silhouetted against the lighter sky. Jak could see from his position that there were only two occupants in the wag. They wouldn't be able to see him, as they were showing no lights in an attempt to disguise their position from where they thought a patrol might be. In the quiet, it was impossible for a person to truly disguise his or her position in a wag, but at least with no lights it would take longer to locate…unless it was already known where it was headed.

Jak smiled as he readied for attack, a humorless smile, his lips drawing back over vulpine teeth. His Colt Python was still tucked in his camou pants. Speed was essential in getting out of concealment and into space to move freely. If he needed an immediate weapon, he always had a leaf-bladed knife ready to palm.

The wag rolled to a halt, and the albino heard a muttered exchange between the two occupants as the engine cut out. One, called Murphy, was the driver. Greenberg was the name of the other mercie, and they exchanged a few comments about getting the job done before the sec had a chance to get over to them, and get the hell out. "We were lucky the other night," he heard Greenberg say, adding, "Those bastards are too good. Let's hope the big score really works."

The two mercies climbed from the wag, taking in the surrounding area and judging it to be empty. They were wary, but beneath that they betrayed the security they felt by a certain relaxation of posture. Despite the wish to be wary, everything told them that they were alone, and they wouldn't be prepared for attack.

Jak tensed every muscle in his body, every sinew taut and ready to explode. His eyes darted from one prey to the other, and also around the surrounding area to judge the best places to move, to duck and cover if necessary. Not that he would need it.

The two mercies had both looked into the back of the wag to remove the plas-ex they would need for their bomb when Jak moved. Although his clothing was dark, it was only the shadow of cover that had kept his startling white face and stringy white mane out of view, and as he leaped from his hiding place, it seemed to the two men as they turned at the sudden sound as though a white bird with a terrible beak and eyes of fire had sprung from the darkness.

The sight was so unexpected and so terrible that it froze them for a second.

A second was all that Jak needed. The man named Murphy caught a leaf-bladed knife, thrown while in flight with such accuracy and force that it entered his left eye, spinning in the air and skewering into his brain, entering the frontal lobes behind the eye socket and rendering him devoid of movement but with enough awareness to know the terrible fact that he had been chilled.

Greenberg's attention was then fatally torn between the apparition in white and his chilled friend. Torn fatally because the albino landed on the hard-packed dirt floor and in one bound had flattened the mercie against the side of the wag, Jak's combat boots thudding into his chest at the culmination of a flying leap. Greenberg felt one of his ribs crack as he bent against the metal edge of the flatbed wag at an unnatural angle, and he was unable to drag himself upright, his breath driven from him and the ability to draw any more denied by the pain in his lung from the fractured rib piercing the organ.

Jak landed a little way back from the mercie, having used him as a springboard to get some distance. Rolling, the albino was on his feet again and moving in for the kill against his almost defenseless foe. Greenberg fumbled for his blaster through the mist of pain, but felt his wrist crack and another agony add to that he was already enduring as Jak took his wrist in both hands and cracked it, leaving it limp and useless. The albino followed this with a straight-fingered chop to the open throat, crushing the thorax and leaving the mercie unable to breathe.

Greenberg fell forward, exposing his neck. The bones of his vertebrae stood out against the corded muscles of his neck, and it was little more than an exercise for Jak to take one clean chop at them, shattering those that attached his skull to the rest of his skeleton.

Greenberg was chilled before he even hit the dust.

Jak stood back, pleased with his work. The threat was over. Barely out of breath, he turned to where the refinery buildings became an explosion of light and sound. Dean and Doc were making progress.

But what of the others?

MILDRED KEPT HER WATCH on the far side of the storage tank, remembering the action she had seen there previously. It was a good place for the saboteurs to come, as it was sheltered from view if there was a patrol on the near side, taking in the pipeline, as well as the tanks. Although any wag would have to come the long way around to tackle the tanks in this way, it would be worth their while as they could buy valuable time installing bombs and booby traps.

But this night there was a booby trap waiting for them.

Mildred had a secure place in the shadows between the two tanks. There was nothing but metal at her back, and it would be impossible for anyone to take her from behind. The same was true of both sides. The only way anyone could come at her was from the front. And it was the only direction in which she had to focus her attention.

Mildred heard the wags come in from along the blacktop, heard the change in pitch of the engine notes as they separated and went in their differing directions, and waited for the one that she could pick out as coming near to her.

It looked as though the wag had three occupants. They weren't easy to spot as the wag came around in a semicircle and approached the tanks from the blind side, as the wag itself was outlined against the horizon. It was a jeep, like the ones she had seen used before.

Three against one weren't good odds. Ryan wanted one of the saboteurs kept alive to use against Baron Silas Hunter? Hell, it'd have to be one of the saboteurs from the other wags, as far as she was concerned—unless one of these bastards survived by accident. Because with odds of three to one, there was no way she could take a chance on trying to keep one alive and chill the other two. While she was paying attention to the live one, the others might get her before she could move.

There was only one way to play this.

Ever since she was a child, no one had ever accused Mildred of subtlety. Sure, she could hack that if it came her way. If she had to be diplomatic and sensitive in the past, she could fake it. Sometimes you had to, like in her prefreezie days when she had been a doctor and had to handle people who had terminal illnesses, or whose loved ones had passed away under her care. That was fine. But most of the time, being subtle, diplomatic and sensitive meant kissing some poisonous little snake's ass, and it meant deferring to someone who would walk all over you given half a chance.

It was a lesson from the predark days that had stood her in good stead since she had emerged into the Deathlands.

Mildred wasn't going to let these bastards even get out of their wag. She took from a coat pocket a gren that J.B. had given her, for use in an emergency situation.

She pulled the pin and stepped forward, focusing her eyes on the wag that was almost at a standstill. She took a firm stance and, without leaving the safety of her shadows, she threw the gren.

It was a good pitch. Hard and true, with just a slight amount of lift to it. It flew at the wag before the mercies had a chance to register what it was, and clipped the top of the windshield, just enough to break its path and momentum, and tip it into the interior, where the men still sat.

The gren went off in a flash of light and a roar of sound. It was a shrapnel gren, and Mildred hit the dirt, covering her head with her arms against any debris.

Inside the wag, the mercies didn't have a chance to realize what had hit them as the shrapnel ripped them to shreds seconds before the explosive charge triggered off the plas-ex they had with them, and ignited the wag's gas tank.

Threat nullified by the second big explosion of the night. Mildred looked up to see a smoking chassis and little else where the wag had been standing.

She wondered how John was doing.

J.B. WAS, in fact, a man whose almost infinite patience had been stretched unnaturally thin. There was little he could do in his position out near the blacktop that fed a side road to the refinery and well. A small hut there held building materials for the road, and the Armorer had been able to secure a hiding place. But this supply hut was the target for this point, and if it was to be hit, he was directly in the firing line. He just hoped that the mercies would want to lay a bomb and not just use a gren. If the latter was the case, then J.B. was dead meat before he had a chance to bite back.

He was the first to see the wags approach. Five of them, in convoy. There was something about someone in the leading wag that seemed oddly familiar, but he dismissed the thought. Let whoever got that wag deal with the problem. Then four of them peeled off the blacktop and down the side road, past the hut where he was hidden and off across the desert to their allotted tasks. With the amount of grens he had on him, plus the M-4000 and the Uzi, it was tempting to try to take them out as they passed. But before he could have got them all, his position would have been identified and bombarded.

Better to let them pass.

That had galled him, but now he sat waiting for

the last wag, which still stood on the ribbon of black-top. He didn't dare risk firing until it started its run toward him, as then the crew would just have to concentrate their blasterfire on the hut or pitch a gren at it to completely obliterate him. But leave it too late, and he would be blasted out of existence before he could pick them all off.

Did they know he was in there? It certainly seemed to him that they were mounting a war of nerves...and winning.

The Armorer felt sweat bead on his forehead and trickle down the bridge of his nose, past his spectacles. He blinked as the sweat stung his eyes, but kept his Uzi, set to rapid fire, trained on the wag. That was his best first-line defense.

Finally, just when it seemed that his nerves were screaming at him, the wag began to move. He could only assume that they had been waiting for the other wags to make distance so that they could time their raids in unison.

Through the small window hole of the hut, the snubbed barrel of the Uzi stood out. If he let them get too close, they would see it and start to fire. But too far and they would be out of effective range.

J.B. blanked his mind. His grasp of weapons was so instinctive that he wanted to go with it, and trust his gut feeling.

Now.

He squeezed the trigger of the Uzi and started to spray the oncoming wag. There were sparks as bullets ricocheted, and the wag swerved as the driver tried to take evasive action. But he swerved too hard, and the front wheels hit a ridge of rock at the side of the road. The wag tilted and tipped, the near-side wheels turning on air.

Slugs from the Uzi sprayed the underneath of the wag, severing the fuel line and igniting the fuel. The gas flickered to flame, spreading to the tank and making it combust. The explosion was doubled in a fraction of a second by the plas-ex that the wag was carrying.

"Dark night!" the Armorer cursed, flattening himself in the hut to take cover from the force and heat of the blast as it swept over the structure.

He picked himself up as it subsided and looked out of the window at the blazing hulk of the wag.

So much for trying to take a mercie prisoner. Maybe someone else was having that kind of luck. J.B.? At least he was alive. There was nothing more important than that.

Chapter Twenty

Ryan and Krysty made their way to the well and derrick on foot, having tethered their mounts in their rostered positions. Both moved swiftly on foot, keeping a watch for each other as they approached the site. Krysty was sure that the saboteurs were at a safe distance as her hair flowed wild and free, not curling to her neck in the manner it adopted when there was danger present.

So it was that she knew instinctively that the approaching footsteps—light and almost inaudible on the still night air—were Ryan's.

"So you got here, then, lover," she said softly.

"Yeah, and with time to spare, I'd say. There's no sign of anything going down yet."

Krysty shook her head. "When they come, how the hell do we take one alive to nail Baron Silas?"

Ryan shrugged. "I don't know. In the middle of a firefight it's not going to be easy to just stop one of the coldhearts and say 'Excuse me, would you mind coming with us.' Guess we've just got to hope, and mebbe hope that one of the others can get us a mercie."

"Not much of a hope, is it?" Krysty queried.

Ryan shook his head. "I reckon we might just

have to battle our way out of this, like every other fireblasted situation.''

''At least we're ready for it,'' she replied.

Ryan pointed out the two areas of the wellhead where there were hiding places. One was the small blockhouse used to house the main valves and stopcocks for the wellhead pumps—where J.B. and Jak had previously encountered saboteurs—and the other was in the heart of the derrick itself, over the hole where the main shaft of the pump would fit when it was restored. A smaller, test borehole stood to one side of this, and the casing around it would provide cover for the one-eyed man to use in the event of a firefight...which was an inevitability.

The two companions took their positions and waited. They didn't have long to wait before the distant roar of the wag engines became audible. As with all their companions, they were able to hear the change in pitch and harmony of the engines as they veered off toward their differing destinations, and were able to pick out the sound of one individual wag as it moved toward them.

From his position on the derrick, Ryan was unable to see the wag until it was upon them, but Krysty had been able to observe its approach, and identified it as yet another of the jeeps that the saboteur parties seemed to favor. She could tell that it had three occupants—a driver and two passengers, one of whom was holding what looked like a Heckler & Koch G-12 caseless rifle. Even in the darkness, Krysty was able to identify the shape because Ryan had once used such a blaster.

Krysty waited in the blockhouse, her Smith & Wesson .38 in hand. She was sheltered in the shadows cast around the doorway, but had enough of herself showing to be able to get a good view of the outside.

The occupants of the wag climbed out. They were brisk and businesslike, but not hurrying, men who knew exactly what they were doing and that they had but a little time in which to do it. So every movement was to maximum efficiency. The driver of the wag was short and fairly stout; he looked powerful but not too fast, and carried a snub-nosed handblaster that could have been anything in this light. The second man was taller, but just as broad. He had long dark hair that made the line of his head flow smoothly into his neck in the dim light, making him appear to have no neck. He looked very powerful, as his torso tapered to a tight waist. He would be quick.

But it was the third occupant of the wag that took Krysty's breath away. She got a clear view of him as he moved across toward the derrick in the moonlight, suddenly becoming illuminated as he moved across patches of shadow and into the light. There was no mistaking the Stetson hat, snakeskin boots and rangy figure....

Although distracted by the surprise of seeing the baron, Krysty soon switched her attention back to the two men by the wag. They were unloading a cache of plas-ex, and also something that could be timing devices, although in the poor light it was difficult for Krysty to tell. The baron was moving over toward Ryan, so it was up to her to take these two out.

Krysty leveled her blaster and aimed at the shorter, fatter man. If she took him first, then the one with the Heckler & Koch—the one who looked leaner, fitter and faster—would have time to turn and loose a few rounds at her. Whereas his companion, if he were to be the one left after the initial shot was fired, would probably be slower, and would be using a handblaster that would be less powerful and less accurate from a distance.

That settled it. The taller, more muscled saboteur would be the first one chilled. For there was no doubt in her mind that she would take them both out. Ryan had to keep Baron Silas alive, as he was the best chance they had of proving their own innocence in the bedlam that was bound to erupt.

The two saboteurs were now hunched over the plas-ex and timers, the taller one holding a lamp that illuminated the work the fatter man was involved in. He was manipulating the wires of the timing devices, rigging up a bomb. Krysty knew she would have to strike soon, and so she drew a bead on the fat man. Her finger tightened on the trigger, pressure increasing as she squeezed gently but firmly...then stopped suddenly.

Baron Silas Hunter walked back into her field of vision, stopping in front of the two saboteurs and blocking her shot. There was no way she was going to risk taking out the baron.

RYAN STOOD behind the cover of the borehole shaft, the SIG-Sauer in his hand. His amazement at seeing the baron walk toward him had lasted only a moment. It was incredible that Hunter would risk everything by going on one of his own sabotage missions, even if it did confirm for Ryan that the baron was indeed behind it all. It had to mean that this night's attack was the last gasp by Hunter to stop the project going any further. Why was something that Ryan would have liked to know, but ultimately that was unimportant. The only thing that mattered now was getting Hunter alive and keeping him that way.

As Ryan shifted J.B.'s M-4000 across his back, Hunter suddenly stopped in his tracks, causing the one-eyed man to also freeze. Was he aware of Ryan's presence?

Hunter turned and walked back toward the wag, passing out of Ryan's view and causing the one-eyed man to curse to himself. It would have been a whole lot easier if the baron could have been kept separated from the other saboteurs.

THAT SENTIMENT WAS ECHOED by Krysty as Hunter bent over the other two, muttering in a voice too low to be clearly audible. He straightened, nodding as he did so, then ran across to the derrick, passing from her field of view.

All yours, lover, she thought as she closed in on the two saboteurs, who were set to their task with more speed than previously.

The saboteur with the lamp and the Heckler &

Koch had no idea what hit him. Although Krysty wasn't an accurate shot to the degree that either Mildred or Jak were, she was still the possessor of a keen eye. The bullet took the tall and muscular saboteur straight between the eyes, shattering his skull and the bones of his nose, driving splinters into those frontal lobes that weren't eviscerated by the hot lead of the slug. He fell backward, dropping both lamp and blaster, not knowing that he was even chilled.

The fatter saboteur was momentarily stunned into shocked stillness. Then something in his brain clicked into gear, knowing that he would be chilled unless he acted. He went for his blaster, trying to turn....

Too late. Krysty's second shot took him at the top of the cheekbone, in the area between the ear and the eye socket. He screamed as the bone acted as a shock absorber for the slug before shattering under the impact. It was the merest fraction of a second longer that he lived, but a fraction of a second that was of the acutest agony.

Knowing they were dead, Krysty emerged from the hut, keeping low in case Hunter should have turned back. She checked the chilled saboteurs to be sure, then turned to the derrick.

What she saw made her blood run cold.

RYAN HAD LOST TRACK of the baron when the first shot was fired. Somewhere in the shadow, Hunter had disappeared. He couldn't have gone far, but knowing he had to have realized what had happened, and that he knew the wellhead better than anyone, Ryan knew he'd have to be on triple red.

Even so, Hunter's voice from behind still shocked him and made his blood run cold.

"Drop those blasters and turn around slowly, or else I'll chill you where you stand," the baron said softly.

Ryan had no doubt that Hunter had his blaster leveled at him, and so he complied, making sure to be triple slow and buy some time. The baron had to know that there was someone else at the wellhead, but he couldn't keep his attention perfectly divided. Ryan just hoped that Krysty would be able to do something before the baron decided it was time for him to buy the farm.

"So tell me," Ryan said calmly as he turned. "Was Crow involved?"

"No. Shame he had to tumble to what was going on, as he was an okay guy and a damn fine worker. That I do regret, if I'm honest."

"I regret that, too," Ryan said. He wanted to keep the conversation going as long as possible, to buy time for himself, and for Krysty to try to attack the baron. He'd be less likely to hear her approach if he was busy talking. Ryan continued. "I don't get it. Why do you want to destroy the well?"

"Want? Hell, the last thing I want is to destroy it." Hunter laughed bitterly.

"Then why are you doing that very thing?" Ryan asked.

A tinge of genuine sadness entered Hunter's voice.

"I don't have any choice. I spent years searching for a well. Years. And it was part of my father, too. When I found this one, I couldn't believe that it was still operable. The test drilling found that there were sizable deposits—or that's how it seemed."

"How it seemed?" Ryan interjected, trying desperately to see if Krysty was in view anywhere, trying desperately to keep Hunter talking.

"I guess that some old deposits had been trapped by rock shifts, making big enough pools to drill into. But soon after we started work here it became clear that there wasn't anything really left in the well, and those deposits soon dried up."

"Shit, that's one beauty to explain to the other barons," Ryan said.

"Explain? After all the jack and supplies they've pumped into this? They figure that they own me, and they'd take it out on my ass. So I had to delay the project somehow, until I had enough jack and an escape route to make a run for it."

"And now you have."

Hunter nodded. "And the perfect setup, with you getting the blame for tonight's disaster. 'Cept you were too clever. Which is why I'm gonna have to chill you."

"Go ahead. It isn't going to help you," Ryan said calmly.

"You're one strange fucker, Cawdor," Hunter remarked as he leveled his blaster.

It was then that Krysty leaped from the shadows, having made her way into a good position. She didn't

want to fire at Hunter with Ryan so close, so instead
threw herself forward and took the baron from one
side, driving into his ribs with her shoulder and using
her incredibly strong arms to grab at his blaster hand
and force it up. Hunter fired harmlessly into the air,
then dropped the blaster as the nerves deadened in
his fingers.

The force with which Krysty hit the baron propelled them both across the edge of the borehole for
the main shaft and into the empty space.

"Fireblast!" Ryan yelled, bursting into action as
he saw Krysty and Hunter disappear into the blackness of the hole. It was a bore sunk several hundred
feet deep, with nothing to break a fall.

The one-eyed man reached the edge of the hole.
Peering over the edge, he could see that Krysty was
clinging to the edge by her fingertips, which were
slipping painfully as there was little purchase, and
she had Hunter clinging to her heels, even though
she was trying desperately to kick him loose.

"I go, you go with me lady," he yelled.

"Not if I can help it," she yelled back, loosing
one of her feet from his grasp and pulling it up before
thrusting down hard, the heel of her boot cracking
hard against the side of the baron's head, catching
him above the ear and stunning him...just enough
for him to lose his grip and plunge into the depths
with a wild scream.

"Hold on," Ryan gasped as he reached down and
gripped her forearms in his strong fingers, using his
boots and the edge of the lipped wellhead to gain a

counterforce before pulling with all his might, dragging Krysty upward as she scrabbled for a foothold to help him.

It took a few seconds, but she was finally able to pull her arms over the lipped edge of the wellhead and drag herself upward as Ryan pulled, until she was out of the borehole and lying on the derrick, gasping for breath.

Both of them were silent for a few moments as they regained their breath, before Krysty gasped, "What now...lover?"

Ryan shook his head. "We'll take the wag and round up the others. Head out on the blacktop and hope for the best. Get J.B. to get a direction and try to head back for the redoubt, get the fuck out of here and somewhere else."

"Try and explain to the barons?" Krysty hissed through painful breaths.

Ryan shook his head once more. "No chance...look at it."

Krysty raised her head. There were several fires across the work site, and she could hear the scattered sounds of battle coming to a close. The well was in ruins, and there was no Baron Silas Hunter to stand accountable to the other barons. Just a bunch of outsiders that no one would trust.

She raised herself to her feet, leg muscles still trembling from the effort. Fixing the one-eyed warrior with a stare, she said, "Yeah, you're right. No one'll believe us. Let's get the wag, round everyone up and get the hell out."

Ryan grinned. Despite the situation, he couldn't help saying it.

"Yeah—and out of hell."

A state-of-the-art conspiracy opens the gates of Hell in the Middle East....

PRELUDE TO WAR

A team of brilliant computer specialists and stategists and a field force of battle-hardened commandos make rapid-deployment repsonses to world crises. But now even Stony Man has met its match: a techno-genius whose cyber army has lit the fuse of war in the Middle East. Stony Man's Phoenix Force hits the ground running at the scene, racing against time to stop an all-out conflagration that promises to trap America in the flames.

STONY MAN

Available in June 2002 at your favorite retail outlet.